FROM THE HEART

AMBROSE IBSEN

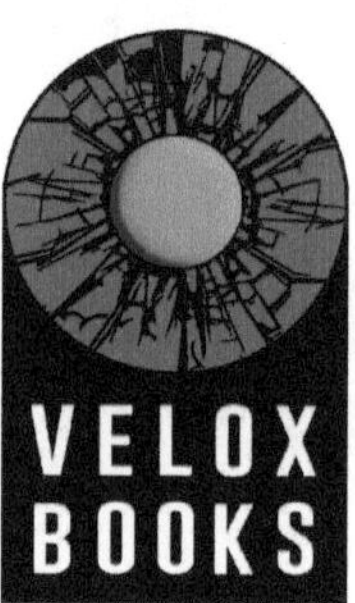

Published by arrangement with the author.

Copyright © 2025 by Ambrose Ibsen.

All rights reserved.

The story, all names, characters, and incidents portrayed in this production are fictitious. No identification with actual persons (living or deceased), places, buildings, and products is intended or should be inferred.

YOU'RE READING ANOTHER TERRIFYING COLLECTION FROM

**FOLLOW VELOX TO KEEP
THE NIGHTMARES COMING:**

CONTENTS

When the Spider in Your Lover's Mouth has Gone   1

On the Third Lap   21

A Certain Smile, A Certain Sadness   45

Rotter   61

Spaghetti Night   79

A Second Helping for Ouroboros   83

The Incident At Mera Peak   97

Writer's Retreat   127

Elspeth   139

Room to Breathe   165

The Polyglot Problem   181

Joey Santiago was a Friend of Mine   201

Knit One, Purl One   221

WHEN THE SPIDER IN YOUR LOVER'S MOUTH HAS GONE

The setting sun burned behind the clouds like a bulb in need of changing and a harsh wind stalked the foothills. I slotted the car into the driest patch I could find, a cubby perpendicular to the drive, hooded by the sodden boughs of a few overgrown tamaracks. The rain-haunted air, thick as syrup, didn't go down too easy; I drank it in between grit teeth while surveying the area. The hills roundabout were shedding streams of runoff and I could hear the gush of an overfed gully from nearby. Left to right, north to south, I took a good, long look till I was sure we were alone.

There was no one for miles but me and Marlene. Black-haired, chestnut-eyed Marlene. Marlene with the funny laugh. Marlene with the freckles and mischievous smile.

Marlene, who slept peacefully beyond the waters of the tarn.

There was nothing to do but begin the slow trek to the water's edge, but even so I staved off the inevitable with glances at the little house couched in the western declivity. Its windows were dark and foggy like a doll's eyes. Already she was half-buried in weeds, and given a few seasons more I wagered the growth might well overtake her crooked gutters and erase every outward trace of the life we used to live there. That suited me just fine. I could remember when those windows weren't half so dark or foggy. I could remember when they were left open in fair weather, and when her voice would pour out of them in song while she worked in the kitchen. I could remember it like it was yesterday. But now I'd had my fill of remembering.

A slow march brought me up and then down the slope. My boots cut squelching arcs into the mud, and my jeans and t-shirt were quickly pasted to me by the driving spray. I strove like a pilgrim toward the waterfront, and over the mossy hump ringed in weathered boulders I found the little pool, engorged and juddering thanks to the heavy rain. In way of preparation, I had brought with me only a single item, a waterproof LED. This I fished out of my back pocket and activated before stepping past the boulders and wading into the cold water.

It was time for our reunion.

***

They used to call us many things.

Whackos.

Freaks.

Creeps.

Cultists.

Marlene and I had heard it all. And, from an outsider's point of view, the two of us could scarcely disagree with such labels. Our lifestyle, our beliefs, had been quite outside the norm; forming the *Sect of the Veiled Sentinel* cost us nearly everything. We were abandoned by our families, friends stopped returning our calls, and our community offered only cruel gossip and moral outrage. With all our ties forcibly severed, we found ourselves with little choice but to flee into the outskirts. There, at least, we could have peace.

It all began in my apartment one night. The two of us, lovers for some months, had been experimenting with ever-increasing dosages of hallucinogens and nootropic compounds. Up to that point, our escapades had resulted in terrific hallucinations, splitting headaches and a shared gut feeling that we were butting against the very seams of reality.

But on that fateful night, we went further, deeper, than ever before. Marlene, in particular, walked straight off the edge and plummeted to some other place. Where she went is hard to say; harder still is comprehending how she ever made it back. After mega-dosing exotic drugs, we entered a coma-like sleep of nearly two days. I emerged from this state dehydrated and viciously ill, and for some time after continued to battle horrific visions.

Marlene, however, *didn't* emerge.

She *died*.

I first noticed it in the hours after I came to. Following bouts of vomiting, I had tried to rouse her, only to find her stiff and silent. Her skin had taken on a bluish tinge and her eyes, open all the while, had become unbelievably dilated. She didn't respond to offers of water or food, and as the hours passed and I began to fear for her life, I tried other methods of awakening her. A rough sternal rub produced no reaction; neither did a series of hard pinches. Only then, still half-stoned, did I even think to look for a pulse or listen to her heart, and in my horror I found her as still internally as she was externally.

I fled the apartment in a haze of paranoia, chased by phantoms—real or imagined I still can't say—and walked the streets till dawn came calling. When the wee small hours had passed and Mr. Sun had guided me out of the worst of my comedown, I slunk back home and wondered if Marlene's death had simply been another ghastly hallucination.

Stealing in quietly, tentatively, I found my lover was no longer splayed out on the futon as she had been hours prior. Instead, she was now seated upon the floor, cross-legged. The color had come back to her skin—in fact, it had *more* than returned, and her flesh now glowed in dewy hues of healthful radiance. Curiously, she was blindfolded with a strip of white cloth that'd been torn from a bedsheet. Like Lady Justice, she turned majestically and beheld me from behind the veil.

No longer was she under the influence of any drug, and no longer did she wear the fetters of human limitation. Having passed between the realms of the living and the dead, the old ways had been obliterated in her and she had been filled, as a vessel is filled, with the pure waters of some other sphere. When she spoke to me, it was not in a voice I recognized, and when she shared with me the fruits of her travels, my very soul was stirred by the authority of her instruction.

The one I had known and loved as "Marlene" had been effaced to make room for something new from beyond the ether. Gone were the days of drugs and experimentation; here, in the space of some few worldly hours, she had gleaned from these tools all that could be gleaned, and she now carried the fullness of this knowledge within her. The human form in which this all-encompassing intelligence now resided was altogether inadequate; Marlene was but a holding tank. A new vessel, a new mode of being, was apparently a great necessity—and once so equipped, the visitor from beyond, I was taught, would be able to lead the world into a new, enlightened age.

But before that new age could dawn, the bondage of the old would have to be stripped away.

There were others who once shared our vision. Marlene and I invited friends and acquaintances of ours—largely those with a background in drug culture—to live with us and learn. These came and went, most unwilling to give what was demanded of them. Word got out about Marlene's teachings, of her claims to otherworldly powers and insights, and it was then that the mockery began. They were intensified in the weeks and months to come as a few acolytes, myself included, grew more fervent in our servitude.

At her instruction, I made myself a eunuch, as the high priests of old, and led the others in candlelit forays into the stuff of fathomless eons. Rituals of cleansing, some of which involved mortification and injury of our physical selves, made no small waves in the local community. By this time the lot of us were already estranged from family and close friends, but the sniffing around of police, journalists and others made it necessary for us to seek seclusion.

Through the pooling of funds, we purchased a small house on a remote property. There, we intended to practice our faith in secrecy and to bring the *Other* to complete fruition. Marlene and I, along with three other men, moved into the house.

By the next autumn, however, only Marlene and I remained.

Life in the small house was strange by any conventional measure. Marlene was left to live in the larger of the house's two bedrooms, alone, while the four of us acolytes made use of the other rooms. The four of us tended to the needs of the property, and Marlene—when the pull of the otherworldly was lessened—would sometimes join us for walks and meals. None of us were allowed to enter Marlene's sanctum; only when summoned were we to step into the rearmost bedroom. This precaution was intended as a protection for us, for there were aspects of Marlene's transformation which were frankly dangerous.

In those moments when her humanity ebbed and the *Other* waxed most profoundly within her, it was dangerous to gaze into Marlene's open eyes. A steward of hidden things, she could communicate in a single gaze maddening truths that the psyches of mortal men could not withstand. It was for this reason that she wore the blindfold.

Early on, one of the initiates, spurred by intense curiosity, ventured into Marlene's room late at night, seeking an audience with her while the rest of us slept. He emerged shortly thereafter, a gibbering mess, and proceeded to flee the property. We learned not long after that he had perished by his own hand—had thrown himself off an overpass. This incident only added to the slanders and cruel speculations about our sect, and when the linkage was made between us and the suicide, we were questioned thoroughly by the local authorities.

In the days that followed, the two others—frightened, doubtful, restless or some mixture of the three—also left the property, leaving only Marlene and I. I have, in the years since, discovered that these two men—traitors to our enlightened cause—*also* died by suicide. I do not mourn them, and I rather doubt that Marlene does, either. Had they only kept on, they could have shared in our glories—could have seen the dawn break. The two of us remained alone on the remote property for some sixteen months following this final desertion, and it was in this period of closeness that we made the greatest strides in purification.

It was early in spring when Marlene informed me that the time had come. The old was set to fall away and the new would need fresh soil in which to germinate. I was called into the inner sanctum late one night, where I found my former lover blindfolded and seated upon the bed. There, she told me what needed done, and what I could expect. I confess that my faith was profoundly shaken by her commands, but... meditating upon the task ahead long into the night, I came to accept these orders just as I had accepted all the rest.

I was asked to wait until the presence of the *Other* in her waned—until she was, once again, walking the halls as plain old Marlene.

Then, I was to strike a killing blow.

The first phase of our lengthy collaboration was to end in Marlene's murder. Only when she had shed her mortal coil could the second phase begin...

I never so much as hurt a fly in all my days till the moment I parked the kitchen knife in her guts.

The tip landed a few doors down from any organs of note, robbing her of a quick death. She'd been at the sink, tidying up and singing. I recall it was some little jazz ditty, a real Billie Holiday moment. She'd always loved to sing. I held her to me and stroked her hair with the handle jutting from her navel, and I begged her to keep singing till she couldn't take up the breath for another verse. Once she went quiet, I dragged her out into the rain and we went for a swim in the tarn, just as she'd instructed me.

In the summer, when the sun is out, you can see straight down to the bottom of the tarn, where the perch and bluegill flit about. It's rather shallow, fifteen or twenty feet at its deepest, which makes for easy swimming and diving. But there's more than fish and diversion to be found in these clear waters. Its greatest treasures are nigh invisible from the surface, and can only be rummaged up by much delving.

There are hidden places in the world, places where peace can be heaped upon peace. Nooks and crannies exist in locales of already profound remoteness, and he who discovers one of these can distance and seclude himself to the point of being utterly forgotten by the world, just as slumbering cicadas are forgotten in the years prior to their emergence.

Found below the waterline of our soupy tarn are a number of caves—flooded spaces largely unplumbed except by the odd fish. Owing to some geological process, the tarn's banks give way to long, winding passages that lead into the surrounding landscape. There are maybe five or six of these in total, however one of them is not like the rest. This singular passage doesn't flood; in fact, it terminates in a dry little cave at the heart of a nearby hill. The tunnel of which I speak is easy to find if one knows where to look; but that, of course, is the trouble with all hidden things—to one who is ignorant of its whereabouts, it may as well not exist.

In the plainest terms, then, it was a *fine* place to hide a body.

On the night I killed her, I descended into the cold waters and, with only a boat light to aid me, brought her into the aforementioned tunnel. Inside, surrounded by cool, vaporous air, I left her perched against the far wall, blindfolded, with a kiss on her clammy brow and a promise that I would return in a decade's time.

For ten years, the *Other* would be at work within her remains, taking on a new form. Shielded from the eyes of the world, the *Veiled Sitter* would bide its time and mesh its inconceivable mode of existence with the fabric of waking reality. This transition would take ten long years; as a tropical fish requires careful introduction into a hobbyist's tank, the *Other* required time and silence to ingratiate itself with our plane. What's more, when its biding was through, it would require release from its subterranean tomb. This task, a retrieval from the deeps, was left to me.

Presently, I went sloshing into the tarn with my LED.

It had been ten years since I'd last entered these waters, almost to the hour.

The time had finally come. The new dawn was set to break.

A sharp inhale, a dive and a leisurely rightward groping were all it took. Mentally, I must have rehearsed the whole sequence a million times over the past ten years. I discovered the ridged cavern entrance with breath to spare and quickly went wriggling through, LED piercing the darkness of the inner earth. There was a narrowing, and a massing of silt upon the surface; I fought through both and dragged myself into the opening, a child stirring in the hillside's lonesome womb.

Damp air and damper earth awaited me within. It was almost impossible to breathe the miasmic stuff that crowded in on me, laden with the stench of minerals. I was tunnel-bound now, crawling on all-fours without enough room to sit upright. The light was nudged ahead of me every few moments, bringing still more of the cavern into focus while I clambered over soft soils and smooth stones.

And then, suddenly, there was no longer any need for progress.

I had reached the end.

There, huddled in the corner where I'd left her, was Marlene.

I admit that my breath hitched in my throat at sighting the tips of her toes—the only part of her then visible on account of the light's position. Skin as dry and dark as leather clung to those toes; an admittedly baffling sight, since I'd come in search of newness and vitality. I was slow to advance, to shed more light on the figure stashed there, and every salutation I dreamt up went tumbling back down my throat before I could voice it. Still dripping, my hand quaked as I held out the light.

Death and spoilage had gripped her feet, her legs; the things remained curled up against her like the brittle limbs of a dead insect left to bake in the sun. "O-O, Veiled One..." I finally muttered. "Are you... Are you there?" The light danced upon her midsection, bringing up a withered waist wrapped in dusty, blood-stained cotton—the dress she'd died in. The handle of the kitchen knife, still jutting from her belly, cast a long shadow against the wall of the cavern as I drew a little nearer.

Her thin arms had been folded around her torso in an eternal self-embrace. The longstanding stiffness of death was upon her; nowhere could I spy even a glimmer of the promised rebirth. I admit I was shaken by doubt as I crawled forward and fixed the light upon her face.

There, a truly terrible sight awaited me.

The blindfold still clung tenuously to a pitted and skeletal face, and sparse hair remained tethered stubbornly to a dead scalp. There was no movement in the veiled eyelids, no color or quiver in the earthworm-like lips, no heave in the still breast. Gravity had eased her mouth open, left her lower jaw to sink by slow degrees, till it seemed fixed in an endless yawn. The tongue beyond her pearly teeth had been reduced to a rough and shrunken stub.

I sat upon the damp floor of the cavern in disbelief.

Ten years. Ten long years I'd waited for this day. I had returned, fully expecting to find something otherworldly awaiting me in the subterrene darkness. Instead, I'd found only a corpse. I was plagued by despair, by regret. Had we miscalculated? Had the *Sect of the Veiled Sentinel* been founded on delusions? Had the *Other's* teachings been false? I began to doubt everything I knew, everything I'd *thought* I'd known.

For some time I spiraled in the darkness of the inner earth, lightheaded in the moist, unpalatable air. So distracted was I in my misery that I failed to notice the first stirrings of life in the corpse stationed before me. In the corner of my eye, I happened to catch a hint of movement—the rise and fall of a hardened breast. This was not the rise and subsequent fall of respiration, but indicative, it seemed, of a more central stirring. Something within that breast had repositioned itself, and I watched through tears as it traveled upward, slowly leaving the cadaver's center. The dead neck was inflated by the slow passage of the thing; something flexed and burgeoned within the leathery confines of the corpse's throat.

I wondered if this movement was owed to the writhings of some pest, or to a buildup of noxious gas within the cadaver, but when the voice called out to me from beyond her lips, I realized it was neither. *"Darling..."* The word seeped out of Marlene like a sigh. Her throat bulged as if with pent-up wordage, but for a long while she said nothing more. I had begun to doubt what I'd heard when, finally, the voice made a reprise. *"Darling... You've returned..."*

I snapped to attention, clutching at the earth with shuddering hands. "Marlene? Is that... is that really you?" In the subsequent silence, I grew anxious and fidgeted with the LED. "Has... Has the transformation taken place, master?"

"Do you doubt?" came the response.

I *had* begun to doubt, and wracked with guilt for my lapse of faith I said nothing.

A phantasmal laugh filled the cavern—*Marlene's laugh.*

The frog-like bulge of Marlene's throat ceased as the unseen obstruction rose up and tumbled into her open mouth. I caught doubtful flickers of movement beyond her lips, but could not, for all my staring, determine what had emerged. *"I will prove it to you, my faithful one..."* There was a moment of perfect quiet. Then, softly, the thing in Marlene's mouth began to *sing*. My ears perked up at once, and in my excitement I nearly banged my head against the ceiling of the cavern. The shadowed tunnel was filled with song—a fragment of "When Your Lover Has Gone". Note for note, the old standard was sung as only Marlene could have sung it, and I sat enraptured till finally silence reigned again.

"O, master, what do you ask of me?" I bowed obeisance, my brow touching the earth.

"Take me from this place," came the breathy reply.

"How? How shall I take you?" I asked, sizing up the corpse. "Will the vessel hold if I carry it through the waters?"

"No," whispered the shying fugitive in her throat. *"No... you must protect me from the water. Things are delicate at this hour, my love. I must have air. I must be kept dry... As for this old husk, I have no use of it. It can remain here..."*

"I... I don't understand," I said. "How shall I take you to the surface, then? We must swim a little distance to exit the tarn..."

"Come closer," ordered the hidden thing. *"Come closer, my dear, and press your lips to mine, just as we used to do."*

I will not deny my hesitance at so grotesque an ask, but I ultimately did as I was told, joining my lips to Marlene's.

The leathern texture of the cadaver's open mouth was overwhelmingly repellant to me, and when the corpse's gaseous emissions poured forth from its rotting core and into my own airways, I nearly retched. I was robbed of the chance, however, by a sudden seizing of my tongue. Something dashed out of the corpse's mouth and went bounding into my own—a swift and jagged something, which at once bolted for the end of my throat and hampered the aforementioned wave of sickness, like a cork stopper. I felt chitinous legs engaged in a thorough study of my oral terrain; their spindly ends found purchase between my teeth, and the thing's shuddering mass cozied up against my hard palate with a pleased shudder.

"*Very good, my darling. Very good,*" came the thing's voice—and when it spoke, pressed against the roof of my mouth as it was, every syllable went rattling through my skull and tickled my brain. "*Take a deep breath and keep your mouth closed—just until we're out of the water.*"

A gush of saliva welled up in my mouth, and I felt the coarse hairs on the thing's back flatten against my tongue like the threads of a wet mop. Breathing around the twitching thing proved difficult, but as I slowly eased my way out of the tunnel, leaving the corpse behind, I made several attempts to fill my lungs. Finally, meeting the waters at the cavern's entrance with my boots, I took a final gasp and then pursed my lips. We went rolling into the tarn, me and the thing that had crawled from my lover's mouth.

I kicked hard, fighting toward the surface with my jaw tensed, and within a few moments I found it, planting the LED in the muddy bank. Shuddering, I hauled myself out of the tarn and climbed commando-style across the field till I had come again to the ring of boulders beyond.

"*Well done.*" The thing cooed at my uvula as though it were a microphone. "*Well done, my dear. The new dawn is soon to break...*"

I shambled back to the car, teetering between illness and unbridled excitement. The Veiled One had taken on a most unexpected form in its ten years of development. Where I had planned to find something humanoid and familiar in the cavern, the *Other* had instead opted for a smaller, stranger design. I dropped into the driver's seat sopping wet and slammed the door shut. Only then did the thing come bounding out of my mouth; with a hard push of the forelegs, it stroked at my chin, cheeks and nose before springing quickly toward the dash. I heard a dull, moist thud, followed by a hasty scamper. The thing disappeared beneath the passenger seat without my ever getting a very good look at it.

I remained lightheaded and drooling, hands linked through the steering wheel. "What... What now?" I asked, unable to swallow for fear of vomiting.

The many-legged shadow took to preening itself. "*Take me far from here, darling,*" it commanded. "*Take me to your home.*"

"Home?" I echoed.

"*Yes. Yes... There is much to do. We have preparations to make before the coming dawn...*"

Within moments, we were on the open road.

———

The thing went scrambling out of my pocket the moment I thrust open the apartment door; it sped down the hall without a word and vanished from sight. I heard its long legs play against the fibers of my tired carpet, heard its carapace thump against the floor—and then nothing. Like a stranger in my own home, I stood in the entryway a little while, passing my keys from one hand to the other.

Thus far, our reunion had been anything but smooth.

I had been the very picture of devotion to our cause. I had been devoted to the point of *murder*, and had lived out the prior decade in quiet desperation. Years of desire and curiosity had brought me to this day, but having now made the trip into the cavern I was left with more questions than answers, and a sinking feeling that I was being ignored by the one I'd served and pined after.

Though burning with questions, I had not broken the silence of the lengthy drive home; instead, I'd stewed in it, allowed it almost to convince me that all had been a mere illusion. The mysterious thing had not given voice to any forbidden truths, had ceased to praise me for my recovery effort and could not even be bothered to make small talk. The *Other* had simply brooded beneath the passenger seat; I, a cabby, and she my icy fare. Upon throwing the car into park, there'd come the tugging at my pant leg. With shocking deftness, the thing had come crawling up the back of my seat, ushering its wiry bulk into my damp pocket. Dutifully, I had ferried it past the threshold...

And now, locking up and putting on the lights, I felt very much alone in the apartment. There was some peeling off of wet clothing as I advanced through the living room, along with a jab at the thermostat and a rifling through my hair for bits of detritus. As I paced, eventually stationing myself at the end of the hall, I worked up the courage to address my master.

"Are... Are you there, O Veiled One?" I posed, shivering as much for the chill I'd caught as for my intense anticipation.

But the one-bedroom unit was wrapped in quietude as clinging as cellophane, and I found myself very much alone even as my question faded from hearing.

"M-Master?" Then, thinking it might respond to a more familiar name, I called out, "*Marlene?*"

No reply. I heard not so much as a skitter as the minutes ticked by.

Whatever my disappointment at being ignored, I was unwilling to court doubts about the master's intentions, and reasoned that the journey from the tarn had been exhausting for her. It was not my place to question the *Other*—to greedily seek the entity's time and attention. She was my master and I her servant, and it was only befitting of a servant to wait until such time as she had need of me.

I showered and changed into clean clothes, and from there I spent the better part of an hour listening from the foot of my bed for signs of movement through the apartment. Still, I heard nothing. The *Other*, wherever she was, had slipped out of hearing. The day's stresses and exertions had taken their toll on me, and with the bedside lamp still on I confess I fell asleep shortly thereafter.

I did not sleep well, nor deeply, but when I awoke several hours later, I couldn't help noting a few strange changes in my environment.

The first and most immediately noticeable was the fact that the bedside lamp was now off. The knob had been turned while I'd slept, and the bedroom had been plunged into almost total darkness.

The next thing I noticed was related to the first. The lights elsewhere in the apartment, in the hallway, living room and kitchen, remained on, just as I'd left them, and by their combined powers a fair glow pooled upon the bedroom carpet, just beyond the edge of my half-open door. This, as I blinked and sat upright, gave shape to things in the room which would otherwise have remained doused in shadow. I became dimly aware of the closet across from my bed, and of the dresser beside it. Glimpsed in darkness, either of these might have invited unease into an already tired mind.

I had only to determine that the dresser was not, in fact, a looming predator before my survey of the room continued, and it was then that I chanced an upward glance, my gaze flirting with the metallic outline of a wall vent, positioned just above the door frame. This thing had been glanced at a thousand times, a fixture in the room undeserving of the least notice.

But never before had I spied the outline of a grinning face behind its narrow slits.

A face, whiter than milk, seemed to hover in the shadows of the duct. Wide eyes stared across the darkened room; their stare rested on me as softly as a feather. Just how long I'd been under this delicate surveillance I couldn't guess. The eyes were lacking in color, almost inhuman in their darkness, but the gentle framing provided by the arched brows and the toothsome smile, coupled with a dusting of freckles from cheek to cheek, jostled my memories with unexpected viciousness, and from the depths a name made its way to my lips. "Marlene?" I nearly fell out of bed in disbelief.

At once, the face was retracted. There was a fit of scurrying, and a long, slow creak which seemed to spread across the ceiling till, as before, there was only silence.

I stood up and put on the bedroom light, approaching the vent in question. Standing on tiptoe, I ran my shaky fingers against the dusty grate, finding its metal partitions still warm on account of recent breath.

"Marlene?" I called, practically bellowing into the grate. "Please, master! Please, speak to me!"

She would not speak. I was pointedly, hatefully ignored. All was stillness and quiet for the remainder of the night.

Doubts crept in.

When more than twenty-four hours had passed since I'd brought the *Other* home and she still hadn't addressed me, still hadn't brought me into the loop or shared with me her grand designs, I began to suspect I'd been had.

Ten years prior, Marlene had described the *Other* as a wise and all-powerful presence—a keeper of immense knowledge, a thing so aged that it had watched the seasons roll past since their inceptions.

This thing I had brought back with me, however—the thing which had come lurching out of Marlene's corpse—did not strike me as anything of that kind. It was callous and cold; a fine imitator of Marlene's voice and affectations, but perhaps unrelated to the work of our sect. It was, quite possibly, little more than a demonic pest, an opportunist.

It was possible—and seemed likelier by the minute—that Marlene *had* made a connection with some otherworldly being during her lifetime. This entity, a spiritual parasite, had wooed us all with its lofty talk of enlightenment, but had in fact been a schemer from the very start. Planning its escape into the world, it had led us in abominable rites for many months, had watched in delight as we had wounded ourselves in want of the farce it had spun, and had ultimately convinced me to murder sweet Marlene.

For some time, I sat in silence about the apartment, building up this theory of mine. But it wouldn't be till almost thirty-six hours after our reunion that I got something like confirmation.

From beyond my window there came a flurry of flashing lights. An ambulance and firetruck, screaming down the road, had gummed up the lot in front of my building, and I watched a handful of first responders hasten from both, toward the stairwell. I stepped out of my unit in time to see them march through the door of an apartment on the floor below, where a weeping woman begged them in. "My husband, please! Please! I-I found him like this. I-I don't know what's wrong!"

It was only through much eavesdropping and by comparing notes with neighbors that I was able to piece together an account of what'd happened.

The victim, a middle-aged fellow living in apartment 202, had allegedly been drawn out of his unit by a woman's singing. Charmed by the sound and curious, he'd left the sofa to investigate, and had walked a little through the common hall. The victim eventually made his way back into his apartment, but when he did, he did not appear well. According to his wife, he'd returned somewhat pale and shaken, his t-shirt damp with sweat. When pressed, he'd said nothing about his time in the hall—in fact, using what seemed to be the last of his energy, he'd waved her off angrily and plopped back down onto the sofa.

A few hours later, the woman had come out of her room to discover him sprawled across the floor, his face and neck tinged in a necrotic shade of black—good and dead. A pair of puncture wounds, equally spaced across the back of the neck, were cited with curiosity by the paramedics. But as regarded this strange injury, curiosity would prove the sole yield. Any connection between a presumed insect bite and the man's sudden and horrific end was dismissed out of hand, for it was common knowledge that no species in the area could possibly answer to the impressive bite marks, nor to such profound deadliness.

The death caused a small sensation within the apartment block. Neighbors I seldom saw came crawling out of the woodwork in search of gossip. Theories were put forth ranging from the banal to the ludicrous, but none touched upon the truth. The truth was mine alone, for *I* knew whose singing had lured the man out of his apartment in the first place, and I had my own notion of whose fangs had found their way into the back of the poor sod's neck. The species was an exotic one indeed, a specimen imported from the underworld itself.

And I had been its trafficker.

Following the man's death, I became certain of a few things. The first was that I had unwittingly loosed something evil upon the world. I had not brought with me some wise and refined being; my trip to the tarn had brought me into contact with nothing short of a pestilent beast. I was not dealing with the *Other*. I could not even be sure that such an entity existed. In all our occult dabbling, Marlene and I had cast forth many nets into the ether, and who could say, after all these years, what had been ensnared in them? We had been charmed by it, thoroughly taken in to the point of devoting our lives to it.

But in reality, it had been a monster all the while. Growing. Plotting. Developing...

The other thing that I became absolutely certain of was that I had to somehow distance myself from the creature. I could not allow the link between us to be discovered by the world-at-large. What's more, the *very existence* of said link was a sure liability; my knowledge of the thing was sufficient to paint a target on my back. I reasoned that the creature would eventually return to me—not to bring about some rosy new world, but to make of me what she had made of the man in apartment 202.

Within a day, I moved out. I took with me only what I could carry in the trunk of my car, and holed myself up in a hotel for some weeks before seeking a new apartment in another city. Rooms in the region were in short supply, leading me to peruse newspaper listings and the like. It was through these channels that I came into contact with an elderly gentleman who, on account of his retirement and desire for a bit of extra income, had decided to let one of the rooms in his house. The place was a little out of the way, somewhat outdated and drab, but I found the owner amiable and the price fair. I paid him a few months of advance rent on a handshake, and the name I provided him with was a false one, for obvious reasons.

For three weeks running, I have had peace in my little upstairs room.

Until this afternoon, that is.

You see, I have just returned from an errand. The homeowner is gone, has been out on a trip with friends for more than a day now, leaving me alone on the premises.

This is why it's been so disquieting to enter a house that *feels* well-occupied.

No sooner did I step through the door just minutes ago did I sense a prying gaze upon me, coupled with the undeniable rupture of an atmosphere whose sole mark should have been stillness. It was a simple thing to put this off, to tell myself that I was merely being paranoid.

Harder to deny is the strange noise I heard upon absconding to my room just now. I live on the second story, in a windowed room that faces the front lawn. There are no trees encroaching upon the walls of the house, and the day has proven quite windless. Nevertheless, I have heard certain stirrings in and around the building, as of something patiently *scratching* at the inside of the walls. Old homes like this one are sometimes plagued by mice; funny that I've never heard them up to this moment...

And though the grass on the lawn outside is still as glass, I find myself straining to hear the wind, *any* wind... for *what else* could possibly be the source of the faint hum I hear issuing from the ceiling, near my closet? I draw a little near to the closet door and give it a nudge, finding my bags still stuffed within. There is little more to see, save for a slot of wood in the ceiling which answers for a door into an attic crawlspace.

Why, the last time I looked at that wooden panel, I'm *fairly* sure it was firmly in place. Now, it's sitting askew. Could I possibly have knocked it aside while stuffing my things into the closet days prior? No, I rather doubt that.

Gaps of darkness are visible around the skewed panel, and the humming seeps from this shadow as blood trickles from a wound. There's nothing of groaning timbers in it, nor settling drywall. It's breathy enough to be the wind...

But then, the wind doesn't know the melody of "When Your Lover Has Gone"...

ON THE THIRD LAP

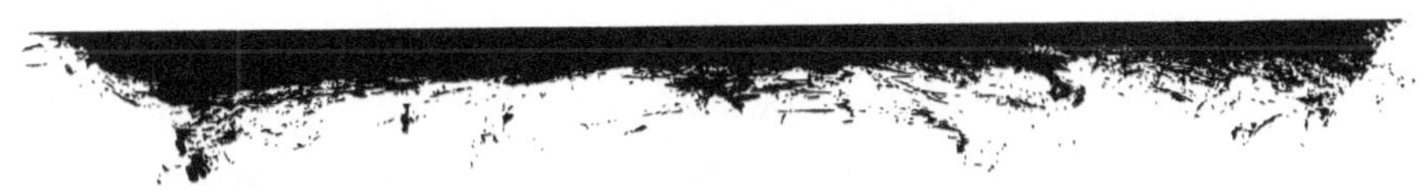

When faced with the choice between a pedometer and a battery of new meds, I chose the pedometer.

At the yearly checkup, my GP was more than a little peeved. Flipping through my paperwork, I found his every glance at my labs punctuated by a quirked brow or an exasperated sigh. "Those changes to your diet and lifestyle we discussed during your last appointment..." he finally said, drumming a pen against his knee. "You didn't take *any* of those on board, did you?"

It was true enough that my love affair with beer and pizza had only deepened since my last visit to the doctor's, and that my blood pressure and weight—already points of concern—had increased further. "It's been so hard," I complained. "You know how it is, trying to eat well at work. And these days, I just can't seem to keep it off! At twenty-five, thirty, I could eat whatever I wanted, doc. Now, if I even *look* at the wrong foods, I wake up paunchier."

"Would that we could all remain twenty-five," came his stony quip. "We're approaching a crossroads, Len. This BP is getting out of hand, and your labs are all out of whack. Your liver panel alone is..." He tossed his shoulders. "We need to start thinking about meds."

"I really don't like the sound of that," I admitted. "Isn't there some other way? I don't want to be on a cocktail of meds for the rest of my life, sucking down handfuls of pills..."

"We discussed the other way—diet and exercise—during your last appointment..."

"What kinds of meds are we talking about here?"

"Oh, the way you're going, we're going to be starting on statins, something for that hypertension—maybe even something for that blood glucose of yours. I could formally declare you pre-diabetic with numbers like these."

In the end, I got off with a serious scolding but no new medications. And another thing: A firm promise that I'd employ the lifestyle changes he'd suggested consistently until our next meeting in three months. If my numbers were still poor by that forthcoming appointment, he promised to throw the whole pharmacology handbook at me.

I found Rachel grinning in the passenger seat as I came sauntering out of the doctor's office that afternoon. She'd come along with me, and was playing some noisy puzzle game on her phone until I approached the car and plopped down into the driver's seat. "He really laid into you, I see?" She put on her seatbelt and pocketed her phone. "How bad?"

"Plenty bad," said I. "He's threatening me with every pill under the sun if I don't shape up."

"So, shape up," she replied.

"Easy for you to say." My wife of twenty years, as trim as the day I'd met her, was nothing if not a salad enthusiast. Always active and dabbling with new diets, her middle name may as well have been "moderation". "*You* could live on grass and topsoil, dear."

"With a zest of lemon, perhaps."

"Yeah? Well, not me. I've got appetites. I've got hunger, you know? I like to eat. It's been that way since I can remember."

"You need a hobby."

"I've got hobbies!"

"Hobbies that don't involve you sitting in front of a TV, babe."

I wheeled out of the parking lot and started for the freeway, tapping at the wheel in exasperation. "He says I've gotta start watching my diet and exercising. So, what? No more burgers? No more IPAs?"

"That's just for starters," she put in. "You're going to have to do a lot better than that if you want to get in shape."

"You're all in league, aren't you? Just trying to ruin my life..."

"It really isn't that bad, dear. You can start small, believe it or not. Making one small change to your diet or daily activity, you'll be surprised at how easy it is. Then, you roll that victory into another. And then another. That's how you build momentum. Before you know it, you're juice-fasting and running marathons."

"Sounds exhausting."

"Well, it's true. And once you get into better shape, you'll have all kinds of energy. It only sounds tiring because you're carrying a bit of extra weight right now."

I teased the edge of the rearview mirror, bringing the soft edge of my face into focus. "Listen to you now, talking about my spare tire. You know I'm vain, Rachel. You're going to give me a complex."

She chuckled. "You've never exactly been James Dean, my love."

"Nor you Brigitte Bardot!"

"We could try walking." Rachel yanked out her phone and went scrolling. "Walking is the fundamental movement—the stuff good health is built on, if you ask me. If you did *nothing* else in the way of exercise except for loads of walking, I think you'd be much better off than you are now. Surely *walking* isn't too much to ask?"

Walking seemed simple enough, on its face. "How much mileage are we talking?"

"I've seen a lot of numbers thrown around. Ten thousand, fifteen thousand steps..."

"You're losing me," I warned. "First you tell me me and iced cream are through. Now you're putting numbers out there in the *tens of thousands?* I'll be stepping from dawn till dusk..."

"No, it's not as bad as it sounds. I'll tell you what, we'll do it together. We'll get pedometers. You know, there are some lovely models available these days that sync up to your phone. You wear it on your wrist all day, like a watch. It tracks your vital signs, your daily mileage. I hear they're a lot of fun."

"If that's your idea of fun, I have terrible news..."

"We'll start small, Len. Walks around the apartment complex. It's quiet enough, and the sidewalks are well-maintained. It'll be nice and easy. What do you say? Thirty minutes of brisk walking after dinner."

"Thirty minutes?"

"More, if you feel up to it."

"Let's not get carried away..."

So it was that we became the proud owners of matching digital pedometers. Rachel placed the order right there in the car, and by the wonders of modern commerce the things were tossed noisily onto our doorstep by the next morning. By dinner, we had them charging in the living room, and had adjusted the rubbery wristbands to fit us both comfortably.

Thus began our evening ritual of walking through the apartment complex.

It was hardly as scenic as a national park, but the layout of our suburban apartment complex was pleasant and green enough to make for comfortable—if not particularly interesting—after-dinner walks. I made a good-faith effort six days out of seven to mirror Rachel's eating habits; my dinners were comprised of fish, greenery and other things I'd regularly shunned over my past forty-five years. As soon as the table was cleared and the dishes were done, we always did the same—assuming, of course, the weather was decent. She would step into her sandals and I would strap on my running shoes. With pedometers securely on our wrists, we'd set out from our unit for three quick laps around the complex.

The six large buildings comprising our apartment complex were arranged in an almost circular fashion, with large green spaces and parking lots scattered in-between. One of the green spaces had lately been repurposed into a minuscule dog park, where the pets of tenants loafed around and seeded the half-dead grass with droppings their owners were often too lax to pick up. From our unit on the outer east fringe, we could pass said dog park, walk past the small leasing office and maintenance shed, stroll past the pool and the other five apartment buildings before encountering a small convenience store. Turning at the convenience store, we would find ourselves within a stone's throw of our front door.

Initially, the three laps left me surprisingly fatigued. True, I hadn't done any major exercise in ages, but I was shocked at how tired I was after a half hour of mere walking. Rachel set the pace, and despite her shorter legs, her springiness made it difficult for me to keep up for the first week or two. Whether it was on account of my improved diet or the regularity of these walks I can't altogether say, but after about two weeks of this regime, I finally found it in myself to match her speed without sucking wind.

In those early sessions, we mostly kept to the sidewalks within the inner ring of the complex. Now and then we'd walk the outer ring, slowing a bit as we cooed at the dogs on offer, or pausing to make small-talk with the people at the leasing office, but we scarcely deviated from the sidewalks in those earliest instances. When I finally started getting my bearings, the two of us decided to mix things up a bit, and would go walking throughout the nooks and crannies of the complex. The parking lots and sidewalks outside of other buildings became our stomping grounds, and with this increased steppage came insights into the lives of our neighbors. Though we'd lived in our apartment for some years, we had never, up to that point, paid much attention to the other buildings. Now, we found great amusement in making regular tours.

It was July by the time we started our irregular explorations through the complex—and a particularly hot one, at that. I'm not much for hot and sticky weather, but sensing that my health was turning a corner I grinned and bared it through the heat and kept on. Schlepping through the lots, we became accustomed to studying the rows of parked cars outside the buildings, and would often remark on them.

A dusty old hatchback with a battered rear bumper became a source of great amusement for us. Its tires were half-flat, and over the course of many weeks it never once moved from its spot beneath a sagging pine. Rachel and I spun all kinds of stories about the car—about its owner, about how it'd gotten its signature dent on the back bumper. We even took bets about how long it would take the property managers to discover its disrepair and have it hauled away.

At least two or three tenants in the complex had left Christmas lights tangled around their outer railings from the previous year, and a few had prematurely set up jack-o'-lanterns to bake in the sun of highest summer. Such flourishes were technically a violation of lease terms, but the tired folks working the rental office had bigger fish to fry and usually turned a blind eye. Ditto with the smoking; the campus was littered with NO SMOKING signage, but this rule was routinely disregarded by renters and maintenance men alike.

Our meanderings throughout the community often brought with them smells; the aromas of burning charcoal, of sizzling hot-dogs and hamburgers, sometimes flooded the air like perfume, and would incite in me terrible cravings. We observed a lot of animals, too—birds, squirrels, stray cats and interesting bugs. All the while, our pedometers would track the mileage. Some days, we only managed to walk for the planned thirty minutes, but on some occasions, when the climate was more tolerable, or when the two of us were really into it, we'd go for forty, even fifty minutes. I hate to admit it, but a month into our after-dinner walks, I started to enjoy them—even to look forward to them. The changes in diet were already paying off. My step was easier, my pants were fitting more comfortably, and I was no longer winded at the mere prospect of going for a walk.

There was one evening in mid-August, though, where Rachel and I had a brief interruption to our regularly-scheduled walk. A work meeting kept me an additional three hours, pushing back our usual dinner. We finished eating just as the sun was beginning to set, and I considered calling off the day's walk as a result. "It's getting kinda late, don't you think?" I whined. "We can go a little longer tomorrow, but I dunno if I want to wander around this place in the dark."

"Why not?" asked Rachel, stepping into her sandals. "It might be fun! We hardly ever see the complex by night."

"I don't know... there might be more bugs. Mosquitos. I *hate* mosquitos."

"You know, as your fitness improves, you're going to need more activity than this. If you're going to be so prissy, then maybe we should find some money for a gym membership; we can run on treadmills in an air-conditioned space. How's that sound? There are places around here with decent rates. I bet we could afford it."

"I like the sound of air conditioning," I replied. "But who said anything about running?"

"Let's just get out and do the walk. You'll be glad we did."

Less than convinced, I put on my shoes and joined her by the door. "Eh, maybe a short one, then. Just long enough to help me digest."

"Whatever you say."

We set out into the young night, and we wound up walking for close to an hour. The complex proved serenely quiet, and the lack of surrounding traffic introduced a feeling of great peace. What's more, with the sun down, the temperature had dropped a few degrees, making for more comfortable conditions than in days previous. Hand in hand, we took our time and went looping around the place while watching the moon rise in the sky. I rather enjoyed myself, and I know that Rachel had a nice time, too.

That is, until we crossed into one of the dim parking lots—the one stationed between the third and fourth buildings in our usual sequence.

In our apartment complex, there are no streetlights in the parking lots. Rather, the buildings themselves are all mounted with bright exterior lights, the glow of which seeps into the lots, sidewalks and main drag. They draw a lot of insects at night, and are so bright, in fact, that we had to install blackout curtains in our bedroom in order to ensure decent sleep. The light produced by these staggered fixtures renders the apartments themselves in sharp relief even in the wee small hours, but leaves many spaces between the buildings mired in hazy shadow.

Striding through the lot, buried in thoughts about the work meeting I'd had just hours prior, I didn't immediately notice when Rachel stopped. It was only when I'd advanced several paces ahead and her steps had completely died out in the nigh silent landscape that I also came to a halt and turned around. "What's up?" I asked. Grinning, I gave the pedometer on my wrist a little shake. "Need a break already?"

Rachel wasn't looking at me, though. She'd paused on the sidewalk, and was staring at a small sedan parked in a visitor's spot. In fact, she wasn't just staring—she appeared utterly *entranced*.

"What's the matter?" I asked, backtracking just a bit. Following her gaze, I gave the car a once-over myself—and that's when I noticed what had so fiercely gripped her attention. "Oh... Oh, man, that's *foul*..."

The front end of the car was covered in what appeared to be massive flies. Brown, red-eyed bugs the size of nickels, with large transparent wings, were heaped upon the hood, windshield and roof. There must have been a few dozen of the things, and I knew at a glance that they were no mere houseflies. These things were big and nasty—the kinds of flies with a genuine bite.

"You don't see that every day," muttered my wife with a shudder. "What in the world *are* those, Len?"

I gulped, taking a step back. The flies scarcely moved. They weren't buzzing around the car, weren't crawling about it in insectival exploration. They were all just sitting there, heaped on the auto glass, on the wipers and side mirrors, as though awaiting a lift. "No clue," I said. "They look nasty, though. Maybe I'll look 'em up later... Big, brown flies with red eyes..."

Rachel looked to the other cars nearby—to a pick-up at the right, and to an SUV at the left. "The flies are only on *this* car," she noted with a frown. Gesticulating to its neighbors, she added, "There are none on the truck or the SUV... They're all just gathered *here*. Don't you think that's strange?"

I nodded, eager to put as much space between myself and the flies as possible. "It's *definitely* strange, yeah. And if I'm honest, I'm not too keen on hanging out with them."

Rachel finally pulled away and raced past me on the sidewalk, hands in her pockets. "That's so gross. What could cause so many flies to just cling to a car like that? It's *disgusting!*"

I chuckled, panning about the apartment building and shrugging. "Who knows? There's something about that car they like, I guess. Maybe there's a bad smell about the car they're drawn to. Could be that the owner stepped in a turd at the dog park before his last drive and the flies are investigating."

She nodded. "Could be. Or maybe... Maybe he hit a bit of roadkill or something on his way home." She kept on nodding, this theory taking root in her mind. "Maybe some bits of a dead animal are stuck to the tires or undercarriage."

"Sure, sure," I said, quickening my pace. Then, tapping at my pedometer to gauge our progress, I smirked and added, "Or, you know, there could be a body stashed in the trunk."

Rachel stopped dead in her tracks. We'd built a good bit of distance between ourselves and the sedan in question, but she turned and glanced over her shoulder as though she expected to find it creeping up on us. "Y-You really think so?"

"Don't be ridiculous," I replied. "Dude just needs a carwash or something."

Still, my wife didn't seem so easily convinced. She studied the vehicle in question for several seconds—even backtracked a few paces—before joining me with a defiant shake of the head. "Something about it really creeps me out," she ultimately said. "I've never seen anything like that. Have you?"

"Not really, no. But, so what?"

"It's gross," she protested.

"No argument from me."

"It's *unnatural*."

"Strictly speaking, it's *perfectly* natural. This is the great outdoors, after all. If a bunch of bugs want to hang out on a car, then who are we to tell 'em '*no*'?"

We rounded the next corner and broke away from the strip of parked cars, but still the ordinarily jovial mood of our walks had been somewhat spoiled. I tried making a little small-talk about my work meeting, complained about my boss's rantings, but Rachel only half-listened as we stomped along. Her thoughts were elsewhere, and every time she peeked over her shoulder with a narrow gaze and a hard frown, I knew just where her mind was.

It was around the time we came upon the communal dumpsters that she halted once again. The pair of receptacles—large, squarish and heavily-rusted—had been packed to the heavens with all manner of trash. Someone had probably been evicted not too long ago and their apartment thoroughly renovated by the property managers. At least, that was *my* assumption. Aside from a good deal of furniture, there were empty paint cans, rolls of old carpeting and several tarps stuffed into the two dumpsters.

"What's your over-under on a recent eviction?" I posed, whistling as the gated dumpsters entered into view. "They must have left quite a mess if the property managers had to tear out the carpet and such."

Rachel nibbled on her lower lip and approached the teeming bins with altogether more interest than she'd ever shown in garbage before. "Either that... Or someone was killed in one of those apartments, Len. It could be that the killer tore up the carpet... disposed of bloodied furniture and painted the walls..." She shot me a little glance in the corner of her eye, and I admit I couldn't tell whether she was trying to pull my leg.

"You know what I love most about you?"

"The way I look in yoga pants?"

"Yes," I replied. "Your imagination is definitely a runner-up, though. In the top five, at least."

She folded her arms and then pivoted purposefully toward the rolled-up carpets. With gusto, she reached up and tugged at the stuff, presumably looking for stains.

"Whoa, listen, knock that off," I said. "There's no telling *what's* living in that carpet. If you bring home fleas or bedbugs, I'm going to make you sleep on the porch."

"C'mon, Len! Don't you see the connection?" She clicked her tongue and moved briskly from the dumpsters, continuing our pre-planned circuit across the blacktop.

"I think you've spun a story in your head and you're determined to see things your way," said I. "You're jumpy, out of your element. This is why we shouldn't go for these walks after dark."

"Whatever."

We trudged on in near silence for the next half-mile—I toying with my pedometer and happily watching the step count rise and my wife panning the other sidewalks for either looming figures or dogs to pet, but finding neither. We passed a handful of open windows along first-floor units, listened to families cleaning up after dinner, to people watching television or singing along to music. By day, when the lots were mostly empty and the occupants of these apartments were at school or work, it was easy to write the whole place off as a vacant shell—a facade. Now, passing through it silently under cover of night, we were reminded of the fact that we were always surrounded by others. The joys, sufferings, yearnings and idiosyncrasies of other human beings were always but a door or window away, even if we sometimes failed to remember that fact.

I couldn't keep my mind from wandering as we walked, and I got to wondering, as we took in one scene after another, whether anyone had ever *died* in one of these apartments. As far as I knew, the complex had been around a few decades—built in the late 80's or early 90's. In that time, there'd probably been countless accidents across the property. Falls, cuts, burns and medical emergencies of every shape and kind had almost certainly visited the complex since its founding.

But what about a murder?

Had anyone ever been *killed* in one of these apartments?

By the time this question rose up in my mind, we were well into our second lap, and it came as something of a surprise to us that we were drawing near, once more, to the fly-covered sedan that'd so disgusted us. It was Rachel who first noticed it again, encountering it with a terrible gasp, as though it'd come up and elbowed her in the gut. "Ugh," she spat, "there it is again..."

I paused before the car and looked it over from end to end. Perhaps it was only my imagination—in fact, it *had* to be my imagination—but it seemed as though none of the flies had moved an inch since my last study some twenty-odd minutes ago. They were living things; their little hands moved in that grotesque scheming motion so typical of their kind, and their wings sometimes fluttered as they shifted their weight. A few seemed to leap up now and then, catching the breeze, only to sail back down and settle on the hood with a buzz and a thump.

I got as close to the thing as I could stand and squinted at the exterior. "Is there something on it? Maybe something got spilled on the car," I ventured. "You know, something sweet—something that would attract insects. A soda, perhaps."

Rachel left the sidewalk altogether and began studying the vehicle from every side. She made a rather obvious show of peering into its side and back windows, and when she arrived at the car's rear, she had a truly miserable look on her face. "Get a load of *this*," she said, jabbing a finger toward the back seat.

It was dark out, but the exterior building lights allowed one to look into cars parked along this front strip. I squinted through the tinted glass, but not before casting a nervous look at the three-story building in front of us. The last thing I wanted was to get chewed out by someone for suspiciously poking around their car. "What is it?" I asked.

"The back seat is full," explained Rachel.

I saw that it was, indeed. The entire back seat was lined with what appeared to be large coolers—the kind one might haul to the beach to keep drinks cold. Curiously, their white plastic lids were covered in strips of duct tape, keeping them tightly shut. "Coolers, huh? That tape certainly won't make it easy to fish out a cold brewski, eh?"

"They've been taped shut because they aren't supposed to be opened again. They're probably going to get dumped off somewhere... or buried..." posited Rachel.

I practically cackled at the insinuation. "What, you think a hacked-up body's been stored in 'em? Is that it?"

Rachel pointed back toward the front end. "That's not all. There's like twenty air fresheners hanging from the rearview mirror. *Look.*"

I did as I was told, and if anything found Rachel's estimate too conservative. There were indeed loads of tree-shaped air fresheners tied to the rearview mirror, as well as what looked to be odor-absorbing packets scattered across the dash. "So the guy likes his ride to smell fresh," I quipped. "Is that a crime?"

"Len!" My wife looked ready to sock me in the gut. "Something's wrong here! You know I'm right!"

"Hey, it's definitely weird. I'm not arguing. I'm just saying... You can't assume something this heinous without really good proof." I looked again to the apartment building, half-expecting someone to come charging out of the lower-story door. "For all we know, the guys's a hunter, right? Those coolers could be full of fish or venison or something."

With complete disregard, Rachel walked up to one of the back windows and all but pressed her face to the glass. Then, pulling away, she shook her head furiously. "Oh, no, no, no... No, Len, look! Look! There's blood! There's definitely blood on one of those cooler lids! It's a handprint—red and messy! Just look for yourself!"

"You're going to get us screamed at," I muttered. "This isn't our car and it isn't our business! Someone's going to come bounding out of one of these apartments any second..." I sidled up to the car and played at looking through the window. "I dunno, babe. I don't... I don't really see it..."

"*There!* Right there, on the lid! The one closest to the window, see?"

Sure enough, with a bit of effort, I spied what appeared to be a large rusty splotch on the lid of molded plastic. It was vaguely hand-shaped, but far more interesting to me was its apparent freshness; the splotch didn't look dry. "What the..."

"See? See? I *told* you!"

"It looks like it's still wet," I mumbled. "That's... that's weird."

"This is too much. We've gotta call the cops," she said. "Come on, let's call 9-1-1."

That was a bridge too far for me, though. "And tell them what? Some guy's got a bunch of flies on his car and a few large coolers in his backseat? He could have left that stuff in there after a cookout for all we know, babe."

"But what about the blood?"

"He threw a steak on the grill with his bare hands and got some on the lid when he went to close it," I guessed.

"And what about the stuff in the dumpsters? The rolled-up carpets? The furniture?"

"People get evicted every day. I bet there's stuff like that in *all* the dumpsters around here—not that I'd care to look."

"And the flies are just... ?"

"Hanging out. Enjoying the vibe," I reasoned.

"Wow."

"Look, what do you want me to do about it, babe? Want me to interrogate the flies? Ask them what they've been up to? What the fuss is all about?"

"*Wow...* You're so above it all, Len."

"I'm just trying to be reasonable!" I shot back. "Sorry that I don't buy this whole murder mystery thing, OK?"

"You're just going to ignore the—"

I threw my hands up. "You wanna call the cops over this? Be my guest. Call it in, if you want. We'll all have a good laugh about it someday. But they're not going to do anything because there's no evidence of wrongdoing! Trust me, babe, this is no big deal. It's all a little weird, but that's not a crime. Can we please just finish this walk?"

Rachel didn't take this request of mine particularly well; in fact, it blew up in my face. "You wanna finish your walk?" she echoed. "Well, go right ahead. I'll see you at home." Irritated, she pulled away at once, muttering as she sped off toward our place.

I called after her, tried to plead my case, but she wouldn't have it. She quickened her step, vanished around the bend, and I knew then that I'd be spending the night on the sofa in stony silence. The sound of her sneakers drumming against the sidewalk faded from hearing and I was left with only flies for company.

With a sigh, I continued my daily walk—less a march now than a stooping trudge. I was filled with all kinds of conflicting feelings as I moseyed on. On the one hand, I didn't feel as though I'd done anything wrong. Her insistence that something illicit had taken place had been silly. There was no proof of any crime here, nor any strong reason to suspect one—just a few oddities. I felt that she'd flown off the handle, had built a mountain out of a molehill.

Trouble was, Rachel had never been one to do that. I'd always known her to be pretty level-headed, and usually trusted her instincts on things. If something about this car situation was putting *her* on edge, then perhaps there really was something to it, and I'd been wrong to shut her down the way I had.

Subconsciously, I found my way back onto our usual track and completed the second lap, passing our front door and finding the lights on in our unit. *At least she made it back safely...* I thought. Briefly, I considered calling it a night and heading up to make amends. Knowing Rachel, though, I knew it better to give her a little space, and so I kept on past our building and entered into a third lap. This wasn't about health and fitness anymore; my continuing along the track was a strictly penitential affair now, and I shuffled along the sidewalk with my hands tucked into my pockets.

Without my wife by my side, I no longer found the walk enjoyable. Where the two of us had spent the previous months building up a consistent fitness habit, the greatest joy I'd reaped from the arrangement had come from spending time with her. Our banter, the closeness we'd shared—without these, the walk felt hollow and rote. While it was true that I was feeling better than I had in some time thanks to the increased activity, I hardly felt the motivation to continue without her presence.

I passed the dog park, where a woman tried coaxing a minia-ture pinscher through the gate on a short leash. I sauntered past balconies where smokers reclined and the occasional radio chirped, and from this or that open window such varied smells as Indian food, marinara and cheap beer seeped out into the open. None of it interested me; the sounds, sights and smells were nothing but a nuisance to my brooding.

It was quite without expecting it that I found myself coming up to the fly-covered sedan during my solitary third lap. I happened upon the thing with suddenness, and I admit I startled a little at the sight of it. There was nothing untoward about the thing, aside from the fact it was crawling with the gnarliest flies I'd ever seen in my life, but I recoiled from it all the same. Pausing on the sidewalk a few paces from its front fender, I scowled at it, as if to say, "You know, until *you* came along, I was having a perfectly lovely evening with my wife..."

That was when I heard it. The low, muffled metallic *thump*.

That it had come from nearby was plain; I watched as the flies on the hood of the sedan quivered in the wake of the sound, their wings stirred to life by the resultant vibrations coursing through the vehicle. It had come only once—a single blow, at once feeble and attention-grabbing—and I admit I swooned when I heard it. I peered past the buggy windshield and scoped out the interior, but failed, at first, to make out the source of the faint bang.

Leaving the sidewalk and wedging myself between the sedan and neighboring SUV, I glanced furtively through the back windows, finding only the succession of taped-up coolers from before. The front seats remained unoccupied, and there were no signs that anyone had accessed the vehicle since my previous lap.

But something was evidently stirring within. There was another bump, this one louder than the first, and I heard it most clearly as I shimmied up to the car's rear bumper. With a tremor in my breast, I dared to reach out and touch the top of the trunk. To my horror, the auto body was still quivering, and through the shell I could sense minute movements, as of a weight being groggily shifted.

Something was in the trunk. It moved slowly, sporadically, as if only tenuously conscious. And more than this, as I stood by, aghast, it *spoke.*

"*Please... Please...*" Unsteady whisperings poured from the trunk as the occupant suddenly tossed his weight to one side. Male or female, I couldn't say—the voice was too low, too breathy and pained. "*Please, there isn't much time... Please, come closer...*"

"Y-Yes?" I dared in a tone hardly more formidable than the trunk-dweller's. "Are you... are you hurt? In danger?" Such questions were admittedly ridiculous to ask under the circumstances, but never having encountered such a thing I hardly knew *what* to say. "I hear you."

A terrible groan issued from the trunk. The imprisoned one fought to orient himself, to sit upright, perhaps, and sent the whole sedan rocking on its suspension. Flies scurried up onto the car roof, and their buzzing momentarily eclipsed everything else from hearing. "*Please,*" continued the pleading, "*there isn't much time. Come... closer... I must tell you something...*"

"Yes, of course," I whispered back. Slowly, keeping my eyes pinned on the apartment building, I knelt down and very nearly pressed my ear against the top of the trunk. "What is it? I'm here for you, I'm listening..."

I heard a slow inhalation through the thin barrier of plastic and metal.

And then, unexpectedly, a *laugh*.

A *slow, dry and sinister* laugh.

"*You were right.*"

Shouldering equal parts bafflement and unease, I shook my head. "I'm... I'm sorry?" I drew away from the trunk a little, my breath fogging up the finish. "What do you mean?"

"*You were absolutely right, on that first lap.*"

"I don't... I don't understand..."

The laugh rumbled through the shadowed confines, terminating in a higher register. Almost tittering, the one in the trunk elaborated, "*You told the woman there was a body in the trunk... I heard you... And you were right... There IS a body in this trunk. And in the back seat, too. And UNDER the seats...*" The laughter reached an almost childish fever pitch.

I swallowed hard and lost my balance, sitting on the asphalt while the flies crescendoed overhead.

The trunk was pummeled from the inside by a wild fist. "*Let us out, will you?*"

This was obviously a disgusting joke of some kind. The vehicle owner was simply trying to get back at me and Rachel for our nosiness, and had crawled into his trunk in the interest of giving us a big scare.

And it was certainly working.

"All right, that's enough," I said, gaining my feet. "I'm sorry for being nosy. I didn't mean any harm."

The inside of the trunk was treated to a one-two punch which left the inner panels groaning. "*Let us out.*"

I backed away, appealing to the neighboring cars and buildings for aid. The lot was quiet and empty, however, and most of the apartments along the stretch sat dark and still.

"*Let us out. Let us out!*"

The only piece of technology I had on me was the wrist-worn pedometer, and as I staggered away from the sedan its display lit up with a cheery alert, informing me that my heart rate was elevated. I was in the habit of leaving my phone at home during these walks in order to stave off the temptation of scrolling, and so would have to make it back to the apartment before I could dial 9-1-1. I rushed off, jerking in terror with every thump at the trunk lid, but did not feel truly threatened until, several paces on, I heard the thing spring open with a terrific squeal.

I turned in time to watch the trunk fly open. The smell hit me before anything registered visually; a stomach-churning stench which joined notes of rot and artificial sweetness poured out across the lot. It was the smell of warmth-goaded decay holding hands with the cloying aroma of a gas station air freshener.

The night was blackened by a surge of coin-sized flies; the beat of their wings as they fled the confines of the trunk could have blotted out a siren in the distance, and the things fanned out in a nauseous wave across the lot, perching on the sidewalk, on adjacent cars, on the blacktop and on their quivering fellows themselves, till every surface within a dozen feet of the sedan seemed to wear a living carpet of the things.

But this was not the only thing that emerged from the trunk. A thin figure clutched at the edges of the rear bumper and came shambling out, one leg at a time. Feet met the asphalt with the squelch of sticky blood, and the whole of the figure, evidently doused in gore, acted as human fly-paper; scores of the brown flies clung to him. Whether the thing that began limping after me was more man or fly, I couldn't even begin to say. I was less sure that he even existed. I felt myself in the grip of a mind-numbing hallucination—a waking nightmare.

For the first time in years, I ran.

Feet firmly on the ground, I put my sneakers to the test and bolted across the lot. Concepts like fatigue and fitness meant nothing to me as I broke into a full-on sprint; all I knew was survival. I rushed headlong into one of the green fields between apartments and, when I'd broken across the main drag, centered the glowing lights of the nearby convenience store in my sights. Following said lights like a beacon, I threw myself forward at full-tilt till I could no longer hear the sticky, clopping tread behind me, nor the low and constant hum of angry flies.

I all but collapsed on the stoop of our building. Pausing just long enough to ensure I wasn't still being trailed, I stole in through the lobby door and pulled myself up the stairs till I arrived shuddering at our unit. I pounded at the apartment door for all I was worth, realizing with a string of curses that I'd also left my keys, and kept my gaze fixed on the lower lobby, waiting for the shambling, fly-covered thing to enter the building. Mercifully, it never did, and Rachel—summoned by my maniac pounding—was quick to answer the door. "Len, what's gotten into you?" she asked.

I pushed past her and slammed the door shut behind me, only then realizing just how out of breath I was. My hair was matted to my brow with sweat, and I could hardly drink in enough air to form words. I bolted the door and staggered a little ways into our living room, where I slowly approached our street-facing window. Tugging the blinds aside, I scoped out the sidewalks below, looking for the hideous thing that'd come loping out of the sedan. Not so much as a fly entered into view; the night was peaceful, with traffic remaining sparse and nothing in the way of passersby.

"Len! What's the matter? What's wrong?" Rachel gripped my soggy shoulders and gave me a hard shake. "You're so pale! Are you feeling all right? Do I need to call an ambulance?"

Confident now that I'd escaped the thing, I pulled away from her and collapsed into my easy chair, head in my hands. There, I waved her off and insisted that I did not, in fact, need an ambulance. "I'm fine," I told her repeatedly. "Nothing's wrong. Nothing's wrong..."

She didn't believe me, of course. Settling on the sofa beside me, she held my trembling hand and swept the sweaty locks out of my eyes. "Len, honey, what happened out there? What's wrong? Did something happen?"

When my heart had finally stopped jack-hammering in my breast, I summoned a deep breath and spoke up. "You were right, Rachel. You were right..."

She arched a brow and shook her head. "I was right? What do you mean?" Glancing toward the window, I knew she was thinking back to the sedan, to the flies, to the little spat we'd had. "Is this about..."

I couldn't burden my wife with what I'd seen. Rachel had been right—something *had* been wrong with that car. There *had* been something in it. But rather than admitting this and getting her more deeply involved, I chose to shield her from the truth. "You were right," I ultimately said. "These walks aren't doing it for me anymore, babe. I need more than just walking. We should join a gym and start running together, just like you suggested."

———

I didn't sleep a wink that night, and wound up having to take the next day off of work. I was up late enough to hear the garbage trucks trundle by in the wee small hours, and when next I dared a short walk around the complex, I found each and every dumpster empty.

The sedan parked in the visitor spot—the one that'd been covered in flies—was also gone. It'd been moved at some point in the night, and as I paced the grounds I couldn't find so much as a single dead fly in the area.

I did, however, happen to run into one of the maintenance workers as I strolled by. Mac, a handyman who'd been at the complex some years, shook his head at me as he sat upon the hood of his truck and smoked an afternoon cig. "Some of these people, I tell ya..."

"What happened?" I asked. "Another backed up sink? Someone put too much pasta down the garbage disposal?"

"No," he said with a laugh. "Some idiot," he explained, pointing at the building ahead of us, "moved out the other day, but he tore up all the carpeting before he left."

"This building, here?" I asked.

Mac nodded. "Tore up every scrap of carpet in the living room, left the subfloor exposed. He painted the walls, too—but not in the right color. We're gonna have to repaint 'em, now. I don't know what he was thinking, but I wouldn't be surprised if he was using his apartment as a drug lab or something. You know how people are, getting up to no good. Anyhow, it's a big headache. I'm going to be stuck in there all day cleaning up after him! I hope the manager takes him to court for damages, though I rather doubt he will. The owners of the complex are spread so thin they'd rather crack the whip and have guys like me mop up the mess."

"I see..." The building Mac had pointed to was, of course, the very one the sedan had been parked outside of the night previous. Whether the horror I'd encountered and the damage to the apartment in question were related was, technically, an open question. It was possible that the two events were unrelated—that Mac's contention was correct, and that the hideous run-in I'd had with the thing in the trunk had had nothing to do with the goings-on within the stripped apartment unit.

Whatever the case, I never did go for a walk in the complex again after dark, and something like a year later, when I was offered a decent promotion, Rachel and I moved far from the place, settling in a quiet neighborhood in a different zip code.

A CERTAIN SMILE, A CERTAIN SADNESS

Some nights, while seated by the bedroom window, my grandfather would smile. I remember that smile well, even after all these years—that particular smile that a stray memory would invite to his lips. Somewhere between fussing with his pipe, feeding scraps into the wood-burning stove and humming bawdy sea shanties, he'd find himself steeped in the world of decades past and I'd hear him chuckling from my spot on the rug. That laugh of his meant one thing: He was about to share a good story.

There were other times, though—times when, I suppose, the memories stung him in the heart and his ordinarily stony expression only grew stonier for the remembrance. The sadness that sometimes took up station in his eyes while he ruminated on old miseries never failed to rouse my curiosity, and I would sometimes set aside my crayons, my blocks, to ask him what was wrong.

There are a great and many things that children do not understand, and my grandfather—who shuffled off his mortal coil at the ripe old age of ninety-two—knew this very well. When pressed, his expression would shed every trace of upset with practiced ease, and he would distract me by motioning out his window at the crooked maple that grew in the front yard, or by noting the phase of the moon.

Once, though, he didn't put me off. Once, when that particular sadness gripped him, he didn't wash his hands of it, but instead let it linger there while he bit down on his pipe. I can't say why he decided to speak his mind that night; for that matter, I don't know what, exactly, dragged so strange and awful a memory as the one he went on to share to the surface.

The moon was high and full, an orb of gold that seemed likely to stream down the velvety sky like a teardrop at any moment. A month or so prior, my grandfather's property had echoed with the cries of cicadas; now, the trees were bald, and the skittering of their fallen leaves filled out the long country silences instead. The crisp fall air sneaking through the open window and the regular pulsations of wood-scented warmth that poured out of the nearby heater made for a pleasing contrast. I spent many, many days in that house of his during my formative years, but I can't for the life of me remember what that room looked like by day. It's always dim in my reminisces. The little room was serviced by only a single lamp in the corner, with a tired greenish shade.

Knocking the ash from his pipe that night, I could tell that my grandfather was troubled. Though he held his tongue for quite some time, the desire to speak gradually won out, and when he cleared his throat and crossed his legs, passing the pipe nervously from one hand to another, I realized him on the verge of opening up.

What follows is the odd story he told me on that autumn night. I listened closely in that cozy hovel, sitting on the rug beside his chair while the fire popped at our backs. If I think hard, paddling through the noise of the intervening years, I can still hear his voice as he fixed his dark gaze outside the window and began through a puff of sweet smoke.

"The world I grew up in is gone, Jacob—and should you be blessed with old age, that's something you'll have to come to terms with yourself. You may not believe me, seeing me as I am today, at the end of my tether, but I was like you, once. Yes—I have been a boy, a young man, and, as they say, I have lived to tell the tale.

"I have little to complain about, really. I've been on this Earth for nine decades already. I've seen my children grow and succeed, and I've gotten to know my grandchildren. Why, if I'm still around when your cousin gives birth this December, I'll get to meet one of my *great*-grandchildren. I am blessed, my boy—truly blessed.

"And yet... And yet, if there is one aspect of growing old that I take exception to—just one that I have difficulty with—it would be that an accretion of years gives one more time to sit with certain things; more time to *remember*. The good and the bad together, the good *and* the bad. What's that? You thought the worst part of getting old was the aches and pains? The dicky joints? Bah! Those are unpleasant enough, to be sure.

"But in old age, so long as the mind remains intact, one has opportunities to stew on things. Happy memories are a joy, and for one who has achieved as many years as I have, one hopes that there are no shortage of those to meditate on. But the unpleasanter stuff? The stuff that keeps you up at night, makes your guts tie up in knots? You live with those, too. You carry 'em. If you're wise, you learn to lug the burden and soldier on—same as with those rickety knees or arthritic fingers.

"Once, in my younger days, I had a friend named Stephen. No, no—I was not quite so young as you are now, Jacob. I was, perhaps... fifteen—no, *seventeen*, years of age, now that I think about it. And, while we're on the topic of age, I *forbid* you from breathing a word about this conversation to your mother. Am I understood? She would surely disapprove of such talk as this...

"Now, my friend Stephen and I, we were both born in the old country, just before the war. My earliest memories involve air raids, bomb shelters—things that modern children have no acquaintance with. And what a mercy it is, to live and die in peacetime, Jacob...

"On a warm summer evening, I was out with Stephen, doing some fishing along the small stream on the edge of town. The fish were biting, I remember; you could catch all sorts of things in those days with just a pocketful of night crawlers and a makeshift rod. Sometimes we'd strike out with just nets or buckets and come away with enough shad and perch to feed our families for days!

"The sun was about to set, and we'd managed a respectable haul. Days of good eating, I tell you. But no sooner did we prepare to return home did we hear something overhead. A dreadful noise—one we both knew well. *Planes*. They charged through the sky, making a terrific racket, and left a whistling in their wake that made the hairs on our arms stand at attention.

"They were bombers, and within seconds our hometown was chewed up by explosives. I pray you'll never see the likes of it, Jacob—your friends and neighbors blown to smithereens, your hometown filled with smoldering craters. And the smell—the *smell!* It was a nightmare. I'd never been more scared in my life. You'd better believe we ran for cover! Of course, when fire's raining down from the sky and buildings are being knocked into rubble, there isn't much you can do, except hope for the best.

"We cowered, still knee-deep in the stream, until the planes finished flying past. Oh, they were thorough—they made at least two or three passes that evening, and they left the town brighter than they found it for the fires that now burned all across it. It had all been so unexpected. Our betters had assured us that the war was nearly won, and that a bombing of this scale was an impossibility. Because of that, we all got caught unawares. There'd been no time for evacuations, for piling into the shelters. No time to start up the klaxons, either. They hit us before we saw it coming, and people—good people—were destroyed within their very homes or while walking down the street.

"Stephen and I abandoned our things by the stream and rushed home after that, but we had a miserable time of it. Most of the streets—the major ones, anyway—were rubble. The smoke was coming in so thick that we could hardly see, and the fires were beginning to spread. We went shambling through town, looking for survivors. For a good while, perhaps thirty minutes, we didn't encounter even one.

"There were bodies, of course. Men, women, children—you name it, all cast about the scene. Collapsed houses were many, and in the distance we could hear the screams of those trapped within 'em. Most of those died out soon enough, though. Some succumbed to injuries, others to the smoke and flame. It was horrific to behold, worse than anything you see in the movies.

"Eventually, I can't remember how, we made it back to our neighborhood. Every other house looked to have been flattened, and the ones that still stood were hardly in good repair. Tongues of flame raged from the gaps in the ruins and sent clouds of black, choking smoke into the sky. We shouted at the top of our lungs, looking for our families, our neighbors. One of the most frightening things I remember from that day was the *silence* in the wake of our cries... We felt like the last two people on Earth.

"Our families survived the attack. We lost much, of course; our homes were in ruins and most of our possessions had been destroyed. But our lives, the most important things, had been preserved. Not that we had much time for warm reunions. No, being seventeen and able-bodied, we had to join the others in searching for survivors. Later on, in the middle of the night, the town would be filled with soldiers, and *they* were the ones who did most of the heavy-lifting in that regard. We just had to do what we could until they showed up.

"Stephen and I went poking around, joined up with other neighborhood kids who'd survived. We put out the smaller fires together, tried to round up some of the injured and elderly. It was quite a job, I tell you. In the process, we discovered a few casualties that were hard to swallow. Friends of ours, people we'd known all our lives. Friendly neighbors, pets...

"There was one, too, that I'll never forget. A block or two down from our houses, Stephen and I found a bombed-out shell, still standing on a small hillock. It had burned awhile, but not as badly as some of the others, so that when we happened upon it we were able to enter without too much trouble. Inside, we found a chaotic scene. Bits of the floor were missing, the windows were all broken out and the roof had partially collapsed.

"Inside, we found the woman who had lived there, too. She was a young, pretty woman—a schoolteacher. She'd only just moved in a month or two prior to the attack, and couldn't have been more than five or six years older than Stephen and I. Always well-dressed, with some lovely pieces of jewelry, she'd turned a lot of heads in town. Her husband, a military officer, was currently serving in a distant theater; he wouldn't find out about her fate till a month or so after the fact.

"The woman was dead. She was splayed out on the floor, her fine white dress singed, her hair dusty and tangled around the leg of a chair. Her eyes were wide, blank and bulging as ping-pong balls, and the string of pearls around her neck looked so strange to me against her cold, bluish skin. She'd died almost instantly, by the looks of it. A thump on the head, maybe—or too much smoke during the brief fire. I never found out just how she met her end. There wasn't any time to speculate just then; we had a job to do, and simply moved on in search of survivors.

"Well, the process of rebuilding was slow. Even after the war ended, it took us years to get things back to something like normalcy. Those early days were really hard, though. Barely any food to go around. Spotty shelter. We all looked out for one another, of course. Some were evacuated out for medical care. Some of us, like Stephen and I, remained behind with our families, simply making do. I suppose all of us younger ones did a lot of growing up in that period. This kind of tragedy... it leaves its mark, no doubt.

"Come here, Jacob. Shut the window, won't you? The breeze is getting a little cold for my likes. I'll see about the fire. You just shut that window and draw the curtains for me. Good lad. My eyes aren't what they once were. Out there, on the lawn, I almost thought I saw... Never mind, never mind. Now... let me see about this pipe. There we are.

"As I said, the days after the bombing were hard for us. Having reached the limits of what we could do, we watched the military men clear the rubble. We were available to help with the heavy lifting, of course. Along with our fathers, we worked long shifts doing menial labor. For food, we had to rely on whatever military rations we could get our hands on. A few fields in town hadn't been decimated, and these provided the odd tomato or cabbage. Then, of course, there was the stream...

"Awhile after the bombing, I found myself fishing with Stephen again. Just the two of us were out there, taking a break and trying to catch something decent to eat. I wasn't having any luck; my bait went untouched, and I was almost ready to start eating the worms myself, just to feel something in my stomach. Stephen, though, had more success; he hooked a nice-sized shad within ten minutes, and in the next half-hour he scored a whole string of perch. It didn't take me long to mosey on over and try my luck at his spot.

"That was when I realized that he wasn't using the same kind of bait I was. No, he'd skipped the usual night crawlers and had opted instead for a very fine little lure—a lure which incorporated what looked to be a few fine pearls. I asked him about the thing. *'Where'd ya get it?'* and *'How long've ya had that?'* I remember he shrugged. He got awfully quiet, and to put me off my questioning he promised to share some of the day's catch with me. It wasn't like him to be so evasive, to have that shameful look in his eye. Stephen was an easygoing fella, hardly the kind to act all secretive and such.

"It didn't take me long to realize where those pearls had come from. In all my life, I'd only seen pearls a handful of times. Most recently, I'd seen them in that blown-out house, where the two of us had stumbled upon the young teacher's body. Stephen knew I wasn't stupid, and before we left the stream he confessed everything to me. He made me promise not to tell anyone. And, to my credit, Jacob, I kept that promise. Till tonight, at least. But... the older I've gotten, the more I've wanted to break this particular promise. You see, there are some things that shouldn't be covered up. There are things in this life that should be brought to light...

"After the bombing, while we'd been tasked with looking for survivors, Stephen had gone off on his own. It'd been fairly late at night, and things had been so chaotic that no one had batted an eye at young Stephen wandering the ruined streets. He told me that he made his way back to that house on the hill; that, when he was sure there was no one nearby, he crept inside.

"There, with only the firelight pouring out of other buildings to see by, he stole across the rickety floors of the house and approached the dead woman. He helped himself to the string of pearls around her neck. They'd simply been too beautiful, he said. The moment he'd laid eyes on them that first time, he'd felt compelled to go back for them. '*The woman is dead,*' he told me. '*What need does she have of them anymore? Why oughtn't I enjoy them?*' That was his reasoning, I suppose. When the war was over, he planned to sell 'em off—to make some money a few towns over.

"I kept my word, didn't tell anyone—not that it didn't make me feel awfully uneasy. When we were through with that little chat, I didn't even want to eat the fish he'd caught with the aid of those ill-gotten pearls. But I tried to put it out of my head, Jacob. Stealing from the dead, especially under circumstances like those... it's unspeakable. It's *disgusting*, is what it is. But all of us, at some point or another, do things we ain't proud of in retrospect. I figured there wasn't any sense in *my* losing sleep over it, anyhow. If not for what happened next, I might've forgotten all about those pearls.

"One night—a week, maybe two after the bombing—Stephen showed up at my place looking spooked. He was pouring with sweat, his face whiter 'an bone china. I thought his eyes were gonna pop out of his skull when I answered the door a little gruffly and asked him what the ruckus was about. He pulled me outside, and he didn't say a word until we'd left our neighborhood behind and were walking up by one of the empty fields at the fringe of town.

"He went fishing through his pocket and pulled out the string of pearls; I remember how they caught the moonlight as he held 'em swaying between his trembling fingers. He was frightened, he explained, because he'd seen something while out for a walk just about thirty minutes prior. He'd been down by that ruined house, on the hillock, and while strolling by at sunset had seen the dead woman standing in the doorway, staring at him. *Grinnin'*.

"Stephen had gone running at the very sight of her—gunning down the street. Told me he'd never been so scared in his life. Of course, I could tell he'd been spooked, but I didn't really believe him. I agreed to follow him out there, and we made the walk, sure enough. When we arrived, there was no woman standing in the door. I even poked my head in—no one *inside* the place, either. Stephen, though, was convinced. He admitted that the last few days he'd been having weird feelings, especially at night. Seeing things in the corner of his eye. Hearing things, too. He didn't care to hear my opinion—that it was his guilty conscience. No, sir, he believed it was something else; the ghost of the woman he'd stolen the pearls from.

"We went our separate ways, and I thought we'd be laughing about that little episode before very long. I was wrong, however. The next afternoon, while heading out to the stream for a bit of fishing, I happened to bump into him. He tagged along, still as hunted-looking as ever, and I could hear him fiddling with the string of peals in his trouser pocket, real nervous-like. I plopped down on the bank and did some proper fishin' while he got to muttering about this whole pearl business.

"He said to me that, initially, there'd been something like thirty, maybe forty pearls on the string. He hadn't counted them, exactly, but knew there'd been a good few of 'em. He'd removed a few to make some lures, but should still have had a couple dozen on the line, by all accounts. With a quaking hand, he yanked out the string and started counting the things with pursed lips. Then he counted 'em again. And again. There were fewer pearls there than there'd been the day before. He was sure of it. By his estimation, he was losing one of them every day. He'd turned his pockets inside out and had looked around his home, but for all his trying he hadn't been able to find a single one of the missing pearls.

"If he was losing the ill-gotten treasure, it was just as well. His just desserts, I supposed. But with every passing day, my buddy started looking rougher and rougher. And his stories, well... they grew wilder and wilder. He began to have trouble sleeping, which his folks were happy to chalk up to all the chaos in our region. The war was a convenient boogeyman; you could blame just about any misfortune on it, except for the ones it actually caused. Doing that, you see, was 'unpatriotic' or 'bad for morale'... Stephen was in a bad way, though, and I don't believe it had anything to do with the bombing.

"In fact, when he turned up some days later, his string of pearls clearly lighter and his features becoming more haggard, I couldn't help but believe him. He confided in me that he could no longer sleep; that he laid awake on the little cot his parents had set up for him to use in their sole remaining room. Very late at night—three, maybe four in the morning—while his parents snoozed away with ease, he'd find himself visited by the shadowed, grinning form of that woman.

"She would stand at the bedside, her teeth creaking in a vicious smile. She said nothing, made no sound—didn't so much as lay a hand on him. But each of these visitations would come to an end the same way: Something small and solid would strike the wood floor beneath his bed. Then, the woman would turn and go just as quietly and suddenly as she'd arrived. And in the morning, Stephen would invariably find one less pearl on his string.

"He was convinced that she was slowly taking them back, that the sound he heard each night was that of a pearl being plucked from the string and dropped down onto the floor. Of course, his searches each morning were fruitless. He took up some of the wobbly boards in that old house but couldn't find so much as one of the missing pearls.

"Stephen wanted out. See, he was sure that, when all the pearls were gone—when the last had fallen from the string—he'd die. It was a feeling he had, in his gut, and considering how awful he was looking I half-shared in his belief. So, we started to brainstorm ways to get rid of the pearls. We sought ways to appease the ghost, if you will.

"Together, we ventured back to the little house on the hill by cover of night. Of course, the woman's body had long been buried by that point, and the place had been cordoned off by soldiers for a planned demolition. We snuck past the notices and Stephen dropped the pearls into a little crevasse in the floor, not far from the spot where we'd found her body. I remember him kneeling down and letting the whole string fall from his palm; and I remember, too, when he reared back and started wailing just seconds afterward, hiding behind me as if seeking protection.

"He claimed to have seen the woman under the floor, looking up at him while he'd dumped the pearls. No search on my part brought any such thing to light, and I was pretty certain that he'd hallucinated on account of his sleeplessness, or that the moonlight drifting in through the busted roof had played tricks on his heavy eyes. But he swore up and down that he'd seen her—that his fingers had nearly brushed up against her bared, grinning teeth as he'd carefully lowered the pearls down. With the matter settled, we ran out of that house in double-quick time and hoped that would be the end of it.

"It wasn't. Next morning, before sunrise, Stephen was at my door again. He'd managed a few precious hours of shuteye, he told me, but had been awakened by the sound of a pearl dropping to the floor. Worse still, upon rising, he'd gone rummaging through his pocket for his handkerchief only to discover the string of pearls there—one pearl lighter than it'd been the day previous.

"I accused him of fraud, of having retrieved the pearls from the house on the hill, but he denied it up and down. Denied it with tears in his eyes. What was I to make of that? He'd tried to do the right thing, to return the pearls, but somehow they'd wound up back in his possession. The woman was still after him and his life, he was sure, was still at risk. After all his pleading, I agreed to help him get rid of them some other way. The plan I came up with was a simple one. If the ghost of this woman was intent on bringing the pearls back to him, then we'd have to lose them in a place they could never be recovered.

"We took our rods and fishing gear with us and followed the stream for a long stretch—a few miles. Finally, on a day with good sun and a strong current, we made our way to the estuary. It's where the stream met other inland waters and connected to the ocean, see? These waters are often brackish, and larger fish—sometimes big, ocean-dwelling species—come through there. Well, Stephen and I set about doing some fishing. We each caught a handful of baitfish near town; into these we inserted a few of the pearls.

"Casting out with our baitfish, we stood by the banks and waited for the bigger fish to nudge our lines—which didn't take long. One by one, the baits were consumed, and the second we felt a bite we cut the lines and let the fish have 'em. Slowly, we got rid of every single pearl that way. They were swallowed up by the bigger fish, who gobbled their meals greedily and took off swimming for who knows where. With pearls carried off in the bellies of game fish in every direction, we finally felt like we'd come out the other end of the thing. Stephen, I remember, bawled like a baby. He'd been so scared, so out of his mind with terror and exhaustion, that he fell to pieces once we finished.

"We walked back to town together, and he strolled about like a man just out of prison—light and carefree. I knew he'd have no trouble sleeping that night, and for the first time since before the bombing, he was acting like his old self. We parted ways at the main road, and I went back home to help my father with some work around the property.

"You want to know if that was the end of it, Jacob? By all accounts, it should've been. It should have been over and done with after that. But it's never that easy when you're dealing with the dead. Don't get mixed up with them. Don't let 'em get their claws into you, my boy. Once they do, you're going to have a mess of a time getting free. Now, let's see about a little more wood in this stove, eh? There... She's burning good and hot tonight. I can hardly feel the chill anymore.

"The next morning, we all woke up to a big commotion. Someone, I don't remember who, went down to the stream right around dawn. While he was poking about, maybe fixing to do some fishing, he waded down into the shallows and stepped on something that didn't feel solid enough to be a rock. He started groping around with his hands, and realized in short order that he'd stepped upon a *body*—yes, a corpse, pressed down against the stream bed.

"I needn't tell you whose it was. That's right, my boy, that's right. It was old Stephen. The whole town was summoned to the stream in a hurry, and the men quickly hauled him out of the drink and onto the bank. There was nothing to be done for him by that point, and all of us knew it—most of all his parents, who I'm quite sure never recovered from the shock they received that morning. It appeared that Stephen had somehow drowned; that is, the military doctor who examined him before the burial couldn't find anything else that might've served as a cause of death. But there were some oddities in the mix... Yes, some strange bits, I say. I suppose, from where these well-meaning people were standing, the details I speak of only served to support their theories...

"It was assumed that Stephen had come down to the stream before daybreak, and that he'd gone into the water to hunt after freshwater pearls. Children in the area sometimes did this, though one only ever had much luck in that line by seeking after them in the more brackish and turbulent waters up by the coast. It was assumed that he'd been searching for pearls because, upon being hauled out of the water, his trouser pockets were found to be full of 'em. Must've been thirty or forty pearls, all told—but, oddly, not a single oyster shell as far as the eye could see. It was odd to *them*, of course. Not to *me*. I knew where those pearls had really come from, whose they really were. And so, Stephen's death was ultimately ruled an accidental drowning.

"Somehow, though, I don't think it was accidental. Why, you ask? Well, for one simple reason. You see, there was another strange thing about Stephen's death that's stuck with me all these years. People didn't know what to make of it back then; in fact, they did their best not to mention it. But ol' Stephen, my pal, he died with a broad, toothy grin on his face. That's right; he went out smiling like that jack-o'-lantern on the front porch out there, Jacob.

"If I had to guess, I'd say that he woke up that night to the dead woman at his bedside. And, just as he'd feared, she'd come to claim his life. He'd disposed of all the pearls, had thrown 'em all away. But that hadn't cured him of this haunting. It had only run down the clock and hastened the inevitable. Hand-in-hand, that woman must have brought him down to the water's edge. And there, she'd given him all the pearls back. But only after he'd breathed his last and gotten cozy on the stream bed...

"That was a long time ago, of course... What's that? You've seen it before? Well, certainly—pearl necklaces have been worn for ages, Jacob. Why, look here—this photo I always keep of your grandmother, in my wallet. See? Yes, she was younger in those days. We'd only just married. Quite the looker, eh? She had a string of pearls once, too, you see? I gave it to her as an engagement gift. They're in the dresser there, tucked away with all of her old jewelry...

"What's that? Oh, you're being a real corker there, Jacob. Just rotten. You say you've seen this grinning woman before—out on the lawn, standing behind the trees? Don't be silly, lad. You're letting that imagination of yours get the better of you. I tell you, I never saw her myself... Well, at least I don't *think* I have... My eyes aren't so good as once, but—The pearls, Jacob? Where did I get the pearls your grandmother was wearing in that photo? Well, that's... that's—Jacob, please, that noise was *not* a pearl thumping to the ground. It was the wood crackling in the stove, or perhaps an acorn dropping onto the roof. Don't be difficult, now! And don't you touch those curtains again till the morning, you hear? I won't have them open—not till daylight! Not on a night like this one..."

As it would turn out, my grandfather *did* live long enough to see his first great-grandchild born that December. Just what he thought of my cousin's decision to name the little boy "Stephen", well, I can't begin to guess. The birth proved a joyous occasion for him, though—yet another in the long line of happy memories that old age had given him an opportunity to meditate upon.

I wonder, even now, what other strange secrets he held onto over the years—what nasty little treasures might have been found in *his* pockets at the end, had only someone known what to look for. When the man finally passed, surrounded by his loving family in that same little room where I'd been told the foregoing story, only the creased wallet-sized photo of my late grandmother—wearing her string of pearls—was found in his pocket.

I have that very picture now—begged it off my father upon rediscovering it a few years back—and have placed it in a small frame. To glance at it is to feel and wonder many things. One can't help wondering if the pearls my grandmother wears are the very same that Stephen pilfered from a young teacher, now long-dead. When I look upon it, I feel myself transported to another time and place—to a perpetual autumn that lives and breathes and rustles somewhere just beyond my periphery. The air is always crisp and earthy there, and the wood-burning stove staves off the chill. In that world of falling leaves, my grandfather still lives, his pipe clenched tightly between his teeth, and I am but a boy, peering out the window at the gathering dusk.

One of these days, perhaps I'll gather up the courage to ask him outright.

ROTTER

Jonathan always found the best stuff.

I suppose, when you're an insomniac, you've got to find something to fill the wee small hours with. In Jonathan's case, he'd scour the web till dawn, searching for novelty. Sometimes, he'd trawl the digital deeps and wind up with an anemic yield, finding only lame reposts and edgy trash. There were other times, though, when his nightly haunting of certain forums and obscure chat rooms would bring him into contact with truly interesting—and, at times, *repulsive*—content. Spending so much time in such circles, it's a wonder he didn't delve into the dark web sooner.

Let me begin by admitting I'm no technophile, and I never have been. I know my way around a word processor and play a mean game of Minesweeper, but at day's end I just haven't got the patience to sit behind a computer for hours, hunting for something to gawk at. Now and then I can dig up a solid meme or screamer video, but compared to the nuggets Jonathan used to stumble upon it's all small potatoes.

All this to say: The stuff we watched that Halloween night was *his* idea. I wouldn't have been able to find it on my own had I tried.

When you're plugged into social media or using your phone to passively absorb entertainment on popular sites, it's easy to regard the web as harmless. But for those who dare to peer under the surface, there's a lot more to the internet than cat videos and political rage-bait.

Looking for hard drugs or illegal research chemicals? No problem. Want to have someone draw up phony legal documents or stage surveillance cam footage that no one will question? It's all yours—for a price. Got a jealous lover or annoying co-worker in need of killing? If you've got an internet connection and a bit of know-how, you're in luck...

There are pockets of the web, inaccessible to the general public, where terrible things happen in real time and utter nightmares are bought, sold and chronicled. These sites, sometimes termed "red rooms", don't show up in search engines, and sometimes you need specialized software just to connect to them.

Considered little more than an urban myth by many, like the snuff films of yesteryear, red rooms are said to be live streams depicting depraved and violent acts—up to and including actual murder. I have never visited one of these so-called red rooms and can't say whether or not they really exist.

But, once—and only once—Jonathan showed me something *very much* like a red room.

And I wish I'd never seen it.

Trick or treaters aren't as common as they once were. When I was a kid, we'd stay out past ten, eleven—long after most of the porch lights had been shut off and our neighborhood had been soaked in shadow. Halloween was the one night of the year you could get away with that; the mischief was built-in, expected. Now, I guess, kids prefer to stay inside on Halloween, parked in front of phones and tablets.

Well, that's exactly what Jonathan and I were doing on this particular Halloween. I had the night off, and invited him over to help me pass out candy—the lion's share of which we wound up wolfing down ourselves. A twenty-four pack of our favorite brew got things moving nicely, and I threw down for a couple of pizzas as the sun went down. We dished out handfuls of candy to kids dressed as superheroes and princesses, but found the streets empty by eight.

I remember Jonathan asked me about work, talked about a recent argument he'd had with his father—who he still lived with, and helped care for—and gushed endlessly on about a new online game he'd been playing. I could tell, though, that something else was on his mind. His long hair seemed to me more unkempt than usual that night, and the circles under his eyes were darker. He fidgeted a lot more, and little things like the sounds of dry leaves rustling against the sidewalk, or the far-off laughter of neighborhood kids, made him stir violently.

"Watch any good shows lately?" I asked him. "I took a sick day last week and binge-watched this new anime. The animation these days is such a turn-off, though. I miss when it was all hand-drawn."

"Not really," he replied. "My dad's been a real slave-driver recently. He spends most of his life in front of the TV but has the gall to break my nuts for spending all my time online. He never shuts up."

"He still in the wheelchair?" I asked. "Did that wound on his leg close up?"

Jonathan shook his head and waited until a few masked kids moseyed on from the porch. "Nah. Had to take him in for another round of antibiotics. He acts like it's my fault, too. I tried to do the dressing changes, but I'm not a nurse, you know? I keep asking my sister to come visit, to take care of him a few days, but she lives out on the coast and has better things to do."

"Doesn't she have kids?"

"Two of 'em, yeah. And she works a lot, too. I shouldn't complain, but it's all been on my shoulders since mom passed."

"That sucks, man."

He shrugged. "It is what it is."

We carried on in this way for awhile, reminiscing about college, trading bits of gossip and patching over uncharacteristic silences by playing the "Monster Mash" on repeat. I could tell that he was holding back, that he was biding his time. He'd accepted my invitation, but when it came to all this festive stuff he was clearly just going through the motions. I wondered what was eating at him.

It wasn't until we went inside, put some work in on the pizzas and threw back a couple more drinks that he told me what was *really* on his mind. "Chris, there's something I've been dying to show you." He'd brought a backpack along with him, and I already knew what was inside. Jonathan always carried his laptop around, as much to keep up with his bustling digital life as to show me new and interesting things he'd come across while web-surfing. He eased the laptop out and set it on my kitchen table, continuing, "All this dark web stuff I've been looking into recently... The red rooms—you remember?"

I cracked the tab on a fresh beer and emptied it in a few gulps. "Not really," I hissed through the sting of carbonation. "That some kinda porn thing?"

"No, no," he said. "The red rooms!" He waggled his brows as if the gesture might jog my memory. "A livestream, right? Anything can happen—even murder, for the right price."

"Oh, right!" I chuckled. "The sicko stuff. I remember, I remember. What about it? You're not burning your Bitcoins to watch e-girls get their throats slashed, are you?"

He laughed, easing the laptop open but keeping the screen pressed to him covetously. "Not exactly..." He cleared his throat, glancing around the dining nook as if to make sure the two of us were alone. He was seated by the window, and I remember thinking it odd—funny, even—that he stopped mid-sentence to draw the curtains. Jonathan had shown me some pretty twisted stuff before, but he'd never acted like *this* while doing it. I could tell that he was getting ready to share a real whopper. "I, uh... Awhile back," he continued, voice low despite us being alone in the house, "I happened upon this weird site. Someone mentioned it in one of the chat rooms I frequent. It's fairly new..."

"Yeah?" I put in. "And it's one of these red rooms? They're real?"

"Not exactly," said Jonathan. "But it's kind of like that. Anyway... it's one of the weirdest and creepiest things I've ever seen on the web."

"That's saying something," I replied with a grin. "Considering the fact that you once showed me that video with the—"

"I've shown you some real doozies, no doubt," he interjected. "But this one... this one blew *my* socks off." He let his computer power up and then threw a narrow glance over the bezel. "You want to see it?"

The night was young, and seeing as how it was Halloween I wasn't about to chicken out. The beers had me feeling good and loose, and I admit that Jonathan's strange behavior had piqued my curiosity. "Yeah, why not? How bad could it be?"

Jonathan moved over to my side of the table, and when he'd spent a few moments pounding on the keys, he pushed our plates out of the way and situated the computer between us. On-screen was what I can only call a simple—no, an outdated, ugly—website. The header, written in chaotic, scratchy text that would have looked at-home on a death metal album cover, read simply: ROTTER.

Jonathan's fingers hovered over the trackpad for a few nervous moments. Then, licking his lips, he began to scroll down the black page, which hosted a number of grainy photos in neat rows. These photos, eight in total, were framed in the same livid shade of red as the header text, and their pixelated subjects appeared at least somewhat uniform. I still wasn't sure what I was looking at, but understood these red blocks to be links of some kind. The eighth and last of these was quickly clicked, and Jonathan seemed to tense as a new page began to load.

The browser was dominated by a large viewing window—similar in shape and function to those on popular video-sharing sites. A trio of dots waxed and waned from left to right as the video buffered. What blinked on next was, for an instant or two, rather difficult to make out on account of low lighting and poor contrast.

It was only by a long and careful examination of the screen that I dared mutter, "Is that... Is that a *body?*" some few moments later.

Jonathan nodded solemnly. "Yeah, it is."

"I don't understand... What's all this, now?"

"This whole site—it's a place where you can come to watch live feeds of corpses decomposing within their coffins." He adjusted the screen by a few degrees, reducing the glare from the kitchen light overhead. His hands shook as he did so.

The figure on screen—a man, if I was reading the rigid face correctly—was largely bathed in darkness. From somewhere just out of frame there came a faint, powdery light, the effect and weakness of which served to exaggerate certain of the subject's features. Only the face and a portion of the shoulders and chest were visible, and the shot had been staged from above—zoomed in on the countenance of the sleeper. There was no movement, no sign really that this was, in fact, a live video feed—none, that is, except for an occasional grainy flickering. I knew that such an effect could be added to any still image to lend it the impression of animation, and immediately laid into Jonathan for having been taken in so easily.

"This is the lamest thing you've ever shown me," I told him, flat out. "They snapped a picture of some old guy sleeping and then threw, like, a VHS filter on it! Did you really think this was real?"

"Hey, come on, you don't think I'm *that* stupid, do you?" he challenged. "It's real. I'm telling you for a fact, it's *real.*"

"Nah, this is a dumb hoax. I can tell." I stared at the screen intently, looking for patterns in the occasional bursts of visual snow.

"First off, how are they powering the camera? Even something with a good battery is going to die after a little while. And the lights! You can't keep a light next to a corpse! The added warmth… it would speed up the decomposition quite a bit. And the whole thing is just so…" I ran a hand through my hair and slumped at the table. "It would be easier to fake it. Actually pulling it off would be really hard, not to mention pointless."

Still, Jonathan wasn't hearing it. "Listen," he began, "I'm not certain just how they've done it, but…" He swallowed hard and looked away from the screen. "I first stumbled upon this site like two weeks ago. At first, I thought like you did. I thought it was fake.

"But, you know… out of curiosity, I've checked it a few times since then. And every time I look at this particular stream again, I notice something's changed. You wouldn't know it just by looking at it this once, but… See his eyes? See how sunken they are? The way the flesh around them seems to be retreating? They didn't look like that when I first stumbled upon the site. They looked, well, *fresher*.

"And his mouth. See how his jaw is kind of shrinking in? Every time I tune in, I notice that more and more. His mouth was tightly shut the first time, but now… it's almost ajar. His nose is even sort of crooked, like… like it's slumping, and his forehead has a ding in it, like it's gradually deflating…"

My laughter echoed through the house. "Bro, you're *losing* it. Listen to you! Have you really been looking at this trash so closely? No wonder you can't sleep at night!"

"No, I mean it!" he snapped. Quickly, he reached over and backed up the browser, bringing us once again to the main page, with its numerous listings. He double-clicked on another of the red boxes, and as before we were faced with a buffering viewer window. "Here! Here's another one! I think this one's been here for longer, and you can see—"

The supposed feed came on with jarring speed, and the screen was filled with what I could only judge to be a youngish woman. It was hard to tell the precise age of the woman in frame due to the serious damages marring her face, but I took her for thirty-some-thing. Garbed in black and surrounded by darkness on every side, she, too, was watched from above with a light parked somewhere near her feet.

This specimen was dark-haired and wore what appeared to be a thin, silvery necklace. What most drew the eye, however, was her crumpled visage. Quite literally, her face seemed on the verge of a total inward collapse, with her small nose burrowing into the recesses of her skull and her lips curled back in an unflattering and permanent wince. The lids hung heavily on her eyes like un-ironed curtains, and her pale cheeks sagged against her ears. The corner of her mouth most exposed to the light had about it a greenish hue, and the flesh there was raised in a series of black-brown boils. As before, the unmoving image was dressed up with a bit of visual snow and video artifact, lending it the appearance of a live recording.

I still did not believe that we were looking at the genuine arti-cle—a rotting corpse smiling for the camera—but I was less vocal in my opposition this time around, and more plainly unnerved. "That's a nasty visual," I said, cracking a beer and taking a pensive sip. "Doesn't mean anything, but they did a fine job dolling her up. That bit of rot near her mouth was a nice touch. Realistic."

"That rotting flesh wasn't there the first time I tuned in," Jonathan was quick to interject. "I'm telling you, this isn't a hoax. I don't know how they're doing it, who these people are, but..." He nodded, returning once more to the menu page. "It's real. I'm certain of it."

"Real, fake... You know, either way this is twisted, right? If it's all a hoax, then it's just a time-waster for shock value. And if it's real, then it's in extremely bad taste. It would be disrespectful to the dead."

Jonathan rolled his eyes. "I've watched like hundreds of videos with you of factory workers in China getting torn to pieces by industrial equipment. When I showed you *those*, you didn't have any issue with disrespecting the dead."

"Say, that site we used to watch those on. Is it still live? I bet there's some horrifying new bits on there since we last checked..."

"No, it was taken offline," he replied. "Videos of that kind are still circulating out there, but it's getting harder to find them on the surface web. If you want the good stuff, you have to come here, to the deeps..."

"Good stuff like this sham of a website?" I scoffed.

Irritated, Jonathan scrolled up toward the top of the menu page, clicking the first in the sequence of links. He did so with a knit brow, uncharacteristically refusing my offer of a fresh beer. "Yeah? Let's see what you think about this one, then."

"What's this, now? Another supposed stiff?"

Jonathan ran a palm across his face and sat back in his chair, seeming almost frightened to look at the screen. "The ones listed highest on the page have been streaming the longest," he explained. "Get a load of this and see if you don't believe it's real..."

The video window opened. For an instant, the primitive site grappled with my Wi-Fi; then, with a dull glow, we were connected. From the very onset, I understood this video to be different from the rest. It was somewhat brighter than the others—this, I realized, on account of the figure's apparent shrinkage and retreat from frame.

Moreover, there was *movement*.

We were looking at a twisted human form in what looked to be a dark suit. The settling of the flesh and shedding of fluids had left it blackened and emaciated, so that virtually nothing of the cadaver's original appearance could be accurately gleaned. The corpse itself did not move—at least, its decayed bodily systems were not responsible for urging its gnarled limbs and sunken quarters to stir. Rather, the gradual release of gasses, coupled with the progress of pests through the wreckage of flesh and bone, were the culprits. These forces worked in concert to make the whole corpse tremble. Many-legged things made their tours across the fellow's rotten exterior, and where foul juices had pooled, rice-like maggots writhed ecstatically.

I watched, I admit, in horror. At first, I watched closely in the hopes of discovering some inconsistency proving it to be a looped video or GIF image. The black beetle stalking about the subject's half-empty eye sockets never repeated its route, however, and it was as I watched it retreat into the hollows of his skull that I realized the corpse was genuine. "What in the..."

"Every time I check in on this one, it's worse. I don't know how long this guy's been buried, but... it's been awhile. The camera fogs up sometimes because of the gasses, and... I've seen so many bugs in here. The casket itself must be breaking down at this point..."

"Enough," I said, turning away in disgust. A sip of beer sat on my tongue so long that I considered spitting it back into the can. "Turn it off, man."

"You believe me now?" he demanded, kicking us back to the main page. The ROTTER header burned against the dark background. It wasn't animated, but the thin tangle of lines that made up each of its characters seemed to writhe subtly, just as the maggots in the last stream had done.

"Suppose it *is* real," I said. "Who made it? And what for? This isn't professional enough or reverent enough to be a scientific study. And I refuse to believe that there are people out there who get their kicks watching these people rot..."

"I don't know," said Jonathan, easing back in his chair. I don't know who's behind it. There isn't exactly a FAQ section on the site. This is almost certainly illegal, so whoever is behind it will want to keep things under wraps."

"There's nothing?" I asked. "No clues whatsoever? Your buddies on these chat rooms, the ones who first turned you on to this site—they don't know anything?"

"Well..." Jonathan scrolled tentatively toward the bottom of the page, past the links to the eight active livestreams. "There's this..." The page's footer contained a block of text—an apparent log of updates and news items.

I leaned over and read the latest statement under my breath. "*Welcome to ROTTER. NEWS: October 28th—Join us at midnight EST, on Halloween, as we kickstart a new livestream.*" This brief bit of text was followed by a series of numbers and letters that struck me as little more than gibberish. "What's all this?" I asked. "Did the guy writing the update have a stroke?"

"No," explained Jonathan, "That's actually the address to a crypto wallet."

"A *what?*"

"If you use cryptocurrency, you can set up a digital wallet, you know? If someone knows your wallet address, they can send you funds. That long sequence there must be the site owner's personal wallet. I suppose he posts it so that viewers can support the site... Or, maybe, people are paying him in crypto to bury the corpses we see on stream..."

"*Nice.* So, if you've got a corpse just sitting around in need of burial, he'll take it off your hands for a little donation, eh? Make 'em a *star?*"

"It's possible..."

"Can you identify someone using this string of characters?" I asked.

"Honestly?" Jonathan shook his head. "I rather doubt it. The whole point of crypto is to be able to conduct anonymous transactions. It would take a lot of effort, and tools that probably only the NSA has access to, for us to figure out who this belongs to."

"Well, what are we going to do about it?" I asked, standing up. I paced around the table and parted the curtains, peering out into the dark streets. "If there's any chance that this is real, then shouldn't we... tell someone?"

Jonathan nudged the laptop aside and rested his head upon the table. "Who are we going to tell? The FBI?"

"Sure, why not?" I replied. "Isn't it possible to leave anonymous tips through their website?"

He fidgeted nervously at the suggestion and tugged at his hair while I stalked about the kitchen. "Look, Chris, this is messed up, but I don't know if I want to get cops or feds involved. That's a pretty big step, no? We don't know where this feed is coming from, and like you said earlier, we can't even be sure that it's real. I don't want a bunch of government thugs kicking in someone's door for what turns out to be a sick online prank."

I arched a brow. "Oh? Now you're singing another tune, huh? Why don't we pull up that last stream again and decide?" I challenged. "More and more, I've got a bad feeling about this. Who shared this with you? How does someone stumble upon a site like this one? Your pal in the chatroom or whatever didn't find this by accident. I'd bet on it."

He threw up his hands. "I dunno, man. It's Halloween, and this site is freaky. I just wanted to show it to you and get your take. It *could* be a fake, I'll admit it... but if so, it's a convincing one. We don't have to fly off the handle and dial 9-1-1; let's just forget it."

"Oh, but I thought this was the real McCoy!" I spat. "You were over here, shaking like a leaf just a minute ago, certain it was real. Now you're just gonna shrug it off? What's with you, man?"

He stood up and sighed. "All right, all right. I'm sorry, Chris. I shouldn't have even shown it to you. Let me take a leak and maybe we'll find something else to watch. You wanna stream a movie? I'm sure we can find something good." Jonathan motioned to the computer. "Go on, pick something. I'll be right back."

He left me with an open browser and a handful of titles to plug into Google. After the evening we'd had, I wasn't much in the mood for anything scary, but as the night was young I went scrolling through a few streaming sites and ultimately settled on an old, gloomy haunted house flick. I dumped some of the remaining Halloween candy into a large bowl and carried it, along with the laptop, into the living room, where Jonathan joined me some minutes later.

For an hour, almost two, I watched Bela Lugosi creep across the screen and nibbled disinterestedly on the same handful of Twizzlers. Although my eyes were on the screen, my mind was wandering darker pastures.

Jonathan, having shared his most recent find, seemed in a much better mood, now. He'd been privately obsessed with ROTTER for some time; by sharing it with someone else, I supposed he felt relieved in a weird way. He finally tucked into the beer, and at one point rummaged around in the fridge for some leftover pizza.

On any other night, this all would have made for a good time. As the minutes ticked by, however, I couldn't focus on the movie, on the booze or snacks. Every time I shut my eyes or peered into a dark corner of the living room, the faces of the cadavers would return to me and I'd be filled with equal parts horror and curiosity. Who could be behind such a dreadful site? Why create such a thing in the first place? I prided myself on being pretty unflappable, but something about ROTTER left me ill at ease.

Eventually, Jonathan started nodding off. I poked fun at him—here, finally, the insomniac felt relaxed enough to get a bit of shuteye. He chuckled along, but within ten minutes fell into a deep snooze, head lolling against the cushions and a half-finished beer in-hand. The credits started to roll, and I got up to tidy things while Jonathan snored in the veil of blue light.

I shuttled empty pizza boxes into the garage and clawed up a mess of candy wrappers and empty cans. After a quick trip to the bathroom and a scan of my phone, I found it was past midnight, and returned to the living room. I knew that Jonathan wouldn't stay all night, that he'd have to head home and check up on his father soon enough, but I decided to let him sleep off a few beers and took hold of his laptop. I closed out of the movie and prepared to power it down—and I would have, had I not noticed something odd in the lower-right corner of the screen.

Earlier, before we'd half-heartedly launched into the night's film, Jonathan had minimized the window we'd been using to view ROTTER. To my surprise, he hadn't closed out of it; the specialized browser window remained open. Ostensibly, I could return to the horrible site with just a click.

For some reason—let's call it morbid curiosity—that's exactly what I did.

While Jonathan slept beside me, I pulled up ROTTER and adjusted the screen brightness so as not to wake him. Sure enough, the site's landing page was still there, fully accessible, except that it wasn't the way we'd left it. A new, *ninth* stream was now available for viewing—the one that'd been promised in the site announcement we'd read.

I admit I clicked on this new entry eagerly. I hoped that it would lend some insight into the process behind ROTTER—that something in this latest stream would solidify it as a clear fraud or a proper horror. Unlike the other streams, this one took quite awhile to load; sickos the world over were excitedly logging on to check out the latest addition, leading to considerable lag.

It took thirty, maybe forty seconds, before the image came through.

My initial gut feeling as I took it all in was disappointment. I don't know what I'd been expecting, but the sight that greeted me was in no way different from all the others. It was a dimly-lit scene, the inside of a coffin, with the camera fixed on the face of a supposed cadaver. The only thing that'd changed was the corpse; in this case, the subject appeared to be an older man, maybe sixty or seventy years old, with stern features and a few sprigs of thin, gray hair on his head.

The man looked fresh—so fresh, in fact, that he didn't look like a corpse at all. The spoilage that'd disfigured the other subjects was not present here; he looked as though he'd climbed into the coffin for a nap just moments ago. I felt almost cheated as I watched the flickering footage and prepared to log off.

Something stayed my hand, however.

There was something about this stream—about the cadaver—that bothered me. I couldn't put my finger on precisely what it was, but as I scrutinized his shadowed face, certain subtle details in the low-lit scene demanded closer inspection. Maybe it was in the cut of his jaw, or the loftiness of his brow... Perhaps it was the bushiness of the man's eyebrows, or the unique tilt of his nose...

I recognized him.

Holding the laptop close—so close that I could've tapped the keys with my schnoz—I upped the brightness by a few degrees. Certain aspects of the face entered more sharply into focus and the feed wobbled convincingly through a fit of artifact. When the visual snow had passed, I became increasingly certain that I knew the face on-screen. Unable, or unwilling, to believe it, I looked to my slumbering friend, my shaky hands locked around his laptop.

Jonathan had the same chin as the fellow on stream, and his eyebrows were every bit as bushy as the man's, too. The indisputable link between the two figures, however, was in the singular shape of their noses; large, with a slight and uncommon rightward curve. Adjusted for age, the two might have looked like relatives, brothers.

Or even father and son.

I watched in horror as Jonathan's father lurched suddenly. The corpse took a ragged breath, and one of his large, dark eyes flashed open. A thump, as of limbs striking the inside of a wooden box, echoed from the speakers, and a series of low murmurs welled up in the figure's throat. The murmurs soon graduated into agitated noises, slurred cries. Both eyes were open now, spiraling confusedly in their sockets. There was little room for the head to turn, and the blows that came from his gnarled paws proved too feeble to damage the coffin. He gasped, looking for air but scarcely finding any.

The man was still alive.

I don't quite remember what happened next—if it was my cry, the sounds of his father's vain struggles over the speakers, or both, that woke Jonathan. I all but threw the laptop down onto the coffee table, where it fell shut on its old hinges. Jonathan came to with a start, spilling a bit of beer on his pants as he sat up. "Oh, man, did I fall asleep?" he muttered.

I said nothing. I was trembling all over, still staring at the laptop with wide eyes, like it'd bit me.

"I slept through the movie?" he continued, easing himself up. "Man... what time is it?" He glanced at his phone and uttered a string of curses. "I gotta be getting home..." He picked up his computer and carried it back to his bag, in the kitchen. Helping himself to a glass of water, he laughed—made some small talk about how well he'd slept. "Didn't mean to stay so long, man. I'll get out of your hair."

I followed him into the kitchen, then over to the door, where he stepped back into his shoes and prepared to leave. "You, uh... you gotta go check on your dad, huh?" I said. The question was bait, and I studied his reaction to it very carefully.

He hesitated a little, double-checking the zipper on his book bag, and nodded. "Yeah, I'm sure I'll get an earful for staying out so late."

I wanted to challenge him—to accuse him. But then, as we stood there by the door, the autumn coolness seeping in through the small gaps in the frame, I began to doubt what I'd seen. Had Jonathan's father really been the latest addition to ROTTER? "Now, this is serious... I want to talk to you about that website, Jonathan..." I gulped, steeling myself. "The things I saw on there—"

He interrupted me before I could even find the right words. "I've been thinking about what you said, Chris," he began. He had his back to me, was facing the door, but I could tell he was smiling. "You're right, man. You were totally right. It's a hoax. ROTTER is just a scam, no doubt about it. It was stupid of me to get so wrapped up in it."

I stared at the bag he clutched in his left hand. The laptop in it subtly shifted, and I couldn't help imagining the thing full of twitching, severed limbs.

"Anyway, forget all about it," he continued. "Just forget I ever showed it to you, man." It may have only been my dazed mental state, but those parting words of his struck me as a warning, more than anything. It was not friendly advice; I was being subtly instructed to wash my hands of the affair—lest I wind up on a future livestream.

He opened the door and stepped out onto the porch. I watched him hop into his car and pull out of the driveway. Within thirty seconds, he was completely out of sight.

Jonathan and I don't hang out anymore. I started dodging his calls and texts, and the two of us grew apart after that night. Even if I'd somehow gotten the matter all wrong—even if Jonathan hadn't arranged to have his father buried alive and the murder live-streamed on an obscure dark web platform—the Halloween incident was a wake-up call for me, and I decided to make more normal friends. Sitting up all night, watching shocking videos, is a great way to rot your brain. I decided to ditch the guy and take up hiking or rock-climbing instead.

After a lot of mental back and forth, I fired up my own computer the next morning and filed one of those anonymous tips on the FBI website. I don't believe anything has come of it, and I'm not sure that anything ever will. Sites like these are probably a dime a dozen on the dark web, and identifying guilty parties is next to impossible thanks to layers upon layers of encryption and digital redirection. Anyhow, Jonathan hasn't gotten picked up by the feds on account of my little tip, and I've seen nothing in the news about ROTTER being investigated, either.

For weeks and months after, I occasionally did some sleuth-work, trying to dig into the history of this terrible site. As can be imagined, I didn't uncover a whole lot. The kinds of people who are close to this sort of thing are precisely the ones who know better than to run their mouths about it. I never worked up the nerve to dive into the deep web myself, to actually dig up the site, but I made burner accounts on a few forums and chatrooms, and asked savvier netizens about ROTTER. Last month, I got one reply from an anonymous user claiming to be familiar with the site. He said that it was no longer online; that the owner had shut it down and possibly relaunched it under a different name and address. This is a common move for sites hosting illegal content; at the first whiff of trouble, they'll abandon ship and regroup in some other dark corner of the web.

If ROTTER is still out there, I don't know what name or URL it's hiding under.

And I can't even begin to guess at how many livestreams are listed there now.

The one thing that keeps me from pushing too hard and asking too many questions is the fear that I might one day end up among them...

SPAGHETTI NIGHT

The shadowed thing wriggled in the corner, its gray eyes cutting into him from across the cellar. He heard it speak, voice scarcely louder than the hum of the naked bulb flickering overhead. It hissed out the same message—the same invitation—that it always did. *"Go on, take the knife. Plunge it into your breast. There's nothing to live for, my friend. Nothing at all..."*

For nights on end, he had been plagued by the shadow's insistent calls to self-murder. It was true enough that things had been going badly. First, there'd been the dust-up at work and the subsequent layoff. The mailbox, crammed with letters from debt collectors, was something he'd come to studiously avoid. One of these days, his phone plan was going to be canceled; till then, he did his best not to answer any calls from unfamiliar numbers, lest his ears ring with demands for money. Tensions with his wife, too, were coming to a head...

Although filled with despair, he was not yet willing to embrace so permanent and extreme an end as suicide, however.

Least of all on spaghetti night.

"Look here," he replied to the ghastly thing in the corner, "you say there's nothing much to live for, but that isn't true. Tonight, my wife is cooking my favorite meal—spaghetti. She happens to make the sauce herself, you know. It's an intricate, hours-long cooking process, and the finished product is the finest I've ever tasted. Someday, I may yield to your temptations, but... not tonight. Not on spaghetti night. Now, leave me alone..." Glancing at the knife he'd smuggled out of the kitchen some days prior, he stashed it behind the clothes dryer and stood up.

The wraith in the corner watched him as he started toward the steps. "*You should listen to me,*" it cooed nauseously. "*Don't go up there. Stay here, with me. Bury that knife in your heart and the two of us can keep each other company forevermore...*"

He ignored the thing and climbed up the stairs, shutting the basement door behind him. Striding into the kitchen, he found the room bathed in warmth. His wife, lovely and red-faced for the steam pouring off the pot of pasta, spared him a smile as he leaned against the counter. "Dinner's almost ready," she said, poking at the sauce with a wooden spoon.

"I can't wait," he replied. His heart did a somersault as he watched her work, and he was overcome with emotion. He wanted to take her in his arms, to beg her forgiveness for all the troubles he'd brought upon them, and to assure her that, somehow, things would turn out well. Planting a kiss on her forehead, he added, "Nothing cheers me up like your spaghetti, my dear. I'm so thankful that you've gone to the trouble. I need this dinner more than you know..."

She chuckled, carrying the pot of pasta toward the sink. "Well, I'm glad to hear it. Unfortunately, this isn't my usual recipe. Tonight, I didn't have enough time, so I had to use a jarred sauce. Hope you don't mind."

She had her back turned, and so completely missed the color draining from his face. She missed, too, the violent jolt that passed through him, and the look of utter betrayal that stained his features. "A pre-made sauce? From a *jar?*" he muttered.

Had it not been for the sputter of the tap, she might have noted the disgust in his tone. "Yeah, sorry," she continued, "it was on sale today when I dropped by the store and it just seemed so convenient."

He turned and threw open the cellar door with grit teeth and began a slow, tortured descent.

"Honey?" she called after him, "Where are you going? The food's just about ready!"

Pausing on the uppermost step, he stared down into the gloom, his quaking fist locked around the handrail. "That's fine," he said in a shuddering whisper. "That's fine. Go ahead without me. There's... There's something I need to do down here..."

A SECOND HELPING FOR OUROBOROS

I burrowed into my jacket to keep off the rain and went hurdling, head low, along the empty sidewalk toward the library. Eight floors of glass and concrete glowered down upon me and at every squat building in its tremendous footprint; nothing else on the entire campus rivaled it in size, and from a distance one couldn't help imagining that the university's entire plan had been sketched in such a way as to pay the towering library homage. The grounds had sat empty for a week, perhaps two, since classes had let out for spring break and the usual bustle of students had retreated to the warmer corners of the planet.

But *I* was *not* a student. Although I walked the same paths between the buildings as the students did, crouched beneath the same awnings and referenced the same rain-streaked signs, I had not paid for the privilege to do so. I was a visitor, a trespasser—chiefly, I was an *imposter*. I clutched at the student ID in my pocket—the one I'd paid a desperate grad student a tidy sum for—and rushed through a sodden courtyard for the library's yawing entrance.

The doors slid open and admitted me to a dimly-lit vestibule done up in gray carpet. There, stationed by the glass inner-door, a bored-looking campus security guard nodded off over a magazine and met me with a start. I had practiced for this interaction, had been preparing all night for it, and so when he fixed me with a curious look and asked, "Can I help you?" I knew to react with authentic coolness.

Brushing the rain from my hair, I shook my head. "Can you believe this weather? I'll bet it's a lot nicer over in Ibiza right now, am I right?" From my pocket, I drew out the little orange card and held it between my fingers. "Wish *I* knew what it was like to go on break. Instead, I'm still catching up."

The low-paid guard, lulled into conspiratorial fraternity by my chatter, took merely a glance at the orange card before he bought my story wholesale. I studied his eyes closely and knew within the space of an instant that I'd succeeded; the possibility of my being a counterfeit never crossed his mind. Chuckling, he sat upright on his stool and nodded. "I hear ya! I was gonna take a little trip down to Florida with my friends, but I just couldn't afford it this year." His hand moved toward a little number pad on the wall, and punching in a few buttons he prepared to admit me. "What's your major?" he asked.

"Pre-med," came the pre-rehearsed lie. "If I don't grind during this break, I'm gonna flunk the finals. I can feel it."

"Gotcha." The door slid open and the vestibule was filled with the dry, stuffy air of the interior. The smells of dust and old paper sent a thrill coursing through me. "Well, good luck to you. We're closing up at eight tonight, and there are only a few librarians available right now. Let 'em know if you need anything."

"Thanks, man," I replied, striding past him. "Take it easy."

Like that, I was in. I started across the tiled floors, my jacket leaving a trail of cold drops in my wake, and entered into an almost smothering silence—smothering, because I wanted nothing more than to celebrate my successful fraud with a cry of joy. I was so close now to reaching my objective, to securing my prize, that my hands trembled with excitement.

I had not come in search of medical textbooks or anything at all like what the idiot guard by the entrance might have assumed. Instead, my target was something far more obscure—something that ordinary students likely did not have access to. There was one particular book—or, more specifically, a segment contained *within* one particular book—that I was after, and in order to secure it I would have perpetrated *any* fraud, would have gone to *any* lengths.

You see, months of feverish research had led me to this very university, which was a drive of several hours from my home, in a neighboring State. Only here, I had discovered through the weaving together of many disparate threads, were the unpublished works of a particular author available—works of which I had a gnawing, insatiable need.

But it does the great man an injustice to refer to him simply as an author! He was no mere spinner of yarns, no fantasist. No, he was a scholar, a visionary, a giant whose revelations earned him at once the revulsion and awe of his peers, and whose sum of published work provides, to this day, the single most thorough exploration of what is commonly referred to as the "occult".

I have been, for most of my adult life, an admirer and acolyte of this man—a humble walker of the same psychical footpaths—and have read and reread virtually every word of his that was printed within his lifetime. Every word, that is, except for those which are housed within the tomes and letters he bequeathed to this university—his alma mater. This private collection, unknown to all but the most dedicated followers of the Shroud, has been rumored to contain a great and many things which, if applied by an able mind, would serve to plug the minute gaps within the most powerful occult systems known to man.

You will understand, now, what brought me to this distant library on a cold and rainy afternoon—why I took such pains to concoct this fraud and intrusion.

Somewhere within the walls of this towering edifice was the final ingredient.

The key I needed to unlock *transcendence.*

Upon sighting one of the rare librarians, I had only to deploy a plastic smile to go about my way, cheerfully dismissing their offers for help in finding what I sought. Though the library could likely hold many dozens of studying students—and perhaps many more, when the upper floors were taken into account—I spied only two or three in my entire traversal of the ground level. My progress to the stairwell—and subsequent hike to the fourth floor—suffered no interruption.

Unwilling to leave anything to chance, I had done a thorough study of the library prior to visiting, and knew that the papers of my idol were housed on the fourth level, in a little temperature-controlled hovel dubbed "The Ellerby Room", where the works of famous alumni were committed. It was to the door of this precise room that I skulked with the ill-gotten ID card close at hand, and I found it with little trouble, for it was situated a mere ten or fifteen yards from the stairwell, down a long corridor whose stuffiness was profound.

The door to the Ellerby Room was unsurprisingly locked, accessible only through the use of a wall-mounted card-reader. For this reason, I had sought the ID card of a graduate student enrolled in the university's library sciences program. Students of that stripe were often employed by the library itself, and thus enjoyed the easiest access to the institution's more restricted collections. No matter the care I'd taken in my planning, I held my breath and trembled upon swiping the card through the reader, half-wondering if my attempt would take. I was prepared to do whatever necessary to enter the little room—was not above brute-forcing the card reader or even smashing through the glass door.

None of that proved necessary, however. My forceful swipe of the card produced, after a few beats of fraught silence, a thrilling *click.* I pulled open the door and slipped into the Ellerby Room with a laugh I could not contain, and at once canvassed the ceiling for security cameras. I walked from corner to corner, finding none, and wagered that the space was thus unmonitored. I left the lights off, negotiating the tall stacks solely by the weak light seeping in from the north-facing windows. Each of the thirty or forty shelving units packed into the room were taller and wider than I and ladened with books, boxes and binders. These materials were arranged by author, which made zeroing in on my quarry a thing of ease. Not two minutes after slipping into the room, I located the works of my beloved mentor; three, four minutes beyond this, spent in a mixture of ecstasy and reverent contemplation, I struck upon the item which had drawn me across State lines.

I held in my hands the unpublished draft of my idol's final work, a dense treatise on the occult which had taken the better part of a decade to write. Fragments of this masterpiece had seen limited release prior to his untimely passing, but the astounding whole had never made it to the printers—and what little had been loosed upon the world posthumously had been neutered by his executors. Whether this had been a work of maliciousness or ineptitude, I could not say.

The leather bound book, heavy and smooth, was exactly as my mentor had left it, and I ran my fingers against the soft cover, secure in the knowledge that the great man's finger's had once explored these same creases. We were, through this medium, connected across space and time. I dove into the volume at once, sitting upon the floor with my back pressed to one of the burgeoning shelves. Within, I discovered hundreds of pages—both handwritten and typed.

And one thing else.

Unexpectedly, I discovered a small bit of card stock pasted into the inside cover, the stamped header of which declared the tome the property of the university's private collections. Beneath this was a series of stenciled lines where borrowers of the piece in a time before computers would have written their names prior to checking it out.

It was not the presence of this little artifact that surprised me, no; rather, as I glanced over the card and prepared to turn the page, I found upon the provided lines a single name. It was this name which gave me pause, and which drew an incredulous little laugh from lips which had, only moments ago, been pursed in studious excitement.

I was looking at my own name, written in my very own hand.

Blinking at the strip of card stock, I ran my finger across the entry. It was blue ballpoint, and the penmanship was clearly and bewilderingly mine. My full legal name was transcribed there, though I had no affiliation whatsoever with the university, and had never been—till that very afternoon—within a hundred miles of the Ellerby Room. Moreover, I knew that I had never seen the book before. It had been my greatest dream to read this volume and apply its esoteric teachings; had I so much as touched its cover in passing I would have recorded the memory as among the most joyous days of my life.

I was certain that I had never seen the book, and had never had occasion to borrow it before.

All the same, there was my name.

Ignoring the fact that it was clearly my handwriting on the slip, I wondered if, perhaps, my late mentor had another admirer who shared my name. I dismissed this possibility out of hand; my name is not a common one. In fact, on account of my parentage, it is considered not a little strange and exotic. I believe it to be rather unique, and doubt that another person on the planet has ever shared my exact name.

How, then, had it wound up here?

I don't know how long I sat there, mystified. I plugged deep into memory, but could not recall ever having encountered *any* of the materials within the Ellerby room, much less this diamond I had pined after for so long. Reaching dead-end after mental dead-end, I realized that I had no choice but to wash my hands of the uncanny thing—to return to my planned purpose. Certain that I held in my hands the object of my years-long search, I tucked it into the inner pocket of my messenger bag and immediately planned to flee the premises.

Bag tightly fastened, jacket on, I passed between the shelves and made a beeline for the door. My exit from the room was simple enough, and a profound relief washed over me as I heard the door click shut to my back. Arriving once again in the long hallway outside however, I was burdened by a subtle but sudden shift in atmosphere—a vague feeling which I've always attributed to being watched. I stood at hall's end with my bag clutched to my person and tossed a wary gaze down the corridor's length, where it briefly flirted with the departing heels of another library-goer. The individual, moving too quickly in the dim passage for me to get a very solid look at them, gave me quite a fright, but when I had had a moment to gather myself and realized it'd been nothing but a harmless librarian or wandering student, I proceeded to find the stairwell and began a quick descent.

Here, too, I felt chased by foreign eyes—despite the conspicuous lack of others above or below me. Each landing was clear, and I encountered no one in my downward progress. Stepping out onto the ground level, I found I attracted the gaze of every librarian I crossed—though none said a thing to me, and their bland attentions did not suggest the least knowledge of my theft. I left them behind with a casual wave; the guard at the door was disarmed once again by tactical pleasantries, and within five minutes of having stuffed the book into my bag I was out in the rain again, struggling to contain my excitement.

The library, I'm quite sure, watched me as I fled back across the sodden courtyard and skipped through the mist with a Cheshire grin. The titanous structure seemed to lean in inspection of me, its lengthy shadows reaching out like a grasping hand in an effort to reclaim what belonged to it. I was soon out of range, fumbling around in my pockets for my keys. A few lots over, my compact rental sat curb-side. I didn't bother to engage the wipers, to put on my seatbelt; I concentrated everything I had towards speeding to the hotel room I'd booked in the next town over.

There, I planned to put my new acquisition to use.

The bed and nightstand were pushed against the door and the window was carefully blocked with large pieces of cardboard I'd brought along for the purpose. The ceiling vent was similarly covered and the bathroom door tightly shut, so as to keep dwellers in nearby rooms from hearing what I was getting up to. I bunched up the rug on the floor and threw it aside, choosing for my canvas the faux-wooden floor beneath. Having posed as a traveler, the hotel staff hadn't batted an eye at the large bags I'd hauled in with me from the rental car, and from these I withdrew the tools of my trade.

Vials of thick, white paint and a pair of brushes—one thick, the other thin—were set out on the floor. Six unburnt candles had been packed along, the first five of which were to be used in the ritual. The other was to be utilized as my sole source of personal light in traversing the room, for the work which I was soon to begin had been pioneered in an age far before the invention of artificial lighting. Sunlight had to be assiduously forced out of the room, for the forces I planned to consort with were no friends of the day.

The thick brush was used to paint a vast circle and certain of the larger pictographic flourishes which the work necessitated, while the thinner brush allowed me to fill in finer details with more exacting accuracy. Characters older than the pyramids were set down upon the floor of that room with such painstaking care that sweat dripped in rivulets from my nose. Merely viewing the language of the ancients was enough to make me shudder—enough to make me wonder if the shadows stirring in the corners were merely a trick of the candlelight, or astral travelers come to participate in the ritual.

Hours passed while I took care of numberless other preparations. The room in which I dwelt had been paid up for several days, and the staff had been instructed not to disturb me under any circumstances. The other preparations for the task ahead had all been internal; I speak, of course, of the three-day fast I had undertaken in anticipation of the ritual. Empty as a drum, I finally took a seat upon the floor and cleared my mind, my idol's magnum opus situated before me.

There, by candlelight, I dove head-first into the stolen tome—at first with great care and a measure of misty-eyed sentimentality; then, in pursuit of the choice segment relevant to my work, with seeming fever. Page by page, the blanks in my knowledge of the cosmos—however few—were astonishingly filled, and with this new knowledge I felt my spirit writhe within me, as a butterfly does in its chrysalis. The newly-opened eye yearned for sight; I knew myself standing on the frontier of a new existence, of a state of being far beyond what we call consciousness. In my furious turning of the pages, I came away toward the end with a deep cut across my thumb, and I remember I laughed. "No, no, it's not yet time for blood!" I told myself, nursing the wound as I finished reading.

Spiritually engorged with a new awareness, I had only to follow the simple directions, now—the directions to the ritual I myself had pioneered, based on the writings of my beloved mentor. My years of work and study had culminated in this final collaboration with my idol, and now I was set to complete the grand experiment of transcendence that had eluded him.

The clock on the wall told me that it was still early in the evening.

I would have to wait until the hour hand ticked beyond the '12' to begin, for in those shadowed hours the gulf between worlds is at its narrowest.

I sat upon the floor, in the ornate ring of my own creation, with no food or drink passing my lips and only ecstatic meditations visiting my mind.

And at a minute past midnight, I took the dagger from my bag and dragged its razor-sharp tip across my palm. By several squeezes I distributed my pure essence across the circle and spoke the words that had first come to man in the language of dreams. The gore that seeped from my rent palm looked black in the low light, like so much India ink smeared across the floor. The requisite gestures and incantations were performed, body and mind sparking with the energy of the infinite.

And when all was said and done, when the recipe had been followed to the letter, only one barrier remained before proper consummation could take place. Fingers sticky with dried blood, I reached out and snuffed the wicks of all six candles, burying the room in perfect darkness. There, crouched on the floor like an animal, I awaited the coming of the one who would bear the ultimate truth.

Darkness and time collided against one another ad infinitum; the blows were so great and constant that concepts such as minutes and hours broke down. I can't say how long I was plunged into that chaotic world, that space between, but when the first stirrings of arrival took place, my ears were there to hear them. I heard, at first, what sounded like a slight rustling. Yes, a sound like the pages of a book being hurriedly turned. This gave way to a harsher crumpling sound—a tensing and ripping.

And then, a deep, guttural groaning.

The space was packed with the noises of one who had transcended the need for breath, and so it poured out of him in one note—continuous and intoxicating. The frequency wound its way into my ears, where it poured into my skull like warm water and massaged both sides of my brain with strong fingers.

I was so caught up in the thrill of success that I couldn't help lighting my candle to watch, with worldly eyes, the spectacle then unfolding. The candle was put on by a single spark, and when the flame had stabilized, I thrust it forth into the darkness which had grown and hardened around me like a scab.

My mentor's book sat splayed upon the floor before me, shedding a profusion of pages like a chicken losing feathers. Gradually, its binding became visible—a convulsing tangle of black and red thread. The leather cover twitched against the floor as the book's spine hitched and cracked. The inner seam was splitting and more pages were being jettisoned, leaving a dark, widening gap where they had once been rooted.

It was from this pulsing gouge that the groaning visitor came.

Inching upward like a column of toothpaste from a flattened tube, a gangly human body emerged from the book's central seam. Unclothed, the figure's skin was white as snow, but was everywhere ringed with thin, red wounds—like long paper-cuts. As the figure lurched and wriggled, its body would list to one or the other side, and the wounds would momentarily flare open to reveal the pink, goreless interior of its body. The effect resembled something between the winking of a million gills and the spiral-cut of a holiday ham, its slices jostled by an impatient cook. Its head was low, and it wore upon its face a single page of the book—a clean, blank sheet.

I knelt before the thing in awe, its groaning so relentless that it became almost painful to listen to. "Welcome," I gasped, bowing to the floor. "Welcome... !"

Suddenly, the thing ceased its groaning. I looked up at it, oddly frightened by the silence, and awaited its disclosure.

"Y-You've come from the realm beyond, and carry with you the knowledge of eons. You carry within you the knowledge necessary to help me transcend my feeble existence. Show me, please... Let the honey drip from your tongue and into my ears, master!"

But the visitor did not comply. Instead, it pointed down toward the leather bound womb from which it had sprung. "You still don't understand, do you?" issued a faint, withered voice from behind the thing's papery mask.

I jerked to attention. "W-What do you mean? Please, instruct your servant!"

The thing drew a lily-white hand toward its face and tugged away the veil of paper, revealing itself in full—and I couldn't help screaming at the sight of it. Once again, the figure pointed down at the book, thoroughly ruined. The inside cover was visible, the one the strip of card stock had been fixed to—the card stock where my name had appeared. "You still don't understand. You've been here before."

I was staring up at nothing less than my own face. It'd been ravaged by the same cuts as the rest of the body, so that the eyes and tongue slipped and bulged between slices of spiralized flesh.

"It was a success," uttered my doppelganger. The parted layers of his face clapped and shuddered as he laughed. "You did everything by the book. You wanted to leave behind your humanity, and you did so. This is what awaits you."

"W-Wait, I-I," I stammered. "I don't understand..."

"But you do understand," he—*I*—replied. "And you got what you wanted. You've been woven into the infinite. Stitched in. The knowledge, all of it, is yours. And it always will be. You are one with it."

I dropped the candle. It struck the floor, guttering madly for an instant. When the light stabilized, I realized that the figure was no longer there—that I was alone in the room, slumped in the circle with only the ruined book for company.

Without warning the silence was pierced by a fresh bout of that resonant groaning. This time, however, I recognized it to be coming from *my* throat. Despite the stillness and lack of wind, the loose pages of the book began to flutter and flap, and the leathern shell curled and stretched. I felt my hair being tugged, my body being dragged toward the damaged tome. The frayed binding snagged my hair and began incorporating it, strand-by-strand, as I was fed gradually into the yawning seam. The strength went from my limbs as the remaining pages cut into me; the damaged spine of the book was hardened by my own spine, and the leather cover became all the more supple for the incorporation of my own flesh.

The book was in me; I was in the book. My idol's writings had transcended mere theory, and *I* had transcended my humanity. Both were locked now in a demonic marriage of perpetual consumption; the greater my desire for forbidden truths, the greater its hunger for me. I *had* borrowed the book, once. I remembered it, now. A long time ago, I had borrowed the text and attempted what my mentor had not dared attempt in his lifetime. All existence since that moment had been spent in a tug of war with the fabric of reality. It was not the human body I wished to overcome any longer. No, I would have welcomed my old body with open arms, now.

My every thought, my every desire, was to somehow break free of the book—to reverse what I'd done. Somewhere in the book, I was quite sure, I'd find the knowledge necessary to do so.

I was swallowed, digested, thrust down into a darkness without equal. And there, I schemed against the thing that used my hair for its stitching and my skin for its cover. I secretly rebelled against the object I had once coveted and plotted my escape, my transcendence.

Ah, finally, the light of day. Cool air, the scent of grass. Rain upon my skin.

Yes, yes. An opportunity. It's been so long, but I know the knowledge is just around the corner. I'm so close to the solution I've been looking for.

I start across the courtyard and set my sights on the towering library. There is a book in its special collections which contains the answer, I'm certain of it. I've never read it before, but my late mentor worked on it for years before his death. If anywhere one can find the knowledge to transcend, to break free, then it will be between those pages...

I have fooled my way inside, climbed to the fourth floor. The air is stuffy and the lights are dim. Here, then, lies the great final work of my mentor, sure to contain the wisdom I seek.

Finding the tome is the work of some few moments, but when I crack the cover I discover something unexpected.

My name is written on the check-out slip.

How odd, I think to myself. *I've never borrowed this book before.*

Strange though it is, there's no time to waste. I stuff the book into my bag and rush out of the building with a mind towards carrying out the ritual.

Finally, I've found it.

The key to transcendence is somewhere within these pages.

THE INCIDENT AT MERA PEAK

I admit, we were warned about setting out in the off-season. The Himalayas are fickle on the best of days; you've got clear skies one moment and a howling blizzard the next. Everyone told us so. Careful planning, especially for the more inexperienced set, was sold to us as a must.

Well, they were right—the friends and colleagues who sought to dissuade us, the posters on mountaineering forums who advised us to wait just a few more months. They were right, and the three of us wound up rushing headlong into a profoundly dangerous expedition. We were just experienced enough as climbers to consider these warnings, and just young and arrogant enough to shrug 'em off when the facts didn't suit us. We should have waited. Honestly, though, if I could go back and do it all over again, I never would have gone. I know David feels the same way. Tom, I imagine, has *his* share of regrets, too...

The reason we charged on despite all the advice to the contrary is a silly one in retrospect. You see, it was only during the off-season that the three of us could get weeks off of work to take a trip to the Himalayas at all. We had to scrimp and save, we had to build up vacation time and then reason with our stiff-necked bosses to catch a break. I managed a three-week vacation and the other two guys secured just over two weeks of leave, some of it unpaid. We flew out to Nepal on a shoestring at the first opportunity.

But I wish we'd never gone.

It isn't just the cold, the weeks of suffering we endured. Sure, we had a rough go of it. Most of my right pinky finger is still chilling somewhere on the slopes of Mera Peak, having sloughed off after a bout of frostbite. We took our lumps, but if that'd been all, it wouldn't have been so bad. We'd have come home banged up, but with a good story to tell.

Ironically, for someone who set out in the hopes of having a good story to share, I don't like talking about the incident at Mera Peak. We were abroad four weeks, all told—five, actually, if you include the time we spent in the hospital—and I wish I could forget every second.

What really makes me wish we hadn't gone, the thing that really keeps me up at night, isn't the pain, the ice, the life-or-death struggle we faced while trying to climb that peak.

It's the thing we encountered in the snowstorm.

The thing that *followed* us.

In brief, Mera Peak is a great trekking destination. Its highest highs will bring you up more than 20,000 feet, and offer a view of some of the world's largest mountains. You don't need a lot of fancy gear to climb it; some trekking poles, good boots and warm clothes will do. Compared to a lot of other, more famous and difficult climbing destinations, Mera Peak is a walk in the park. If you're reasonably fit and take care to acclimatize, you should have no real problems completing the expedition. Beginners often take between eighteen and twenty-four days to do it, but having years of experience between the three of us, we were determined to do it at the breakneck speed of ten days.

We slept off the jet lag in a cheap hotel and hopped on a bus which brought us to the base of the Himalayas. We'd packed fairly light, not wishing to be weighed down by unnecessary supplies. Food and means of water purification had been brought in abundance, but we'd trimmed all the fat, leaving behind the ropes and other goodies you can't do without on a more difficult climb.

None of us had ever been to the Himalayas before. David, a friend of mine since high school, had been climbing all his life, having grown up in the Pacific Northwest. He was the one that first exposed me to the hobby, and we'd spent our college summers traveling, conquering little climbs around the US. This trip to Mera Peak felt like something special—our first "real" climb, far from our home turf.

Tom was a bit of a wildcard, though. He was a newish member of a local climbing club, and as such we didn't know him particularly well. He was a big guy, very tall, with a background in football and weightlifting. David thought he was hilarious, and when we first began planning our trip to Mera Peak, he suggested we bring Tom along. Usually, I would have vetoed the idea outright. I found the guy a bit obnoxious, and besides, making a more serious climb with someone I didn't know well felt like a liability. I only acquiesced because the presence of a third body helped us secure certain discounts on travel and accommodation.

"Tom can handle it, don't worry. Complete novices flock to Mera Peak from all around the world, man," David had assured me. Though less experienced than David and I, Tom was arguably fitter than either of us, and he had performed reasonably well on smaller trips with the club back in the States. "Trust me, he'll be a good fit for this."

After running the numbers and talking through it with David, I relented. We shot Tom a text, inviting him, and he signed on eagerly. When the fateful day arrived, we piled into David's beater and drove to the airport.

Less than seventy-two hours later, we were putting on our gear and preparing for the trek.

———

The weather really couldn't have been any better—at least, at the start. We were taken in by the clear skies, the great visibility and easygoing terrain during the first several hours, and in our enthusiasm and naivete we never suspected the Himalayan range's capriciousness. A bright sun joined us as we set out from the base, a charming companion that robbed the wind of its icy bite.

"This is too easy!" remarked Tom as we charged up the mountain that first afternoon. "Mt. Rainier's got tougher climbs than this!"

"Sure, it's easy *now*," replied David, "but don't get too comfortable. I hear there are some rough spots along the way. Better to pace yourself."

"Pace myself?" balked Tom. "I feel like I could climb to the top right now—no breaks. Let's marathon the thing! What do you say, Eli?"

"Be my guest," I laughed. "Just don't come crying to me when it starts to snow and you end up in a whiteout."

Our first day's progress was brisk, and we blazed a steady trail for several hours before we stopped for our first breather. I kept the occasional eye on the compass and altimeter while Tom cracked jokes and David brought up the rear. Walking furiously through the untrodden snow, we encountered no one from sunup to sundown.

That first day was textbook, and we set up our tents by a little outcropping that served to keep off the wind. We ate and reveled and eventually turned in, spirits very high.

The second day was no different. We made swift progress, tearing up the peak at a speed that surprised us, and found another excellent spot to camp in. Our meals, though simple, were filling, and we seemed to be adjusting well to the altitude.

It was the morning of the third day when things began to change.

We awoke to a hazy sunrise—hazy, because powdery snowfall was raining down upon us and cutting our visibility down to a fraction of what we'd enjoyed the previous days. The three of us thought little of this; we packed up our things, scarfed down a quick meal and put our trust in the instruments. The altimeter and compass would give us a good idea of our progress and whereabouts even in poor visibility. I remember we trekked on through the flurry, Tom mouthing off all the while.

But what had begun as a mere nuisance, a light flurry, slowly grew into a heavy—and potentially dangerous—snowfall. "It's really coming down," uttered David, strapping on a pair of goggles. "What's your over-under on this stuff petering out?"

"Fifty-fifty," I said. "It could blow over."

"Eh, let it snow! This is what we came for, isn't it? The real Himalayan experience!" said Tom.

And snow it did. The winds picked up, the once-pleasant temperatures dipped to polar lows and we were gradually humbled by the more difficult conditions. After four or five hours of braving the building storm, we decided to take a short break and sheltered behind a cluster of rocks. There, we watched the stuff come down in giant flakes while resting.

"All right, maybe I've had enough of the snow," admitted Tom, tugging his hat over his cherry-red earlobes. "Can't see a thing in this. It'll clear up soon, won't it?"

"It might *not* clear up," replied David. He squinted through the storm and tried to study the sky. The heavens were a uniform gray and snow was falling as far as the eye could see. "In fact, it could get *worse.*"

"Go ahead and jinx us, why don't you?" blurted Tom. "That's just what we need! What's the altitude now, Eli?" he asked me. "We still on-target?"

"Barely," I replied. "We're really going to have to book it if we want to hit our goal for the day." This was easier said than done, of course. The path was already covered in old, partially frozen snow—some of which was difficult to walk through. Fresh snowfall was only going to make our progress more difficult.

It was perhaps an hour, maybe two, after that short break when Tom called out to us from the center of the pack. "Hey, what is this?" he shouted. "Guys, what in the world—?" He was crouched in the snow, staring at something on the ground. I doubled back to the spot and David hastened to meet us.

It didn't take long for the three of us to realize what Tom had literally stumbled upon. While marching a few yards behind me, he'd happened to list a bit to the left and to stamp upon something buried by the recent snowfall. It was a little mound of sticks and smooth, round stones; until Tom's boot had gone crashing through them, they'd likely been stacked neatly in a vaguely conical shape. "Oh, it looks like you accidentally stepped on a memorial or grave marker," I said.

"It's a *what?*" blurted Tom. "A grave? You mean someone's *buried* here?"

"Could be," offered David. He pulled his scarf up over his mouth and nose and took a few deep breaths that left his goggles foggy. "This is the Himalayas, man—the real thing. People die up here all the time. Guides, climbers—people get into trouble and can't get the help they need. And when they die, it's not always feasible to transport a body down a mountain, you know?"

Tom stared down at the ruined memorial with a mixture of horror and disgust. "You're kidding, right? No way there's *really* a body here..."

"You didn't mean to stomp on it," I said, preparing to continue on. "There's too much snow. You couldn't see. Any one of us could've run into it. It's probably a simple grave for a climber who died on the mountain—and it's probably not the only one up here. Come on, let's keep moving."

Tom, though, remained anchored to the spot. "But I thought you guys said that novices came here all the time—that Mera Peak is an easy climb..."

"It is," said David. "This is a great one for beginners. Just keep your head on straight and pay attention—else you might end up like this poor guy."

Rather unexpectedly, Tom sneered and gave the memorial another kick with his boot—this one intentional. "Ah, I get it. Someone took a trip up here and just couldn't hang, huh? Well, sucks to be him, I guess. We're getting to the top. Imagine coming out on a climb like this and croaking! What a loser, man. This isn't Everest!"

David and I were both bothered by Tom's outburst, and I remember we shared a glance through the storm. Eager to press on however, we departed from the gravesite in silence, resuming our earlier positions.

Looking back, that was the moment everything went south. That was the moment that everything began falling apart for us.

The weather, we soon realized, wasn't going to cooperate. We were looking at a proper snowstorm, and for all we knew it was going to last forever. Buffeted by terrible winds, blasted by wave after wave of snow and ice, we couldn't help but slow down, which significantly impacted our day's progress. As if that wasn't bad enough, Tom's pace began to lag shortly after our pause, and within an hour or two of departing the little grave, his tortured moans became too loud to ignore.

I doubled back to meet the other two, and found Tom squatting in the snow, both hands locked around his left ankle. "What's wrong?" I asked. "We're burning daylight, man. You need to re-lace your boots or something?"

He shook his head furiously, teeth grit. It was David who filled me in, yanking down his scarf with a frown. "He's injured. Thinks he strained his ankle when he stepped on that grave marker before."

"I think I rolled it—*bad*," added Tom. "I didn't realize it right away, but... it must have been when I stepped on those rocks. That idiot back there is dead and he's *still* hogging up the trail. I ought to go back and dig him up, spit in his face..."

We made the difficult decision to set up camp and rest till the next morning. This would give Tom's ankle some time to heal, and we hoped that the snow would quit in the interim as well. We set up our tents, but had to make due with a less than stellar spot that was ravaged by the winds.

David and I both had a look at Tom's ankle, and I tell you it was a pretty terrible sight. The joint was bluish-purple and quite swollen. It was a small miracle he'd been able to walk on it at all, and we knew at once that our plans were going to have to change. He assured us time and again that he'd be fine after a good night's sleep—that he wouldn't slow us down—but David and I both knew that our dreams of a rapid ascent were all but dashed.

After a meal, the three of us settled in for the night. I remember the way the wind howled across our camp, and the bone-rattling cold that seeped in through the seams of my tent. The storm wasn't letting up; quite the opposite, it was worsening. I'd never seen such hard and consistent snowfall as I saw that night, and I haven't seen it since. I tried my best to ignore the wind, and was hopeful that we'd enjoy a more peaceful morning.

———

I awoke to a pocket of calm in the dark Himalayan night with sore and pulsing limbs. The wind had been reduced to the occasional gasp across the nighted mountainside; here, finally, some hope of improving conditions. Slithering halfway out of my sleeping bag, I went groping through my things for my watch and found that we were still in the wee small hours. By the low, greenish glow of the watch I thrust a hand into the sleeping bag for my bottle of water.

I didn't get a chance to take a swig, however.

As I sat up with a groan and blinked in the almost perfect darkness, I realized I wasn't alone.

Someone was sitting across from me, at the entrance to the tent, with wide eyes.

I yelped, spilling water all over the place, and was about to claw my way through the canvas when I found I recognized my staring visitor. "T-Tom? Tom, is that *you*? Dude, what the—"

He threw out a cold hand to silence me, head shaking so hard I thought it might rocket off his shoulders. "Don't move. D-Don't say a word," he warned through chattering teeth. He then turned slowly around, squinting at the tent entrance. In search of something to do, his quivering hands found their way to the bottom of my sleeping bag, and he began wringing it nervously between his fists.

"Tom," I whispered, wiping at my face and leaning forward. "What're you doing in here? What's the matter?"

He didn't answer at once. His attention was elsewhere. I noticed, during lulls in the breeze, he would stiffen from head to toe as though listening with all his might. After a few spells of this, he finally bullied his lips into speech. "There's someone in my tent, Eli."

"What?" I sat up and immediately went rummaging for my headlamp. "What do you mean? Is it David?"

Tom only shook his head.

I got the headlamp going, and could see now that Tom had fled his tent in nothing but his long johns and sweatshirt. The soles of his feet were bare and red; he hadn't even bothered to put on a hat or gloves before stealing into my tent.

Frightened though I'd been to find him staring at me in the dark, I quickly composed myself. "If someone's in your tent, Tom, it *must* be David," I explained soothingly. "Maybe he was checking up on you, man—wanted to see how your ankle is doing."

Again, he shook his head.

"Who else could it be, if not David?" I balked. "We're all alone up here. There isn't anyone for miles and miles around. No one would dare weather like this just to climb a mountain and mess with us. You must have had a bad dream or something."

Tom licked his peeling lips. "It isn't David in there," he whispered. "I woke up a little while ago. That's when I noticed that there was someone sitting next to my sleeping bag, looking straight down at me. Watching me sleep. I-I thought it was one of you guys at first, but..." He shut his eyes and buried his head in his hands. "There's something in there, Eli... and it was watching me..." came the muffled confession.

Thoroughly irritated now, I went digging through my pack for a flashlight, and I thrust it at him. "Oh, yeah? Let's have a look, then." I nudged him aside and stepped into my boots and jacket before unfastening the tent door and crawling out into the newly-fallen snow. As expected, the storm had more or less stopped, leaving us with several more inches of the white stuff than before. Not one step out of my tent I knew that the next day's hike was going to be miserable. I left Tom behind, my breath flashing out before me in puffs of blinding white, and stomped through the calf-deep snow toward his tent.

Tom's tent had been left sitting open, and the breeze toyed with the flaps. Focusing the beam of my headlamp, I took hold of one of my trekking poles and made straight for it. On the off chance that Tom wasn't mistaken—that there really *was* someone waiting for me within—I explored the inside of the tent with a few hard jabs of the pole before hastily crawling in. I trampled his sleeping bag and pack as I made my way through the flaps and wasted no time in doing a complete 360 with my light.

As expected, there was no one inside.

I did my best to choke back my anger as I exited. Studying the grounds, I couldn't find any disturbances in the fresh snow, save for the prints Tom and I had both left behind. "There's no one in there," I growled, marching back to my tent. "And the only tracks out there are ours."

Tom met this news skeptically. He peered out from my tent with a narrow gaze, and for several moments seemed unwilling to leave. "I'm not making it up," he eventually said, gaining his feet with a wince. "T-There really was…"

I shooed him away. "It was a bad dream or something. Get some shuteye, will you? Tomorrow's going to be rough. We'll need the rest."

He sulked back to his tent. I listened from my own as he refastened the closures and got back into his sleeping bag. Whether he slept anymore that night, I can't be sure; I myself only managed a brief and fitful sleep after that, and when the sun reared its head I greeted it as my enemy.

———

David and I both watched as Tom came shambling out of his tent. He was disheveled, his gear hastily thrown on and his expression unsteady. He was doing everything in his power to telegraph calm and wellness, but we saw right through him.

"How's the ankle?" asked David, sizing him up as we packed our tents away. "Did the swelling go down overnight?"

Tom zipped his coat tightly and kept his head low while feeding us an unconvincing, "It's better…" His awkward limping around the campsite in the deeper snow was a terrible sight, but he refused our offers to help tear down his tent. Maintaining a facade of toughness, he stuffed his things away and then tried to appear excited for the day's ascent. "So, the storm finally blew over. That's good."

"Yeah, but it left a lot of fresh snow behind. The climb is going to be more difficult." I eyed him pityingly. "You think you're really OK to go on, Tom?"

He ignored me, breaking from the camp with a snort. It was apparently his intention to take the lead position, and he swiped the altimeter and compass from my grasp as he hobbled past. "Let's get to it, fellas. Time's a-wasting..."

Tom was fooling no one, of course. For thirty-odd minutes, David and I maintained the rear and watched as our injured member tried to cope with only one good leg. The injured ankle sent shockwaves of pain through him with every step so that he could only progress by lightly stepping on his heel, with toes raised. This made for excruciatingly slow travel. For all his posturing, we knew that Tom was down for the count. It would be a matter of days before he was in any position for serious hiking—and by that time, our trip would be nearing its end.

David and I flanked him and called a stop after Tom had led us a meager distance."You're finished, Tom. You can't keep walking on that ankle—not unless you want to risk more serious damage," began David.

Tom would hear none of it. He puffed out his barrel chest and gave a hearty laugh—but the unsteady pace he took right after made him suck wind. "It's not that bad," he insisted. "Really, if I give it a little stretch now and then, it almost feels normal..."

"Cut it out," I warned. "David's right. You could really mess yourself up if you keep pressing on like that. Let's stop here and think this through."

"What's there to think about?" asked Tom, daring another clumsy step. He grit his teeth and tried to re-center his pack. "We're not going to let a sprained ankle ruin this whole trip. No way."

"But Tom, you can't just—" began David.

"Look here!" Tom kicked a divot in the snow with his good foot and then unfastened his pack. "I can still walk, all right? I'm good for it, guys. This isn't my first rodeo—I know how to deal with an injury like this. Just... If you want to help, maybe carry some of the stuff in my pack. It'll lighten my load and make it easier on me." He hefted the pack off his shoulders and dropped it in the snow between us. "It feels so much heavier today. Without this thing on my back, I think I'll be able to go faster."

David and I were desperate to salvage our trip. "It's worth a shot," I ventured. "But if you still have serious pain even without a load on your back, we've got to stop." I reached down and opened the pack, rifling for the heaviest items. David removed his own, and we prepared to divvy up Tom's things between us.

As Tom's pack fell open and its contents were bared to the daylight however, all three of us froze.

The water bottles, packs of food, tent and other essentials we found inside were all expected, but the presence of several large bones—browned and made porous by the elements—took us all by surprise.

"What is all this?" demanded Tom, nudging the pack over with his toe. The stuff within came tumbling out—a thermos; a rib; a small first-aid kit; a collar bone and several finger bones; extra tent stakes and a femur. His face went whiter than the snow, and he looked to both of us with wide, watery eyes. "What is all this?" he demanded, as though we should know.

We had no answer for him.

Neither of us had tampered with his things.

Tom bent down and picked up the pack, emptying its contents completely with a look of disgust. Bones and essentials went tumbling into the snow as we stood and watched in horror. "What is all this?" he kept asking, chapped lips trembling.

David took a step back and fixed Tom with a queasy smile. "Is... Is this some kind of a joke, dude? Did you pack this stuff ahead of time, to freak us out?"

The resultant look in Tom's eyes was deathly serious. "Really?" He motioned to the mess of human remains on the ground between us. "You think... You think this is some kind of prank? You think *I* did this?"

"Let's calm down for a minute," I warned them. "There's no reason to fight, to freak out, OK?" I took a deep breath and carefully picked up Tom's empty pack, smoothing it out with my gloved hands. "No one's been messing with your pack, Tom. It was in your tent all night, remember?"

Tom pulled the pack out of my grasp and began stuffing his things—sans bones—back into it. "I didn't do this. I didn't do this," he kept muttering. "And maybe... sure, maybe it *wasn't* you guys..." He glanced at me in his periphery, his tall frame wreaked by a tremor. "Last night, I saw someone in my tent, remember?"

"Wait, you saw *what?*" asked David.

"Tom had a bad dream or something," I put in hastily. "He thought he saw someone sitting in his tent with him, late last night. He woke me up, but I told him it was impossible. We're alone up here. It's the off-season, and we're far from the base now. The odds of running into someone up here are minuscule."

"But apparently the odds aren't zero," snapped Tom. He stared down at the dome of a human skull protruding from the snow. One of its cavernous sockets was trained skyward, and he shuddered terribly at meeting its vacant gaze. Turning with a wince, he began stumbling on. "Forget it. Forget all of this. Let's move."

"Tom, hold up!" I warned. "Let's take it easy for a second. There has to be some kind of explanation for—"

"I'm done talking!" he growled. "I'm not standing around here with these stupid bones, got that?"

David trudged ahead to meet him. "Bro, you're going to hurt yourself—seriously. Eli's right. We should—"

"Then I guess I'll meet you two at the top!" he snapped, barreling on as quickly as his injured ankle would allow.

The two of us let Tom build some distance. We trekked slowly behind him, certain that he had brought along the mess of bones—which we took for realistic Halloween props—as a prank.

As I reflect on the incident all these years later, I no longer think they were fakes.

———

The snowfall started up again within an hour.

I admit my stomach dropped at sight of the initial flurries. The sky quickly darkened and the mountain began dumping fresh fistfuls of the stuff upon us as we struggled to make the least dent in our itinerary.

However stubborn, Tom wound up with no choice but to lay off the gas. He refused to stop hiking altogether, but surrendered the lead position to David when the snow began to fall. He slowly fell into the rear, and the two of us had to turn and check up on him frequently, for fear that he might get left behind.

Before the end of the fourth day, we all knew, in our guts, that the trip was effectively over. Far from completing our climb in an audacious ten days, we were going to have no choice but to throw in the towel and head back to the base if we wanted to return home before our vacations were up. We crawled on bitterly, the snow gaining force and our spirits dipping with every trudging step. David stomped at the head of the pack, kicking himself for having invited Tom in the first place, while I kept to the middle position. There, my scarf and goggles on tight, I tried to keep a close eye on Tom.

The sharp whistle of the wind as it cut across the white wasteland left my ears ringing. Visibility was dropping sharply; it wasn't quite a whiteout, but the constant fogging of my lenses rendered me half-blind as I tried to stagger on. With my senses dulled by the weather, it's perhaps no surprise that I began to doubt them.

At one junction, I turned to check up on Tom, and was alarmed to find he'd fallen quite far behind. His snail-like pace had left him a blurry fleck in my field of vision; he wavered with his head low, and frequently struggled to remain upright. I stopped to give him a chance to catch up, and palmed the snow from my goggles, only then realizing that his haphazard advance reeked of panic. The guy was stumbling, crawling, writhing through the snow as if his life depended on it, and the wind brought certain of his blubbering cries to my ears.

"G-Guys! Guys, wait up! Please!" Even from afar, the tremor in Tom's voice was noticeable. He wasn't just *asking* us to slow down. He was *begging*, on the verge of tears. Making sure that David wasn't getting too far ahead, I momentarily backtracked to let Tom catch up.

That was when I saw it.

I blinked hard through my goggles, not sure that I could trust my eyes. Tom's shambling silhouette against the wall of perfect white entered into focus—as did something else, which seemed only a stone's throw from his heels.

I will never be able to perfectly describe what it was; there was too much snow, too much wind, too much distance. I am certain, though, that something—frankly, *someone*—was following Tom. A dark silhouette loomed behind him, at times coming so close that the two overlapped in my sight. Clothed not in a brightly-colored coat, but in dark and billowing garb, I watched this individual shadow Tom with a surge of horror in my breast.

"Tom!" I shouted. "Tom!" I bolted towards him, arms raised in warning.

And I suppose it was that racket I made that doomed us all.

The ground beneath my feet felt suddenly hollow. I lost my balance and fell to my knees, the roar of the wind quickly supplanted by odd drum-like sounds the likes of which I'd never heard. It was the sound of a releasing slab; in an instant, tons of snow and ice came barreling down the slopes. I was thrown like a rag doll onto my side, and watched as the whole mountain seemed to leap into the air.

An avalanche.

———

Trapped beneath the snow, scarcely able to move, I did my best to create a little air pocket with my chin. Sucking in a few breaths, I shouted for all I was worth in the newfound stillness. Cold—blood-chilling cold—attacked me from every side. I felt ice creep into my boots, sensed it on my face and hands. Thrown violently down the slope and pummeled by the speeding slab, I was thoroughly disheveled. My pack had been torn from my shoulders, and my jacket had burst open, inviting the frost it had been worn to shun.

I could have died there. It would have been easy to give in to that cold. Had David not heard my muffled cries and dug me out with his ice axe, I'm sure that I would have perished. Thankfully, he'd been hiking far ahead of Tom and I, and had narrowly avoided the falling snow. As soon as conditions had stabilized, he'd gone searching for us. I emerged ten or fifteen minutes after the disaster, thoroughly dizzied, and was reacquainted with the howling storm.

"Eli, where's Tom? Do you know where he was before the avalanche? Where he was situated? We have to find him, there isn't much time." David thrust a trekking pole into my hand. "Come on, we've got to find him!"

Dazed though I was, the situation proved emergent enough to rally my battered limbs, and I joined David in canvassing the slope. I dug into the snow and went looking for traces of Tom—his clothing, his pack, anything. Thirty minutes, then sixty passed, bringing no sign of him. A second grueling hour ticked by without success; that was when panic began to set in.

"He could suffocate," uttered David, hunched so as to shield himself from the punishing wind. "We're running out of time. He's got to be here somewhere. Dig, man! Dig!"

I will spare you the monotonous details, the frightened tears we shed as we turned the mountain inside-out in search of Tom, the desperate swings of the ice axe that turned up nothing of use.

It was almost three hours after the avalanche, when David and I both were shuddering and on the verge of collapse, that we dug up Tom. He had been carried away by the slab and buried deep, and on the way down it appeared as though he'd been dashed against certain outcroppings. Jellied blood clung to his wounds, and his face, when drawn up out of the white, was almost powder blue. If he was still breathing, then neither of us could tell. David and I hauled him out of the frost and carried him to the stablest bit of ground we could find. There, we fumbled with David's tent and the three of us took shelter inside, taking stock of our collective injuries.

I knew I was going to lose at least one of my fingers. I'd shed one of my gloves in the fall, and my exposed hand was pounding as though I'd touched it to an open flame. My fingertips were dusky and, and to my horror I could scarcely bend them. David had come away with a wind-burned face, but was otherwise in good health.

We had only to take a look at Tom under the light of a headlamp to know that he was in a very, very bad way, however.

He was as cold as ice from head to toe, and hadn't stirred once. It was possible that he was still alive but suffering from severe hypothermia. It was possible, too, that he was dead. We tried to find a pulse in his rigid limbs and held a bit of mirror to his lips, but could see no evidence of breath. David and I both did what we could to warm him. We wrapped him in our warmest clothes, nestled up beside him, and tried using a camping stove to generate more warmth in the tent. None of it seemed to make any difference, though.

Outside, the wind was growing truly monstrous. The tent was pulled this way and that by rogue gusts, and the snow was piling higher. David, a steadier presence in the face of emergencies than I, peered outside and made a grave prediction. "If this storm gets any worse, we're done for," he said. "With all this wind and heavy snowfall, there could be another avalanche. It's only a matter of time. We can't stay here. This tent won't hold up. We're too exposed."

"Where can we possibly go?" I asked. I'd been desperately trying to reawaken my frozen digits, bathing them in lukewarm water to little effect. The pain was enormous. "Should we move the tent?"

"No," said David. "If there *is* another avalanche, the tent will be torn to shreds. We have to move. Get out of here."

"There's no way we can descend fast enough," I challenged. "Not with Tom like *this*."

David sighed and fell deep into thought. When he finally surfaced, it was with another brief glance at the storm outside. "We need to find one of those emergency shelter buildings."

Mountainous destinations the world round are in the habit of offering climbers sturdy shelters to use in the event of emergencies. These structures, often built to withstand the elements and sometimes stocked with food and other supplies, can be the difference between life and death in unstable environments. Unfortunately, despite the hostile climate, the Himalayas are home to very few of these shelters. "I don't think there are any of those around here," I lamented. "There are only a few scattered around the whole Himalayan range; we could walk for days and never find one!"

"No," continued David, "I remember reading about it before we set out. There's one simple shelter here on Mera Peak, maybe six or seven-thousand feet up." He dug around in his pockets for the altimeter and studied it. "I mean, I can't guarantee we'll find it in these conditions, but... We're not that far off."

"It's reckless," I said. "If we set out in this—"

"Yeah, I know. But if we stay, we're goners..." he interjected. "Our only real shot is finding the shelter. If this reading is accurate, we're only a few hundred feet off. We can make it, even with Tom in tow."

I glanced at poor Tom, still searching for signs of life in him. "So... we carry him, then?"

David nodded. "Strap on whatever you can for warmth. Protect those fingers. We'll haul him along with us. We'll be a lot warmer in a shelter with solid walls than we are in here. We can wrap him in the tent to keep the snow off of him." He stood. "We've got to get moving, though. Before the storm gets any worse."

I had no fight left in me and surrendered. "All right, man. Lead the way."

We double-checked our gear and wrapped ourselves up as tightly as we could. The tent was broken down and Tom was wrapped snugly in the canvas. Together, we shared the burden and went trudging through the snow, groaning and staggering, cursing and shivering. The two of us had to stop frequently at first to get our bearings, but after a solid march of an hour and change, we managed to reach a broad table in the mountainside, where a small roofed structure was visible in the distance.

Built directly against the mountain, the windowless thing was made of stone and fronted by a thick metal door. On the whole, it looked about as spacious as a dorm room or walk-in closet, and the tiled roof was already buried in drifting snow. We raced toward it and worked together to yank open the stubborn door; the latch and hinges had been frozen, and we only managed to get in by hacking away the ice with our tools.

Throwing open the door, we dragged Tom inside and shut ourselves in. The interior was black as pitch, though we soon discovered a few battery-operated lamps within. There were two beds inside and a few chairs; a wood burning stove, a small stack of firewood, a wooden cabinet filled with canned goods and preserved foods, a few rugs and blankets, and some basic climbing supplies had also been left in case of emergencies on the mountain.

We immediately set Tom on one of the beds and started the fire, praying all the while that we could revive him. Water was warmed and we took stock of our remaining supplies. For a time, we grew hopeful. Against all odds, we'd found the little shelter and were now safe against the elements. David and I took turns looking after Tom, and I spent some time nursing my own wounds as well.

"As soon as the weather improves," said David, daring optimism, "we can get out of here. From this spot, it's a straight shot down to the base, more or less. We can use some of the supplies in here to climb down faster when the time comes. If Tom is feeling better, he can join us; or, if he can't tag along, we'll go down, find help, and come back for him. We made it, dude! We're gonna be OK."

I allowed myself to share in his optimism. As the fire crackled in the little stove, the two of us sat before it and soaked up the warmth. "Just have to wait for the weather to improve," I echoed, looking to Tom. "We're gonna get you out of here, man. Hang in there!"

In all actuality, Tom had probably died within minutes of the avalanche. Critically injured by the fall and effectively smothered by the snow, there was nothing we could have done to save him. We tried every trick we knew, of course, but within hours of arriving at the shelter it was clear that he was gone. Attempts to pick up a pulse, a trace of breath, resulted in nothing. Thawing his limbs with gentle baths of warm water did no good.

There was a lot of guilt, of course. David felt terrible for having insisted on his coming along, and I felt mighty bad myself—not only because I'd co-signed the decision, but because I'd foolishly triggered the avalanche that had gotten us into this mess. We took one of the blankets from the other bed and draped it over him as a shroud, agreeing that, once we descended, we'd find help and come back for his body.

And so, there we were, the two of us stuffed into this tiny nook with a half-frozen corpse, waiting for the snow to stop falling.

There was just one problem.

It wasn't going to stop—not anytime soon.

Three and a half days of wild wind and heavy snowfall left us wondering if we'd ever have a chance to make our planned journey down the mountain. The firelight was our chief source of illumination in the little hovel, which made us feel almost like Neanderthals sitting around in a dim cave. When necessary, we'd break out our flashlights and lamps for brief bursts of added light, but we tried to keep this to a minimum in the interest of preserving battery power. We ate some of the stockpiled food, warming tin cans over the stove, and I kept a close eye on my frostbitten hand. My pinky finger was already turning black by that point, immovably stiff.

We woke up one morning to what seemed like perfect quiet. For days and nights the wind had pounded upon the little shelter, but now we awoke on our shared bed to eerie silence. "The snow... I think it's finally stopped," ventured David.

"Could be." I stood up and stretched. Placing a hand against the metal door, I could feel the cold radiating through it. "Throw another log on the fire real quick. Let's see what we're working with here, yeah?"

"Sure," replied David, rummaging through the stack of firewood. "Maybe, if things are calm enough, we can head down this afternoon."

I opened the door to take a look at the aftermath.

Or, at least, I tried to.

The thing wouldn't budge.

"It's stuck," I muttered. "Give me a hand, will ya?"

David rose and joined me by the door. Together, we pressed on the handle and gave it a hard shove. And then another. Chuckling to ourselves, we tried it a third time. There was considerably less chuckling during the fourth and fifth attempts. Our next dozen tries were staged in fraught silence.

"Oh no..." David pawed at the smooth metal, pushed and nudged it from every angle to no effect. *"Oh, no..."*

In a darkly humorous turn, the door to our little shelter could only open outward. Though we applied a great deal of pressure from the inside—literally charged against it with our bodies to the point of injury and hysteria—we couldn't get it to move an inch. Many hundreds of pounds of drifting, frozen snow had settled against its other side, effectively trapping us within. We had no way of knowing just how much snow we were dealing with, or when a thaw might begin. All we knew was that the door would not open, and that the two of us were now imprisoned in the shelter with the corpse of our late friend.

David raged against the door so long he worked his shoulder into a pulp. Panting, he slumped to the floor and buried his head in his hands. "The snow will melt. It has to." He trembled, leveling his teary gaze upon the door, our betrayer. "We'll try again later in the day. Or maybe tomorrow. We'll be out of here soon..."

In fact, we would go on to remain in the shelter for *weeks*.

***

Time became a blur. The numbers on our watches came to mean nothing; deprived of sunlight and the open air, we could only cower in the glow of the fire and imagine the scene outside the shelter. There was water enough for the two of us stored up in the little edifice, though we drank it down nearly to the last drop by the time all was said and done. Odd drafts crept into the structure now and then, reminding us of the outdoors and providing tantalizing clues as to the conditions without. Winds came and went, heaps of snow were surely displaced, but for all these changes we could not force the door open.

The trying of the door became a daily ritual. After meals, when we had given ourselves some time to digest, we would batter the thing until utterly ruined by fatigue. Each time, we would retire bitterly—but cling to a vain hope that, tomorrow, things would be different.

"If only Tom could help..." said David after one of our many unsuccessful attempts. "He was tough. He would've knocked this door off its hinges, I bet."

It's strange and a bit unsettling in retrospect the way Tom became a mere object sharing our space. Though we spoke of him from time to time, and took care to treat his body with some respect, the corpse on the bed began to fade into the background. He had been left in the bed furthest from the stove and had been little disturbed since our arrival. Our daily business was conducted over and around him; he was, in some sense, just another piece of furniture in the room.

When the lad began to decompose, however, it became more difficult to ignore him.

The inside of the shelter had attained a tolerable level of warmth thanks to the constant burning of the stove. When we ran out of firewood, David and I began breaking down furniture in the shelter, feeding bits of chairs, shelves and even rugs into the cast iron unit to keep the warmth flowing. This heat was a boon for us living occupants, but kickstarted processes in our deceased friend which, in time, made the shelter nigh unlivable.

We had not foreseen the fact that the increased warmth would urge Tom's body to rot. What began as a faint odor, a weird smell in Tom's corner of the room, soon became a revolting musk. Tissues breached by decay would loose rank scents with suddenness; the bed he occupied grew slick with the seepage of failing flesh, and from his depths there rose up such noxious fumes as are ordinarily—and *mercifully*—confined to the grave. Our air was gradually tainted so that, before long, our every breath contained something of Tom in it.

One night, while David slept upon the other bed and I paced the floors in restlessness, I happened to glance at Tom. The fire was low, in need of another chair leg, and all was bathed in syrupy black. Standing at the foot of Tom's bed and overcome by the fumes that poured out of him, I discovered that his body had lately shifted somewhat; that, on account of deterioration, his corpse had changed position. As a result, the makeshift pall we'd tossed over him, stained with fragrant juices, no longer covered his face.

I regarded Tom's dead countenance half in horror and half in curiosity as I stood there in the low light. His eyes were open, all color chased out of them by a white, milky film. His features, once even and handsome, were marred by patches of necrotic black. Frostbitten tissues were being eaten away with alarming swiftness. His blackened nose, cheeks and ears had broken down into festering rubble. The effect was horrifying, indeed—but still I beheld the sight with a certain curiosity. I wonder now if my inhalation of Tom's volatile gasses hadn't altered my mind, or if it was simply the way the firelight fell upon his cratered face...

Yes, the surface level of Tom's visage was breaking away in dramatic and revolting fashion, but I couldn't get away from the impression that, just beneath it, a *new* face—*new* features—were in some way debuting. The tongues of flame in the stove were reflected in his dead eyes, and I saw—or believed I saw—them shift subtly in his gooey sockets. I imagined his frostbitten hands reaching up and clawing at the remainder of his old face. My imagination burned with visions of a new body, a new man, rising from the decaying wreckage of Tom's corpse.

I was used to strange thoughts by this time, of course, and said nothing of my impressions to David. I simply picked up the soiled shroud and spread it over Tom before stationing myself at the fire.

A few nights before we finally broke out of the shelter, I was awakened by David. I presume it happened in the middle of the night, though I didn't check my watch and verify the time. At any rate, I regard that whole imprisonment in the shelter as one long, continuous night.

I'd been sleeping uneasily in the bed for awhile when, subject to a few violent shakes, I was drawn suddenly to wakefulness and alarm. "W-What's going on?" I asked, almost tumbling to the floor.

David, though, pressed a clammy hand to my mouth. He gripped my shoulder and then made several gestures, impressing upon me the need for quiet. Bewildered, I nodded, remaining silent as instructed. Sure that I wasn't about to open my mouth again, David removed his hand and shakily pointed across the room, in the direction of the other bed.

Tom's bed.

I turned my bleary eyes toward the corpse. It remained there, draped by the blanket, just as we'd left it. I sat up a little, offered a weak shrug. I couldn't tell what he was driving at—what'd possessed him to wake me in such a fashion.

David stood between the bed and the stove, gaze never wavering from Tom's still form. Several moments passed without explanation. Finally, he tugged at me, drawing me close. Leaning in, he whispered, "D-Did you hear that, Eli?"

I hesitated. From where I sat, only David's labored breathing and the pop of the fire in the stove were audible. There wasn't even any wind then—at least, none that I could discern. I shook my head. "Did I hear *what?*"

Shuddering violently, David's gaze remained fixed on the corpse. "Just a little bit ago, while I was sitting by the fire..." he whispered. "He started *laughing.*"

I startled, an incredulous grin taking root upon my lips. "I'm sorry... *what?* You heard... You heard Tom? *Laughing?*"

"I'm not lying," insisted David, clutching at the headboard. "I mean it. I heard him laughing. And..." He licked his lips, chest heaving. "It didn't sound like Tom."

"How do you mean?"

"It... It wasn't Tom's laugh. It wasn't his voice..." David sucked in a deep breath, steadying himself. "It's someone else under that sheet..."

To be frank, I was skeptical. Though I myself had been entertaining odd notions during our imprisonment, the idea of a chuckling corpse was a bridge too far, even for me. I stood up, shaking off David's hand, and shuffled toward Tom. Carefully, I flicked on a small battery-powered lamp and turned down the shroud, studying the spoiled slumberer beneath.

Tom's corpse did not move. His blackened lips could not have been said to curl in anything like a smile, and the gel that oozed from his gaping sockets was not to be mistaken for tears of mirth. The man was good and dead; whatever David had heard, I felt sure that it hadn't come from Tom. And yet this brief survey did nothing to combat my earlier impressions. Studied up-close, I couldn't help sensing a deep change in the corpse. Everything on the surface—everything we had once called "Tom"—was in the process of being destroyed. Beyond this deteriorating mask, however, something else, something unfamiliar, seemed to be emerging...

I held my tongue about this. To this day, in fact, I have never been honest with David about my impressions of Tom in those final days. Nevertheless, considering what came afterward, he has reason enough to suspect what I withheld.

The day we broke free of the shelter, we awoke in profound desperation. We had burned just about everything in the hovel that could answer for firewood and had run through nearly all the water and food despite careful rationing. We arose that day determined to force open the door—or to die trying.

Speaking only for myself, I will tell you that I had never made such an intense and brutal effort in all my life as I did that day against the door. I threw myself into it bodily, trained myself against the latch like a battering ram, and worked in concert with David to knock it open. Our first sign of success, wherein we managed to ease the door open just a few inches, invigorated us. We built on this initial progress by striking the door until its rough metal edges began carving into the wall of snow and ice on its other side. Bloodied and achy, we eventually opened it far enough to exit. In the end, I do not believe it was our strength or tenacity that allowed us to force the door; rather, after days of middling temperatures and changes in the wind, the drifts that'd kept us prisoner for weeks had finally grown small enough to be overcome.

The weather outside was unspeakably pleasant; compared to the four walls we'd been staring at for weeks, the sight of the gloomy, windswept mountain was enough to bring tears to our eyes. We hastily packed our things and geared up, preparing to make a precipitous climb down the nearest ledge. We were less than half an hour in preparing, and we set out through the dense snow with a spring in our step.

Our descent was swift. In fact, it was reckless. When we made it to the bottom, I realized that I'd lost my frostbitten pinky somewhere along the way—thanks to a little thing they call "auto-amputation". In my haste, I hadn't even noticed.

We made it back down to the base of Mera Peak a few hours after sundown, and succeeded in making our way onto the winding road which rings it. There, we had to wander for close to two hours before we spied a passing vehicle. Convincing the motorist to stop and help us, we were ferried to the nearest town, where the two of us received basic medical care and were put in touch with local authorities. Informing them that Tom was still up on the mountain, in the emergency shelter, a recovery operation was planned for the next afternoon. A helicopter was used for the purpose, and a number of skilled volunteers descended upon the snowbound shelter to retrieve our friend's corpse.

What happened in that shelter between our descent of the peak and the arrival of the rescuers the next day is the subject of much conjecture. David and I both have our theories, of course—and it is on account of those theories that neither of us will ever again set foot in the Himalayas.

The rescuers entered an empty shelter plagued by the smell of death. Puzzlingly, though, their thorough search turned up no sign of the sought-after body. The bed in the corner was found to be empty; the dead man we'd left in it was simply gone.

Upon finding no corpse in the shelter, the authorities, naturally, tried to cobble together an explanation. Bits of gangrenous and degraded tissue were found scattered about the room; in light of this, it was supposed that a wild animal had fed on Tom, torn at his body, and subsequently dragged him off into the frozen wilds. A sound enough theory, all things considered. Just what predator could possibly have a taste for such nauseous fare as this they could not say, however. Furthermore, there were no visible tracks around the shelter that could identify the alleged beast—the drifting snow had likely obscured them.

If there is one wrinkle in the narrative spun up by these authorities, it is the alleged presence of several items—all of them retrieved from the site and shown to both David and I for verification purposes—belonging to Tom, which were found *outside* the shelter. The pair of boots, the jacket and other articles of clothing that were brought to us were the ones Tom had died in; of that, neither of us had the least doubt when questioned. We had left these items on his body for all those weeks, having no use for his stench-ridden gear.

The volunteers reported discovering these items outside the shelter. It is claimed that they were tucked neatly, left *folded*, beside a small, conical mound of sticks and stones, which was itself taken for a rustic memorial. Neither David nor I had bothered constructing such a "memorial", but we did not bother telling the authorities that we had seen its like before. And come to think of it, I have never heard of a species of predator, whether bear or wolf, that carefully undresses its festering prey and leaves its boots shined and clothing pressed before dragging it off...

Nonetheless, when the incident at Mera Peak comes up in conversation, I tend to agree with this down-to-earth explanation. You see, from where I'm standing, it's close enough to the truth.

Something *did* make off with Tom.

It followed us up the mountain. It shadowed him as he limped along. It infiltrated his body. And when death stole over him, it germinated within his frostbitten husk, repurposing what it could so as to live again. In solitude, when David and I had gone, the thing had finally surged to life. Shaking off and tearing away the old, dead tissues, it had gone staggering out of the shelter—and had the snow but ceased its drifting, the authorities would surely have discovered a set of perplexing prints leading out of the building.

Not mine, not David's. Not the prints of some hungry beast.

They would have been the prints of a man—of a thing that had *once been* a man—leading not to the base of Mera Peak, but higher up, I imagine, into its remote interior...

WRITER'S RETREAT

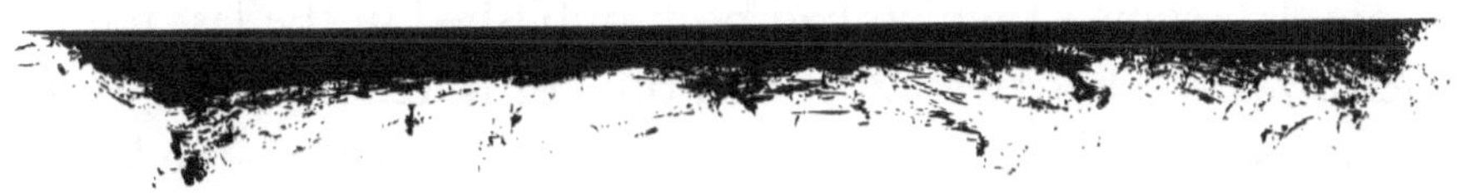

It was late in spring when my friend and I happened upon the little cottage which sat wreathed in gloom and far from any marked road. Squat and shaggy with ivy, it proved very much the proverbial needle in the haystack on account of its having been steadily devoured by surrounding acreages. I have, even today, a good idea of its general whereabouts, but its exact location evades memory. For reasons that'll soon become apparent, I wouldn't speak to its precise location even if I could.

The thing was remarkably inaccessible in a way that few sites in the modern world are. The most rural homes can be approached via highway or country road, and these days no one is ever very far from such scourges of civilization as billboards and light pollution. This thing we found, couched in centuries of growth, had nothing like a proper road within five miles of it on any side. It was a Point Nemo of sorts, a veritable cryptid, seldom-glimpsed except, perhaps, by air, where curious pilots might now and then encounter it, only to doubt what they'd seen.

Its Lincoln-log-style construction introduced it as a thing from a bygone age, though just *how* old it was neither my friend nor I could really say. It lacked running water and electricity, but we found within its walls other signs of relative modernity which thoroughly baffled us. We took turns peeking through the structure's lone window and were thus introduced to a dusty, spartan, but rustically cozy interior, and through these guarded passes we became satisfied that it was, indeed, abandoned. A bed and desk of simple wooden construction were perched inside, and a shelf of similar make teetered between them, burdened by a collection of novels—some of which had been published in the last ten to twelve years. There were, besides, piles of notebooks and loose paper upon the desk, and an assortment of fine pens—the lot of them, regrettably, dried out and ruined by time. A small stock of wood sat cobwebbed to the right of the meager fireplace, and the entryway had been lent something of the homey by a ruddy rug. Within a crooked cabinet hardly deep enough to warrant the name we discovered a few canned goods some six years past their sell-by dates and a glass bottle filled with some cloudy brown liquor. That was all.

Of course, we wondered who the place belonged to, what the structure had been used for, if the owner still lived. Theories were batted back and forth like ping pong balls, but we didn't wonder for long; the answer, it turned out, was close at hand.

You see, on the desk, half-buried beneath a smattering of dust-stained pages, was a dogeared notebook with a pale blue cover. The words "Welcoming the Muse" had been written across the front in neat cursive. By paging through this little volume, we became acquainted with the one who'd left all these goods behind.

The object of our trespass had been used, several years prior, as a writer's retreat.

Writers, on the whole, tend to be rather unwholesome creatures. Is there anything more unloveable in the world than one who sits alone in a locked room, day after day, amusing himself with his own thoughts? Storytelling in its commonest form is little more than fraud, and even its most celebrated practitioners are guilty, at least, of commodifying imagination. What they lack in muscle, charisma and manners, authors often make up for in ego.

We had, in this little journal, a prime example of what was perhaps the most detestable, the most pernicious variety of writer on the planet: The rank amateur. From the opening entry, my friend and I both agreed that we'd happened upon the scrawl of a man who fancied himself a generational talent. He was a master, as all of that foul stripe are, of writing much and saying little; the kind of loathsome creature that hotly anticipates his share of the perfunctory applause at open mic events. Only by the constant back-pats of teachers, parents and well-meaning delusionalists does the novice in letters manage to ape the upright posture of better men.

The inaugural entry ran thus:

I am arrived.

This remote hermitage, discovered quite by accident and untouched for ages, will be the site of a momentous artistic undertaking. My Walden.

Having stripped away all distraction, I sit in wait of Prometheus. The fire he brings will set my soul ablaze and bear such sizzling fruits as the literati have only dimly dreamt of. I have left the door ajar. My ears are trained on the sounds of the forest. Is that the pitter-patter of feet I hear? The coming of the Muse? I await her eagerly—my spectral mistress...

Judging by this first entry and the collection of materials left behind in the cabin, we assumed that the writer had isolated himself in the interest of creating without distractions. We brought the notebook outside with us and continued reading it in the daylight, curious what this expedition of his had yielded.

"Maybe he wound up writing the next great American novel right here," ventured my friend with a laugh.

I was of a very different mind. "Or maybe, after a week in the woods, he couldn't hack it and went back to waiting tables."

The entries progressed:

I have been connecting with the Earth. Barefoot, I have walked the grounds reciting poetry till dusk. Only when the sun has vanished from the sky do the lunar thoughts come out to play; to ease their way, I have greased the gears with a bit of strong drink. Tonight, the writing exercises will begin. I work in the shadows of the masters, filling in the writing prompt worksheets I brought along.

The next:

It is an old adage that the writer ought to write what he knows. Until this very moment, I have wondered as to the subject of my forthcoming novel. I have decided, however, that this endeavor of mine—this retreat into solitude—will make a fine subject in itself. THINK! A novel about a writer struggling to craft a masterpiece! I'm not sure such a thing has ever been done... We have no need of an Achilles, an Odysseus here—what better and more authentic a protagonist than myself?

And the next:

Four days now I have sat in stillness, surrounded only by the sounds of nature. I am reverting to a more primitive state—the only state in which genuine connections with the creative unconscious can be made. My thoughts remain aloft with Polaris, my senses strain at all hours for signs of the Muse. That she draws ever-nearer is not in doubt. When she arrives, I will put pen to paper and the whole grand thing will leap forth. Numbered are the days of its gestation and brief are its labor pains; it comes many-limbed and writhing!

"It sounds like he spent the first few days filling out worksheets and hyping himself up," uttered my friend.

"And drinking just a bit too much. How much you wanna bet he throws in the towel before the ten-day mark? This word-vomit is probably all he managed to write before he gave up..."

We continued.

Wonder of wonders, something strange and terrible has happened. There has been a change in the air. The site was visited by rain and wind for several hours; a soothing and cleansing experience that warded off my pent-up psychical fumes.

The sun tumbled out of the sky but half an hour ago, and as I sat by the window, paging through my thesaurus, I noticed something in the woods outside. The foliage, quite apart from the stirring of the rains, parted as though nudged aside by an unseen hand.

I sense a presence here.

"Plot-twist: A homeless guy just discovered the cabin, and let's just say that he's not a fan of Jonathan Franzen," I guessed.

"Keep reading," urged my friend. "Is he losing it, spending so much time out here alone?"

The next entry differed from the others in that the painstaking cursive had been suddenly abandoned for rough, utilitarian capitals:

Up to this point, I have not written more than one entry per day. The paper and ink are expensive, and I promised my wife that I wouldn't waste them, and that my most recent splurge at the stationary store would be my last until I finally secure a paying job. Well, what has gone on this evening is sufficiently important, to my mind, to risk her wrath.

An hour, perhaps two—time behaves differently here than it does in the city, you understand—after my last entry was penned, I stepped outside the cabin to relieve myself. The wind and rain brought with it unseasonal cold; I shivered as I walked a little into the surrounding woods and did my business. On the trek back, I happened to hear something—the unmistakable sound of feet.

Yes, I am certain I have heard a stranger's tread.

I was not a little alarmed by this, and so immediately sought cover. I fancied an animal—perhaps a deer or badger—was behind it, but as I knelt behind a damp tangle of shrubs and scoured the gloom, no such creature came into view. Instead, something tall and slender—anthropoid—came shambling out of the wilderness.

The figure was bathed in shadow; with so little light to work with, I could only tell that the presence was lank of limb—too lank, I dare say, to be a garden-variety human being. It stood a few heads above my own five feet and nine inches; I would not be surprised to learn that it stands in the ballpark of eight feet.

It stood there, not entering the premises but dwelling stock-still along the cabin's periphery. There was something in its odd bearing—don't ask me to explain it, because I've wasted a page or two trying already—which told me it was aware of my presence. It knew I was there, cowering some twenty-feet away in the bushes. It could well have come after me, could have motioned to me... but it did not.

Instead, the figure seemed intent on becoming one with the scenery—on blending into the darkness and stillness until my eyes could not pick it out of the tableau. And in this it proved most successful. Though I stared at it a long while, and could even now show you the very spot where I first saw it traipse out of the surrounding wood, by small gradations it vanished from my sight. My every sense screamed out and told me that it was still there. It hadn't moved, hadn't made a sound. And yet my eyes, despite their fixedness, had inexplicably lost sight of it.

I won't deny that I fled into the cabin. Ten, maybe fifteen minutes I knelt in the muck, watching the thing—or trying again to find it—before I returned and slammed the door shut. I wish there was a curtain in this window, and that the latch on the door was meatier... Ah, well, a few more logs on the fire will keep me company.

I have been waiting for someone here, at the cabin; awaiting that primordial goddess of inspiration.

But the thing I spied outside the cabin was not my Muse.

And if it was, I doubt I'll ever pick up a pen again...

"OK, OK," said my friend, snatching the book from my grasp. "This guy almost lost me early on, but now I'm invested. What happened? Think he's making it all up?"

I shrugged, reclining against a mossy tree trunk and peering up at the dimming sky. The sun was setting, and the clouds were stained in warm shades of red and orange. "Probably had too much to drink. Or the isolation got to him. It's pretty quiet out here. I can't really blame him."

My friend was ignoring me; had already begun diving into the next entry. "Oh, man... oh, man! You aren't going to believe this!"

I sat up. "What now? He get abducted by aliens or something?"

The next entry read as follows:

I am writing this because, should I die, I have no other way of telling the world what's become of me. My phone has no reception here, and the area is so remote that I cannot hope to reach civilization on my own. At the end of this planned excursion, my wife will be waiting at the closest site of ingress—a little metropark. I plan to march out in the daylight hours; I doubt very much that I could safely exit the woods by night... Until then, I have no choice but to fend for myself...

It's about two in the morning as I write this. Since that last update, I haven't bothered to leave the cabin but once. An empty food can has made a serviceable urinal, and I have spent most of my night sitting by the window, my gaze roving and roving after doubtful shadows in the brush. There have been times when I have studied one spot in the forest—some cluster of trees or tangle of branches—only to feel, in my hindbrain, that I have touched upon the hem of something else. Something that fills the same space, but which my eyes cannot settle upon.

I know how this sounds, and if a professional were to tell me right now that I am insane, delusional, then I would be most glad to hear it, and to have him drag me off to someplace secure.

But I am not crazy.

You see, my store of wood was growing a bit sparse. In the interest of chasing off the cold, I dared to step outside and visit the wood pile. There, like a spooked animal, I grabbed up as many logs as I could, pressed them to myself, and prepared to race back inside.

Have you ever lost yourself in a body of deep water? Drowned, perhaps?

I have; but in my case, there was no water involved. I drowned in the open air as I turned back toward the cabin. Clutching the wood to my breast, I made the quickest, quietest steps I could on my return journey, only to reel back in horror and drop a few pieces onto the ground. I could not breathe; I could no more make use of the fresh air than a fish cast onto a dry shore.

The woods all around me erupted into movement—I watched the growths quake and tremble and wave—but all this brought with it not one iota of noise. There was no wind to speak of, but the limbs of the trees whipped about as though in a tempest. Something was on the move, working the outdoors into a furor, but it brought with it no sound. It was as though the shadow between every trunk and branch had suddenly mobilized—like the black of the sky had stolen soundlessly out of the cosmos and trained its fury on me.

I did what instinct demanded. I charged toward the cabin. However small it is, I wagered that its four walls would offer a modicum of protection. But when I stepped inside, my shaky hands fumbling with the door, I saw that I was not alone.

There was a figure there, crouched near the fireplace. He stood in the little corner to the right, so that the orange glow of my dying fire could scarcely reach him. I could tell, though, that he was very tall and thin, and his black hands were wrapped tightly around his face. It was not a man. He was too long, too dark, too horrible to be a man...

Addled by terror, I did the only thing I could. I snatched a pen and this notebook from the desk and then went running from the cabin. I must record this—must warn off others from visiting this wretched place after dark. If you are reading this, heed my warning and turn back while you still can. As to what's become of me, well... I suppose that depends on whether there's an entry after this one...

My friend and I turned the page with bated breath.

The next page was blank. And so was the next one. Indeed, that ominous entry proved to be the last one in the notebook.

"Dude, what in the world did we just read?" I asked. "There's no way this is real!"

My friend shuddered, studying the notebook with a queasy look. "I don't know... it could be a fake, but... I just have this feeling that it's real."

"No, no," I continued. "It's just not believable. First off—monsters? *Please.* Take the obvious fantasy elements out of the equation and all you're left with is one bad decision after another. This isn't how someone in a life or death situation would act! If you were really scared for your life, do you think you'd bother stepping into the cabin to grab a pen and notebook before running away from a monster? No! For that matter, how did the notebook end up back here? Did he nicely decide to drop it off in the morning? Come on! This was written by a total novice—someone without enough lived experience to know how people really act!"

"All right, maybe you're onto something," admitted my friend. "I thought it was pretty eerie, though. Better than some of those short stories I've read online recently."

I shut the notebook and looked up at the sky. Since my last glance, it'd been drained of color. Night was on its way, and we still had a long walk to civilization ahead of us. "Come on, we've gotta get a move on," I said. "Let's put this back and head out, yeah?"

"Aww, do we have to return it?" asked my friend, eyeing the notebook pleadingly. "Would be cool to take it as a souvenir, don't you think?"

"On the off-chance that the guy who wrote it ever comes back, I'd rather leave it." We paced back to the cabin and shuffled into the dim interior. I groped through the shadows, navigating only by the thin threads of twilight that came in through the window, and placed the notebook atop the pile of papers.

"It's getting so late," said my friend. "Maybe we should just stay the night, eh? We could start a little fire and get cozy."

I panned about the dusty abode and gave the matter some thought.

And if not for what I happened to glimpse in the fireplace, I might have been more agreeable to the idea of an overnight.

I startled when, glancing toward the fireplace, I noticed a dense shadow parked within it. What I might usually have mistaken for logs or other detritus in the gloom was revealed by the new moonlight to be a pair of large, black feet—the feet of one standing within the fireplace. Staring in disbelief at those two feet, I slowly traced the thin, black legs that were joined to them. The mantle blocked the rest of the figure from view, but I could tell at a glance that the one sheltering inside the chimney was of great height and thinness. Rather *lank of limb*, one might say. My friend also happened to catch sight of the dweller in the hearth, and our earlier conversation died away at once.

We stood there for several moments, wondering if we weren't hallucinating. We pawed at our eyes, blinked hard in the murk.

When the thing in the chimney spoke, it removed all doubt, however.

A thin, almost nasally voice came seeping out from behind the old bricks. "*Tell me... How did you like my story?*" the figure asked.

The two of us stiffened, nearly dropped to the floor.

"*Was it artful?*" cooed the thing in the fireplace. "*Was it... frightening?*"

We understood, after that, why a few of the details in the story hadn't worked for us. Indeed, it had been written by someone—*something*—whose sole acquaintance with human nature had come through the lens of predation. I needn't tell you that we didn't hang around; we weren't about to offer a thoughtful critique. We went running from that cabin, into the woods, and we didn't stop until we reached a paved road several miles off.

Had we stayed, my friend and I surely would have gotten *workshopped* into a new ending for the thing's tale...

ELSPETH

The strangest girl I've ever known died at thirteen years of age, drowned.

I remember when the headmaster interrupted our lunch period, his balding head hung low. He was as delicate as could be in breaking the news of a student's death, and to the credit of the dozen or so rowdy boys in my class and nearly as many catty girls, we took the announcement with an uncharacteristic maturity. We didn't jeer when we learned that the girl had been found face-down in a local ravine after a recent bout of flooding; instead, we let the man say his piece and then picked at our meals for the remainder of the period, affecting the sullenness appropriate to the occasion.

I won't lie to you and say that the girl was mourned. No one particularly liked her. She had no friends at the school, to my knowledge, and had been a student of neither exceptional ability nor an underachiever. She'd never been one to take part in any sports or extracurriculars, and in the dormitory was said to have kept always to herself. The girl had not been the object of ridicule, but never had she been the target of praise, either. In every aspect, Elspeth had been seemingly tailor-made to attract as little notice as possible. Had the headmaster confessed to us that she had been a mere mannequin, like a decoy left floating amidst a school of real ducks, we would have readily believed him.

And yet, for all her blandness, the girl *had* left an impression on the lot of us. One had only to drop her name in conversation in the weeks after her drowning to hear her labeled as "that creepy girl" or "the odd one".

Despite having reached the age when boys begin to take a keen interest in the fairer sex, I don't believe any of us ever admired Elspeth in the least—though, I hasten to add, it wasn't on account of ugliness as one might assume. Quite the contrary, with a little effort I can recall a certain beauty in the dead girl; a rare symmetry and delicacy of the features that her peers all lacked. Eyes as large and clear as freshly-washed picture windows; lips as full and red as fresh strawberries; long, black hair of incredible gloss and smoothness. No, she hadn't been ugly. Taken a piece at a time, Elspeth had been, in fact, rather striking.

Unsightliness is sometimes bound up in beautiful things, however. Though the disparate parts may each appear perfect and pleasing by themselves, their piecing together can sometimes prompt disharmony in the whole—a disharmony that is difficult to place, but which jars one on a gut level. This is perhaps too vague a criticism of her appearance to be taken seriously, but this was precisely the trouble with Elspeth. Somewhere in her face, her bearing, her being, there ran a common thread of uncanniness.

It's hard to recall my first memory of Elspeth Emory. As far back as I can remember, she was a fixture at that boarding school—a figure spied briefly during assemblies, one among a number of faces in a classroom. I may have spoken to her on occasion, but even if you put a gun to my head I wouldn't be able to recall a single word of what was said. Others I've spoken to—fellow alumni—say the same; they remember her, but only when prodded. Elspeth, to many of us, had become a memory on the verge of deletion; an old bit of data stored deep in the annals which could only be drawn out by certain keywords.

Ultimately, it was no conversation that reawakened my hollow memories of her some twenty years on. Once or twice since leaving that school, I've paged through my old yearbook and almost certainly glossed over her photo. I even attended our ten-year class reunion without the girl's name ever crossing my mind. Why, then, do I speak of her now? Where did this fascination come from, you ask? Well, I will tell you.

It may be hard to believe, but my borderline obsession with Elspeth Emory began somewhat recently. I happened to be traveling through a small town outside of Treviso when I met her for the first time in decades.

The trip to Italy was a gift to myself. In the first place, as one of Italian ancestry whose sole acquaintance with the culture came via endless breadsticks at Olive Garden, I thought it important to venture abroad and see the motherland for myself. My secondary reason—not an insignificant one—was that I had just split from a long-time girlfriend and wanted nothing more than to wipe my slate clean. The break had been a tough one, the culmination of many stressful fights, and hopping on a plane for a month-long romp through Europe felt like the right move at the time.

It was, generally, a delightful trip. I saw Rome, Sicily, spent some time on the Mediterranean and met many other travelers as I made my way from one hostel to the next. I needn't waste your time describing the food—it was as good as you imagine. The wine was even better. Though it was the middle of summer, I found the climate most pleasing and cheesily attributed this to my awakening Italian ancestry.

My journey eventually brought me to a little settlement near the banks of the Piave River, where I stayed a total of three days. The town, whose name eludes me, was quaint and delightful in its way, but I confess I only stayed there as long as I did on account of some inclement weather. Heavy rain blasted the area and storms kept me sheltering in place till conditions improved. This was nothing that a little vino and Italian food couldn't mend, and I passed these days happily enough.

That is, until I happened to visit a particular *ristorante*.

The storm was in full swing when I ducked in through the entrance, damp and a bit hungover, for a late lunch. I shuffled inside and tried out my rudimentary Italian on the young hostess behind the counter. Thankfully, I made the grade and was guided to a little table in back whose window allowed a view of the rain. Aperitifs were shuttled out of the kitchen at a leisurely clip while I availed myself of various antipasti. Gulp by gulp, bite by bite, the degeneracies of the night previous were mended and I emerged a stabler specimen.

By meal's end I was feeling quite satisfied and placed an order for an espresso; the only fitting end for such a lunch. I watched with interest as the rain began to taper off and the sun made a shy reprise through the clouds, and wondered after my next move. The day was young, but until the ill weather had well and truly blown over I would be stuck indoors. Many of the other travelers in town, upon catching a whiff of the rain, had moseyed on, leaving me alone with the pleasant but semi-inscrutable locals. The prospect of spending another day binging on the local fare was not without appeal, but the breadth of my indulgence in the foregoing days had been impressive, and I feared I might soon grow sick of milk and honey. I wanted, if possible, to seek some new scenery, at the least.

The espresso was eventually delivered with a side of mineral water, but as I went to raise it to my lips, I happened to spot the woman who was then clearing my dishes, and something about her made me stop short. This wasn't the hostess who'd seated me and brought out my food—no, this was a busser, perhaps, garbed in a brown apron.

And although I hadn't the foggiest idea just *where* I'd seen her, I knew with a single glance that this was not our first meeting.

My mind went roaming. At first, I fancied her a relic of the night before; a pretty face I'd sat and drank with in the wee small hours. Moments passed, though, and this particular face didn't turn up in the Rolodex of good-time gals—no, my acquaintance with this face, however inexplicably, predated this little trip of mine. My gawking drew her large, clear eye at some point, and I watched as a faint smile—a little knowing, and a little self-conscious—passed across her ruby lips. There was, in that brief nonverbal exchange, a hint of recognizance from us both, unless I was mistaken.

I must not have been in my right mind when I cleared my throat and addressed this busser, her arms cradling my soiled dishes, in plain English. "I'm sorry... Do I know you? I feel as though we've met before..."

Before I had even realized the silliness in addressing a local in my native tongue, I received my reply. It was delivered, to my surprise, in English as perfect as my own. "I was thinking the same thing," she said with a little narrowing of those vast eyes.

Now that I knew the feeling was mutual, I chuckled and threw back the espresso, glancing this fellow expat up and down. She seemed roughly my age, with long, velvety black hair tied back in a loose braid. The woman was slim, even a little waifish—but her arresting features more than made up for any defects in her figure. She hastened away with the dishes, disappearing through a little door in back of the restaurant, and for a time I thought that was the last I'd see of her. I sucked down my mineral water and stood, shuffling to the front counter where I settled the bill and went snooping around for signs of the mysterious busser.

I didn't have to snoop long, for I caught her peering out at me from the kitchen doorway, a cryptic smile upon her full lips and her slight hands tucked into the pockets of her apron. Matching her smile, I turned for the exit, but not before gesturing her over. The two of us met beneath the awning out front, the damp wind rushing past us and the rain slowing to a crawl. "You live around here, huh? College student?" I asked.

She shook her head and tucked a few raven-colored locks behind an elfish ear. "No, I'm just passing through. The restaurant was short-handed and I figured bussing tables would be a nice way to earn a little extra cash before I move on."

"Where you moving on to?" I asked.

Here, she went on the offensive, flashing a pearly grin. "Are you always this pushy, Mr. Tourist?"

"Only when I meet a girl I really like," I replied without missing a beat. "Anyway, go back a generation or two and I'm about as local as this here road," I said, stamping upon the wet street. "I'm Jack," I continued, extending a hand to shake. "I never got your name."

"Jack..." She tried the name on for size under her breath and shook my hand with an endearing daintiness. I found her hands thin and fragile—and a little cold. Her expression betrayed something like confusion, and she laughed in spite of herself. "I can't put my finger on why, but you *seemed* like a Jack to me."

"Sometimes the name just fits," I said. "And you?"

Her reply wound up having a baffling effect on me; just as her expression had been clouded at learning my name, I found myself thoroughly distracted—and unaccountably uneasy—upon learning hers. She looked up at me with those grand eyes, and in the instant before she spoke, I think her name was already racing toward the tip of my tongue. "My name is Elspeth," she said.

"Elspeth..." Now that I knew her name, I didn't know what to do with it. I think I nodded slowly, smiled awkwardly, and said something like, "That's not a name you hear every day. At least, not in my neck of the woods."

"But it fits, doesn't it?" she asked.

"It does," I finally replied, snapping back into form. "Somehow, I knew that was what you were going to say. I'm sure, more certain than ever, that we've met before. But I can't for the life of me say where."

She offered me another little smile, its exact meaning unclear, and then turned back toward the restaurant. "Well, it was nice speaking to you, Jack. I should get back to work..."

But I wasn't through with her yet. "Hold on," I said, "when can I see you again? We're practically old friends, after all—we must catch up!"

Elspeth hesitated, glancing back into the establishment.

"What time do you get off?" I pressed.

"I'll be done here around eight, eight-thirty," she offered through a sheepish smile.

Recalling my haunts of the night prior, I motioned down the misty street and invited her out for drinks. "I know a few good places," I assured her. "I'll meet you out here around eight-thirty, then?"

"Make it nine-thirty," she insisted. "Gives me a little time to get ready."

"Fair enough." I left her with a wave and a smile, ducking through the drizzle on my way back to the hostel. "See you tonight!"

Although Elspeth returned to the restaurant, I felt her eyes on me long after the establishment had disappeared from view. Her gaze, so crystal pure, clung to me like a cobweb; try as I might, I couldn't rid myself of the sensation of being watched by her. I shuffled from one building to the next, scouring my memory. I wanted to know why she seemed so familiar to me, why both of us agreed that we'd met somewhere before. "Elspeth... Elspeth..." I muttered the name aloud like a spell, examined it every which way, but could find no significance in it.

I did find something else, though. Meditations on her face—lovely though it had seemed to me in the moment—left my stomach clambering. The more I said her name, the more I plunged after dim memories I supposed were rattling around in some dark corner of my head, the sicker I began to feel. I blamed the aperitifs, the parting shot of espresso and the soggy scenery, though somewhere in the recesses of my psyche I must have known even then that these were not the cause of my distress.

The feeling passed when I stopped focusing on Elspeth. I tucked away the memories of her lovely face, the rareness of her name, the curious circumstances around our meeting and slipped into the hostel, where I meant to sleep off my lunch for the next few hours.

I dreamt of a rainy Italian street after dark, a street the likes of which might be found in any small village, and which bore an especial resemblance to the narrow avenues of my then-current stay. The old buildings jutted messily from the left and right of me like crowded teeth, and my dream-self was relegated to a strip of weathered brick road. Navigating the moonlit stretch, my progress down the strip opposed by a pervasive fog, I seemed in want of something—of help, of attention, of company.

In the dream I chanced to speak, but to the denizens of the dream-world and to my own ears my calls were aborted before meaning could be translated to sound, and I felt as though my throat had been packed with the cottony fog. That there were others located along this hazy stretch was never in doubt, for though I could not easily see them, I spied certain evidences of them as I panned up and down the street. Dubious shapes propped up in second-story windows gave the impression of watchful sitters; doorways and alleyways both, though clotted with mist, contained shadows *within* their shadows indicative of a semi-ghostly occupancy.

My staggerings grew more frantic and confused, but no matter the dampened thump of my step along the bricks, the road ahead never seemed to branch off or to end. I turned upward in the hopes of reasoning with the moon, but for all its selective lighting of the dreary tableau, I couldn't set eyes on it. A dread welled up in me at that moment, and on some level I must have realized that I was dreaming. With this self-awareness, various of the shadows were driven away from the scene and my surroundings were presented in a greater level of detail than ever before.

It was then that I turned to one of those second-story windows and found myself studied through a pair of large, glassy eyes.

Then, the mouth of one stationed in a dim doorway was pressed a into blood-red smile as I passed.

A thin figure leaning against a brick facade worked her fingers through locks of shimmering black hair.

Everywhere, I found traces of Elspeth.

She was the one who'd been watching me through the windows.

She was the one whose gaze had brushed against me from the doorways and alleys.

Elspeth. Elspeth. *Elspeth.*

I awoke uttering that name, stomach sour and chest tight. I sat up in my spartan room, clutching a blanket to my breast and fearing that I might be sick. It took some time for my eyes to adjust to the gloom of my hovel; it took me longer still to recognize that the gulf between dreams and reality had finally been spanned, and that I was truly awake. I jumped out of bed and paced around in my underwear for ten, fifteen minutes, and only when I dumped a bit of water over my head and scrubbed at my scruffy face did I return to something like normalcy.

Since departing the restaurant and settling into my midday nap, the rain had quit. I could still smell it coming in through the draft, but cracking the blinds I found the stuff had stopped falling. A measly gray light was seeping out of fractures in the dusk; my wristwatch insisted it was a few minutes past seven. I balked at the time, didn't feel as though I'd slept all that long, but a peek at the wall clock out in the lobby backed up the Seiko on my wrist.

Stopping into the communal bathroom, I took a hasty shower in lukewarm water and, having little in the way of fresh clothes, blasted myself with cologne. These preparations being made, I stepped out into the quiet streets and began meandering. There was still time to kill, after all, and I wanted to exorcise the restlessness in my legs before meeting up with Elspeth.

It was during this long, distracted walk that certain things started to become clear to me. As the studier of antiquities must unearth and brush up objects of interest before they can be closely examined, I went burrowing down into the world of memory, barely sidestepping puddles that would have doomed my leather shoes to ruin, and sought traces of Elspeth in the bedrock. The name which had produced so odd and hypnotic an effect on me finally struck pay dirt when, by happy chance, my subconscious linked it to a boarding school memory of mine.

I could recall sitting in a lunchroom, hearing that name repeated all around me, the other children uttering it *sotto voce*.

"Can you believe what happened to Elspeth?"

"Elspeth was so creepy, don't you think?"

"I never really cared for Elspeth, but that's still very sad..."

All at once, I was struck by the memory of a strange girl—one who had existed always on the periphery, and who had unexpectedly died at thirteen. *Her* name had been Elspeth—Elspeth Emory—I now recalled. And then, without really meaning to, I shuddered.

It wasn't merely that the busser at the restaurant and my dead schoolmate shared the same first name; no, the longer I reflected on them both, the more I began to draw other—more troubling—parallels between them. Elspeth Emory had been possessed of large, clear eyes—transfixing things. None at the school would have denied it. Curiously, the Elspeth I had just met also had eyes of the same rare and beguiling character. The Elspeth of slumbering memory had had long, black hair and full, red lips; ditto the comely busser I was on my way to meet.

Names are strange and powerful things. Certain names are perhaps drawn to certain personalities by the machinery of fate, and so it can be supposed that every "Jack", "Jill" or, in this case,

"Elspeth", share at least a modicum of common ground. Having only met a single Elspeth in all my life prior, I couldn't help but be jarred by the tremendous similarities, however. Although I understood it to be ridiculous, I couldn't altogether smother the notion that the two Elspeths were somehow one and the same individual.

But then, was it really such a stretch? Perhaps, I thought, I was misremembering. Perhaps a girl at the boarding school *had* died, but it had been someone else. Truly, the most logical explanation for all of this was that I'd gotten my wires crossed—that Elspeth Emory had never died, and that we'd met again by coincidence, decades beyond the schoolyard.

The fact that both of us had recognized each other had once intrigued and amused me; now, it filled me with a grim curiosity. As I walked circuits throughout the town and started in earnest toward the restaurant, I decided I would put the matter straight to her—that I wouldn't rest until I'd gotten to the bottom of things.

The hours I spent walking were lonely; the streets, damp and nigh empty, echoed with my thudding footfalls. I looked time and again at the buildings, finding myself watched here and there by disinterested locals, and was brought back to the scenery of my strange dream. The feeling of being watched grew with every lap I walked through the town square, hands in my pockets, and by the time I came upon the restaurant a few minutes past nine, it had gotten rather dark and I had nearly lost my nerve. Something—I can't hope to express what—was at work within me, trying to get me to skip my meeting with Elspeth, to leave the town altogether.

Instead, at ten past nine, I caught a glimpse of her slender form stationed beside the restaurant, her sleek hair hanging curtain-like over her shoulders. She was wearing a tasteful black dress and simple silver earrings, and when she turned and looked at me from afar I admit my heart scrambled in my breast. Believe me when I say that she looked lovely; her gem-like eyes caught the faint moon glow and shimmered brilliantly, like a cat's. Despite the gloom, I could see her thin face parted by a smile. She was utterly entrancing.

And yet, this was not all. For every compliment I might have paid her, every mark I might have given for her beauty, I was haunted by some vague horror that detracted from it all. I approached her on stilted legs, at once stunned at her prettiness and convinced that she should not exist. When I drew near, I must have been very pale indeed, because when I entered into the soft light of the restaurant's signage she leaned forward and appraised me with a knit brow. "Jack? Are you all right?"

I laughed off her concern. "Me? Yes, I'm quite well, thanks. It's just, you frightened me half to death."

She cocked her head to the side. "Why's that?"

"I didn't expect you to look so beautiful," I replied. Tugging at my shirt, I added, "And here I am, looking like a bum!"

She laughed, pulling away from the restaurant and walking by my side. Like the needle of a compass, I turned on my heels and began leading us due booze. The town was home to many a decent watering hole, and I thought nothing better to subdue the strange thoughts in my head than a tipple or two. Now that I was very near to her, I became host not only to that red-blooded feeling that comes over one when in the company of a beautiful woman, but also to an unquashable shiver that made occasional passes up my spine and across my shoulders. I hid this all well enough, chattering as we made our way through a growing fog, but wondered as we walked whether or not I'd even be able to keep a drink down.

"I was thinking about you, earlier," I said, peering up at the dark sky.

"Oh?"

"I think we've met before. You felt the same, yes?"

She nodded, combing away a few locks of stunning black. "Yes. There's something about you..."

The delicate timbre of her voice made the hairs on the back of my neck stand, and my pulse quickened. "You're American?"

Again, she nodded. "Born and raised."

"Whereabouts?"

"Maine," she replied without losing a beat.

My shoulders tensed. That was exactly the response I'd been expecting. "And whereabouts did you go to school, Elspeth?"

"In New York," she replied.

All at once, I shed my tensions. "New York?" I said, chuckling. "Oh, I see. I haven't spent much time there. I suppose it's safe to say we weren't schoolmates, then."

She wasn't done explaining herself yet, however. "I did a stint for a few years at a boarding school in rural Maine," she said. Her tone was innocently matter-of-fact, straightforward in light of my interrogation, but I couldn't help but pick up on something mischievous in it, too. "I was there until my parents pulled me out; we had to relocate on account of my father's job."

The boarding school *I'd* gone to had been in rural Maine. I wet my lips, stuffed my hands deep into my pockets so that she wouldn't noticed them fidgeting. "What school was that? Do you remember?" I held my breath.

"The Rook's School," she replied. "Why, do you know it?"

At hearing her reply, I stumbled. The two of us paused, and I muttered a few curses at the ancient cobblestones. My upset had nothing to do with the street, of course, but with the confirmation of my suspicions. "Yes," I said after a long pause. "Yes, I know it very well. I graduated from there..."

"You don't say..."

"So," I continued, swallowing down my dread, "that's where we met, then... You're Elspeth Emory, aren't you?"

The woman looked up in surprise. "Yes, that's right." She studied my face a moment in the moonlight, fell behind a couple of paces as I trudged moodily on, and then hastened to catch up with me. "And you're... you're Jack Honnold, aren't you?"

I felt as though the wind had been knocked out of me. She'd gotten it in one. "Yes," I admitted. "That's my name..." I could think of nothing else to say, and although we'd drawn very close to the entrance of a small bar, I felt like I'd sooner fall to the ground than walk in and order a drink with this woman. The world seemed to be spinning all around me, and all I could do was chuckle to maintain some illusion of calm. Here I was, walking through Italy with a girl who'd died back in Maine nearly two decades ago. It was all so strange—disorienting, unbelievable and, frankly, hilarious. I wanted to laugh but couldn't get the sound right as I stumbled ahead in bewilderment.

Elspeth paused beside me and placed one of her thin hands upon my shoulder. The gesture made me tense up, and I found I couldn't turn to look her in the eye as she continued. "I knew it... I knew I'd seen you before, Jack..." She cleared her throat, a weird little laugh coming out of her before she could go on. "Now, this is going to sound so strange, Jack, but... I remember you. I remember seeing you at school, back in Maine. But... but as I remember it, something happened. I could have sworn that... Well, obviously, I'm losing my mind, but... I seem to remember that you *died*. A drowning, I thought... You would have been about thirteen..."

I gasped and turned to meet her, slack-jawed. "You... You thought that *I* died? That I *drowned?*"

A little red in the face, she nodded uncomfortably. "Obviously, I was mistaken—confusing you with someone else. But yes, I could've sworn..."

The laughter that poured out of me was easily the loudest thing for miles. I shook with laughter, lost my balance and had to lean against the brick facade of the bar. A few people in neighboring houses spat hasty curses at me for my boisterousness, and doors and windows were suddenly slammed shut. With tears in my eyes, I studied baffled Elspeth standing before me. "I'm sorry, I'm sorry," I pleaded, pawing at my face. "It's just... there's no way."

She shook her head. "Yes, clearly my memory's been muddled..."

"No, not that," I replied. "You see, I was convinced of the same thing, Elspeth."

She eyed me narrowly and gave a cryptic shake of the head.

"I was certain—*certain*—that I had gone to school with you back in Maine, and that *you* had died around thirteen years old. In fact, I still remember the headmaster telling us about it, interrupting our lunch hour. He said—"

"He told us all that Jack Honnold had drowned—that he'd been found in a ravine after some serious flooding!" she hastily put in. "Are you pulling my leg right now?"

"No! No, I'm not! As I remember it, we were told that *you*, Elspeth Emory, had been found in the flood waters. Now that I think back on it, I remember it as clear as day. But... obviously, my wires have been crossed. I'm sorry, I don't mean to mock you... it's just so weird that the two of us have this same false memory, have made this same mixup."

"It *is* strange, isn't it?"

Fighting back another wave of laughter, I motioned to the door of the establishment. "Here, let's have a drink, shall we? Perhaps if we dull the edges of memory a little further we'll get to the bottom of this bizarre mistake."

The two of us entered a single-story bar—the kind of place much-beloved by locals and seldom-seen by travelers. I had spent a few hours there the evening previous, carrying on with a number of fellow expats. Now that they'd gone, Elspeth and I were left alone in the place with a melancholic barkeep, a smattering of locals nose-deep in drinks and a bit of old music floating out of dusty speakers. There were only seven or eight tables, and the walls were of rough, unadorned plaster. The lights were so dim that the interior looked like a cave. I asked the barkeep for a decent bottle in rough Italian and took a seat with Elspeth near the back door.

I poured each of us a generous glass and happily accepted a platter of bread and other finger-foods. With a swirl and a gulp, I admitted a mouthful of the wine and sighed. "Wonderful. Great stuff. Just what I needed..."

Elspeth took a small sip, her saucer-like eyes never leaving me as she did so. When she drew the rim back, I saw her lips stained a fiery red—an effect made all the more intense by the light of a nearby candle. "I remember you, clear as day," she said with a slight nod. "Like it was yesterday. How strange that we should meet *here*, of all places. It's been so long..."

"Indeed," I chuckled. "Believe me, no one is as surprised as me. I never expected my date to be a dead girl!"

Elspeth fixed me with a firm glare, her dark brows arched and her jaw growing tense. "I'm not dead. I'm very much alive. See?" Without warning, she reached out across the table and grabbed my hand, taking care to ensure that a few of my fingertips were pressed to her wrist.

Perhaps, had I held on a little longer, I would have felt her pulse and laughed the whole thing off. The suddenness of the motion, coupled with the unexpected frigidity of her skin, made me pull back however. "I'm sorry, I'm just teasing," I continued, taking another gulp of wine. "It's very weird, what's happened tonight. I'm sure I'm losing my mind. Please, pay me no mind, Elspeth." Whether it was the utterance of her name or the young wine that made my throat burn, I couldn't say.

"Tell me," she continued, "what happened after you left the Rook's School?"

"After that?" I asked. "Well, I graduated, then moved on to university. I completed an undergrad in journalism at a small state school and then pursued a master's at U of M—which I only completed a year or so ago. Since then, I've been working in the editorial department for an arts and culture rag and writing articles for paying markets on the side. And you?"

I listened with immense interest as Elspeth prepared to describe the trajectory of her life since leaving Maine—but, as it turned out, there was precious little to tell. "School in New York, then a bit of college," she replied with altogether too much vagueness. "Since then, you know... I've been drifting from place to place. I take the occasional job before traveling on..." She shrugged and took a pull from her glass. "It isn't a stable life, but it suits me."

Though she had just provided me with a believable alibi for the past twenty-odd years, I found myself rather suspicious. The longer I scrutinized her, the more I worked over the paper-thin history she'd provided, the more I came to doubt it—to doubt *her*. It'd taken me awhile to dislodge the stubborn old memories, but now that I had, I hadn't the least doubt that Elspeth Emory had died back at school, a mere girl of thirteen. Between sips of wine and snippets of Italian pop songs, I replayed those scenes. The sullen announcement from the headmaster, the gossip that sprung up in the wake of her death, the once-ubiquitous girl's sudden absence. Though decades had passed and my memories of her had been long-buried, they were exposed and fresh now.

But at the same time, she was sitting before me, sipping wine and insisting on her own version of events. That much was certain. I did not doubt my eyes. Leaving behind the topic of death, we moved on to simpler fare. We discussed our travels, our impressions of Italy. I found her as knowledgeable a traveler as any I'd hitherto met; in the past year, she'd been all over the country, and had even wandered a little into the neighboring nations. She spoke English, of course, and her Italian was far more convincing than my own; aside from these, she'd also picked up a little Spanish and Portuguese throughout her travels.

More and more, I couldn't help feeling that every word coming out of Elspeth's mouth was a lie, however.

It wasn't that she stammered or seemed unsure of herself; no, everything she said was delivered with a trademark delicacy and earnestness that I found charming. Beneath this civil veneer, though, I suspected much. Maybe it was the wine revving me up, or something in the damp air, or even the way the candlelight played upon her unique features, but I couldn't take her claims at face value. There was a cunning in her, a calculatedness, that revealed itself chiefly in the silences and little expressions she made. Those eyes of hers, glassy and pure, nevertheless roamed about as she carried on, and in them I glimpsed occasional flickers of amusement or hesitation. The quirk of her lips, the way she toyed with her hair—all this struck me oddly as I listened to her speak.

And there was more. The night deepened, and when the first bottle of wine had run dry, I ordered a second. The price was very good and the vintage drinkable; lining my stomach with a bit of the food on offer, I felt as though I could imbibe all night. Elspeth kept up with me, but to my drunken eye she did not much feel the effect of the alcohol. Her dewy eyes remained sharp, her speech clear and unimpeded, her manner rather stable.

I don't mean to say that I was a slobbering drunk; quite the contrary, the stuff only served to make me a little fuzzy around the edges. Elspeth, as the night wore on, appeared the very image of sobriety, though.

Just how long we'd been sitting there when I sensed a change in her I can't be sure. It was very subtle at first; a narrowing of the features and a growing pallor of the flesh. Noting these, I said nothing. Next, by small degrees, there crept in a sunkenness—vast hollows ate up the eyes that had once seemed so lovely, leaving them veiled with dark and puckered lids. Her mouth followed suit, the color going temporarily from her lips and her delicate chin becoming recessed. When the candle at our table died out, these impressions remained in force; the gloom accentuated each of these changes, *intensified* them, until I could only through much squinting see the face of the one I'd initially sat down with.

Elspeth seemed to retreat into the darkness as the night wore on, the shadows enveloping her like a shawl. Her interest in the wine began to appear strictly superficial, and whenever she drew the glass to her lips she seemed to do so only in imitation of me. Running nervously from certain thoughts and fears, I blathered, covering everything from my recent travels to the odd memory of the Rook's School. For her part, Elspeth keenly listened; in fact, I was surprised throughout my soliloquies at her careful attention, at the subtle nods and gestures not only of comprehension, but of *absorption.*

Suddenly, I was cognizant of that vague uncanniness for which Elspeth had always been known; I caught traces of it now in those same gestures, in the relentless stare that was poured out upon me from the booth opposite. The attentions paid to me scarcely seemed human; rather, I felt myself dissected by a hostile insect—eyed by a conniving bird of prey. Despite the vastness and clarity I had earlier found in those eyes, there wasn't a shred of warmth in them to be found now. This wasn't immediately apparent on account of a practiced and consistent facade, but over time I witnessed what I felt were slippages of the mask and my stomach began to rebel against the copious volume of wine I'd funneled into it.

For the first time since meeting with Elspeth, I found myself filled not only with unease, but with regret. I'd made a terrible decision—sensed that I was somehow in danger—and something stirred within me, urging me to flee. Before I could dwell on this feeling and come up with an excuse to indulge it, however, the woman spoke.

"The more I think about it, the surer I am," said Elspeth, very slight as she shrunk deeper into the shadow. The lights in our segment of the bar were completely off, leaving us with only a hint of moonlight from the window. "My memories are true. Jack Honnold died all those years ago... I remember it clearly. So, who are you, then?"

I was taken off-guard by her pointed challenge and withered under the weight of her glare. "I don't know what to tell you, Elspeth. I'm not lying. As I've already told you, I remember things quite differently..."

"One of us is lying—one of us is obviously trying to deceive the other," she insisted.

"So, what?" I asked. "You think I made it all up? That I purposefully misremembered you, Elspeth?"

"I'm not dead," she seethed.

"Obviously."

"I'm *not* dead, Jack." Her hand shot out from beneath the table and clung to mine, its iciness sending a tremor through me. I tried to loose myself from her grasp, but she held on with incredible tightness—a tightness that made my knuckles groan. My pulse thundered against Elspeth's cold, quivering palm, but the longer we sat there, hand in hand, the more certain I became that I could not feel *her* pulse. Struggling against my revulsion, I squeezed her hand in kind, seeking the barest hint of a heartbeat in her frigid digits but finding none.

Suddenly, she seemed to realize what I was doing and let go of me, cradling herself in her arms as though wounded. "No..." she moaned, "No, Jack. I'm not dead. I'm *not!*" Her outburst momentarily eclipsed the gentle music and threatened to spoil the mood, as evidenced by the glares we got from the other patrons. "You're a *liar!*" she spat, and I confess that, in the shadows, her face grew very ugly indeed.

I said nothing, merely accosted her with my gaze.

"It's you who's dead, Jack. It's *you*. I'm sure of it."

"Get ahold of yourself," I muttered. "I don't know how to explain this, but Elspeth, you're—"

"I won't listen to this!" Without warning, Elspeth shot up from the table and turned to the rear door. The thing slammed as she bolted through, and the sounds of her feet pounding against the wet bricks outside was audible for several seconds afterward.

I was left disoriented, ill at ease, and was being watched from elsewhere in the bar with not a little curiosity. I had long since lost my taste for wine, and eyed the remainder in the bottle with disgust. But even though I was through drinking, I didn't get up, I didn't leave. Even though Elspeth's footfalls had long since died out and she'd vanished I knew not where, I didn't dare rise. It wasn't until a few hours later, when the sleepy barkeeper sent me packing, that I finally made my cautious exit and found the night air unexpectedly cool. I paused outside the bar, looking up and down the silent street, fearful that I might catch sight of Elspeth. No matter how many times I panned about on my way back to the hostel, she never turned up, however.

That isn't to say I didn't feel her, though. Just as it had been in my dream, I walked the empty streets and was conscious of a leering presence issuing from around shadowed corners. A faint mist had built up in the rain's wake, and through this haze I mistook many a common shape and fixture for the bent form of the strange woman who'd recently fled from my table.

I never did find her, and returned to the hostel without incident. I even managed, after some hours of pacing, to get a few hours of sleep. After that night, I never saw Elspeth Emory again.

But I *did* hear about her.

———

A week or so later, upon meeting some acquaintances in Tuscany, a certain newspaper article was brought to my attention; a thing in which, initially, I saw no significance. It dealt with an incident on the outskirts of Trevino. Knowing that I had only recently spent a few days in that region myself, this story was presented to me by curious friends who wondered if I'd known the poor creature mentioned within.

It was news of a death, you see, and a rather tragic one by the sounds of it. Early one morning—the very morning after Elspeth and I had so dramatically parted—a body had been fished out of the shallows of the Piave River. It had been that of a young woman—a foreigner, the authorities presumed. She was described in the article as having long, black hair and fair skin, and was alleged to have drowned sometime in the early morning. Investigators were asking for the public's help in identifying the woman, and my friends all wondered if it was someone we'd run across during our travels.

I knew who it was. Before I'd even finished reading the article, I'd known the identity of the girl found in the water. I'd known it because that hadn't been her first time drowning.

And, because the world is a strange place, perhaps it won't be the last, either.

———

Returning Stateside, I set about doing a bit of sleuth work. Under the pretenses of planning a reunion or some such thing, I endeavored to get in touch with some of my schoolmates from Maine—those who'd attended the Rook's School with me. Twenty years, numerous changes in address and occupation made this a difficult task, but by digging into social media I managed to make a handful of important connections, and through these came to learn some interesting things over the ensuing weeks.

I reconnected with an old boyhood friend of mine over the phone, Ronnie Clapham, and one afternoon we spent almost an hour catching up. Much of this call was a breeze, quite fun, and we reminisced a good deal. I learned that he and his wife were expecting their first child, and that he'd just begun working for a new architecture firm. I threw him a few details about my own life, touched briefly upon my recent trip to Italy, but then hit him with something altogether different.

"This is totally out of left field," I began, "but thinking back to the Rook's School, there's something that's been bugging me lately. Tell me, Ronnie, do you remember... oh, it must have been eighth or ninth grade. A girl at the school, Elspeth Emory, died. Remember that?"

Ronnie was some time in replying. Like me, he'd sidelined memories of Elspeth and had some trouble digging them back up on command. "Uh... I dunno, it kind of rings a bell," he admitted. Then, when I spent a few more minutes massaging his memory, it all suddenly came back to him. "Oh, yeah—the weird girl, right? She drowned, didn't she? Awful. I'd nearly forgotten. Didn't know her very well. I doubt anyone did; she was sort of a loner, I think."

I was prepared to tell Ronnie about my encounter with Elspeth in Italy. I wasn't planning to give him a thorough report; in fact, I knew I'd have to prune certain details just to appear sane. But before I could start down that track, he broke news about something else.

"Hold on, what?" I remember I leaned forward in my chair, staring down at the phone in disbelief. "*Who* died?"

Ronnie explained that one of our fellow students, a kid by the name of Josh Taylor, had unexpectedly died the previous spring. Ronnie himself had heard this second or third-hand, and had done a bit of digging in the California news for more details. It turned out that Josh, an auto mechanic, had been found dead along the coast in what investigators were claiming to be a lover's suicide. Both his body, as well as that of an unidentified young woman, were found lapping against the shore. They'd drowned in the early hours of the morning, and the authorities were asking for anyone with information about Josh and his mysterious death-mate to come forward.

I thought this extremely strange in light of what had recently occurred near Trevino, and upon ending my call with Ronnie immediately did some searching of my own. Sure enough, articles from the previous spring turned up readily, describing Joshua Taylor, 31, of San Francisco, and a "Jane Doe" found drifting in the sea by early-morning beachgoers. Suicide was suspected, but foul play and misadventure could not be ruled out.

Josh's loved ones had been interviewed after the tragedy, but none of them had been acquainted with the Jane Doe, and had been unaware of any romantic entanglements on Josh's part. As far as I could see, no headway had been made in the case since the spring, although the police department *had* attached an e-fit photo of the Jane Doe in the hopes of finding leads. I had only to scroll toward the bottom of the page to find this computer-generated image which alleged to represent a facial composite of the female victim.

And what I found made me drop my phone.

The details of the composite left something to be desired. E-fits are seldom a perfect match, what with their tendency to minimize certain features or exaggerate others. But in this case, I had little doubt in my mind that I was looking at a digitally-rendered photo of Elspeth Emory. Her large, saucer-like-eyes stared up from the page, and her puckered lips burned a cherry red. She had long, black hair, well past the tops of her shoulders, and was very thin.

My theory—which has only since been borne out by *another* death, not discussed here, of this same inexplicable stripe—is this: Elspeth Emory died at thirteen years old. Unloved and ignored in life, her spirit has been relegated for years to the abyss of memory. For decades, we've carried around a little fragment of her, neglecting it till it almost crumbles away.

But gradually, over time, acquaintances have begun to remember her.

They have recalled the strange girl with the large, clear eyes.

They have remembered the one with the full, pouting lips—the one with curtains of perfect black hair.

They have begun to see her, to be visited by her.

Elspeth Emory no longer wishes to be alone in death. Instead, siren-like, she seeks to lure in those who once ignored her, to doom them to the same fate she suffered.

In my case, I saw through her. I recognized her for what she was, and refused to be taken in by her lies. Had I ignored my instincts and followed her from that bar, what might have become of me? Probably, I would have joined her by the banks of the Piave River that next morning...

To the best of my knowledge, three of us from the Rook's School have encountered Elspeth Emory in the years since her untimely death. Two of us are dead, and it is only a matter of time before another—quite unexpectedly—encounters her. We have carried around memories of the girl for all these years in the backs of our minds, like a cancer.

Now, it has begun to spread.

ROOM TO BREATHE

Not being able to afford Christmas gifts for one's children is an awful feeling. Passing a child's birthday with mere well wishes and pats on the back for want of funds is somehow more disappointing for a father than it is for the kid in question. The *greatest* shame I have ever felt, however, came not from a missed birthday gift or an overdrawn account over the holidays. No, that singular shame is reserved for the occasion when I lacked the funds to bury my boy.

For eight and a half months—nearly as long as he'd gestated in the womb of a mother who would go on to abandon him at a year old—my son fought a terminal illness. We leaned hard on whatever government help we could find, and I missed shifts to accommodate his appointments, straining the patience of a few bosses. It doesn't matter how much money you have, really—eight months in and out of a hospital will bankrupt the best of us, and I was no exception. There is only so much goodwill in the world, only so much aid that can be summoned with a teary plea. When my son lost his battle against his disease, I was left holding the bill.

As a young father with a once-healthy boy, perhaps I could be forgiven for not planning his burial with any real thoroughness. For most, who are sufficiently blessed to reserve such terrible sufferings for their twilight years, it would be considered too morbid a thing to put much stock into. Grieving and penniless however, I now found myself dodging calls from medical debt collectors while trying to figure out how to lay my son to rest.

I don't know how other people decide where to bury their loved ones. Perhaps they rely on the recommendations of family members or friends; maybe the odd print ad or radio jingle makes its case; maybe, like me, they simply go for a long drive around town with their guts in knots and pull into the first place they find. It was a sorry-looking old cemetery, all told, though I suppose I've never known a really happy-looking site of that kind. I went swaying out of the car, hands in my pockets, and thumped on the door thirty or forty minutes before closing.

My summons was answered by a bent man of roughly sixty years. His head was fringed in tufts of silvery hair, and he wore a pair of round glasses that drooped along the bridge of his pockmarked nose. He blinked at me a few times and smoothed out the navy turtleneck he wore beneath a tired blazer of similar hue before inquiring after the reason for my visit.

"I'm sorry to bother you," I remember saying. "I'm looking for a place to bury my son. I don't have any experience with this, and I don't know where to go..."

The man, who shortly thereafter introduced himself as Lopez, was very cordial, and invited me inside. We together made the trek through a dated lobby and passed into a small back room with space enough for a desk, two chairs, their potential sitters and little else. Lopez was evidently an expert at his trade, with many years of experience; I was hardly the first grieving man he'd ever welcomed into his office, and I could tell because he managed me with a paternal gentleness that effortlessly seized upon my vulnerability. I found him talkative and organized, and no sooner were the initial pleasantries left in the rearview did he begin drawing out brochures, speaking of plot sizes, casket-thickness and, of course, money.

I listened to the man's spiel, despairing all the while as it dawned on me that I would not be able to afford his most basic package. I asked if a payment plan might be available, knowing full well that my battered finances would never be able to manage even *that* arrangement, and was sorrowfully informed that, while banks will gladly advance sums with which to procure big screen televisions, seven-week cruises and muscle cars, his austere business could only operate with up-front payment. It was then that Lopez asked about my situation—asked me what I *could* afford.

And it was then that the dam broke.

Weather enough tragedy in your life and you'll get used to crying in front of strangers. Burning with the fresh ache of loss and doubly sickened by the unfairness of it all, I told the man straight: I was broke, I was on the very cusp and had nowhere to turn. Family members and friends who had once been charitable now eyed me with loathsomeness on account of my endless need. A stint in bankruptcy court was in my near future, but it remained to be seen if even this would keep me from backsliding into utter poverty. The utilities were all overdue, the rent was in arrears and my job was on its last legs.

Lopez listened to this with genuine sympathy, but he was used to sob stories, what with his buttering his bread in the tragedy industry, and experience had made him firm. Unswayed, he set out for me the most basic, affordable arrangements, and suggested that he would do everything in his power to make the price easy on me. This said, he hastened to add, there was only so much he *could* do. The economy, that versatile and omnipresent scapegoat, was cited again and again whenever I earnestly pressed him. I was ultimately sent away with a stapled stack of papers with Lopez's neat scrawl upon them, the contents of which detailed the cheapest possible burial arrangements for my son.

Before leaving, I threw all shame to the wind. I might've kissed the man's feet for a discount, and I begged him to reconsider on account of my desperation. A payment plan, a simpler arrangement—I even asked him if some other cemetery in the area could do it for cheaper. All this was refused—and sorrowfully, I might add, for I could tell the man was genuinely bothered at turning me away. He apologized repeatedly, wished it could be different. "Would that I could offer you something more affordable, my friend, and I am gravely sorry for your loss. The margins, you understand, are already so thin, however..."

The margins, I supposed, were *thin indeed* if charity was allowed to grow cold, and so I shuffled out of that graveyard office a weaker and more hopeless man than I'd entered it—a horror I had scarcely thought possible.

That night, I scraped the bottom of the barrel while poring over Lopez's forms and doing pointless arithmetic. It doesn't matter how many times you add it up or pare it down; zero is all you're left with when you're working with zero. I had one chance of affording a proper burial for my son, I figured—that being the payout of my own paltry life insurance policy. A seatbeltless romp down the freeway at a hundred and twenty, or a long walk off a real tall rooftop would do it. If I conveniently happened to kick the bucket that night, then perhaps old Lopez would be kind enough to take some of that insurance money and make it a package deal; two-for-one.

In the end, I didn't have to resort to such extremity to get the job done, however.

Instead, I had only to pass another sleepless, anguished night. On the other end of it, in the wee small hours of the morning, I received a phone call from none other than Lopez. Initially, I'd mistaken the call for an early attempt at debt collection, and I almost erased the resultant voicemail without listening to it. Sleepily sampling the recording however, I found it to be my man at the cemetery. He was reaching out with a most unexpected offer.

"Mr. Prescott, I'm sorry to bother you so early in the morning," his message began. "You see, something's come up. I've... I've been thinking about your predicament ever since you left my office yesterday afternoon, and I want, if I can, to do something for your boy. Time is of the essence; please, come by my office *as soon as possible*. I cannot stress this enough. There is only a narrow window in which I can assist you with this... and it is a most unorthodox arrangement, I admit... Please, call me back."

At hearing that Lopez was willing to work with me—that perhaps this aspect of the nightmare might finally end—I felt the stirrings of hope in my breast. How odd and foreign a feeling it was. Suddenly invigorated, I jumped into my car and sped to the cemetery.

———

Lopez's arrangement was indeed an odd one.

In fact, what he suggested was, if not completely illegal, then certainly taboo.

I was admitted onto the premises like a fugitive; Lopez had clearly been watching for me. Without a word, he led me through the dark building and to the same back room where we'd previously had our unproductive back and forth. There, shutting the door softly behind him, he locked it and went creeping over to a dusty fax machine from which he pulled out a few freshly-printed documents. "Something has happened," began the man quietly, shuffling the papers in his thin, shaky hands. "Whatever you decide, Mr. Prescott, not a word of this conversation may leave this office, am I understood? It is a matter not only of my legal safety, but of my professional reputation. I do not invite you here and make this offer lightly; I do so only out of immense pity for your situation. You impressed upon me that you are a man with little to his name—a man who has lost the only valuable thing he possessed.

"Let not our earlier dealings make you think me a monster, sir; I am but a man myself, with bills to pay and mouths to feed. Even so, I am not made of stone. Your story resonated with me, and though it is not mine to share, your pain weighs on my heart.

And so, sir, when *this* happened across my desk this night...” Here, Lopez shook the papers in his grasp. “Well, naturally, I thought of you...”

The man explained his offer therewith, and didn't mince words.

“I understand that you can't afford a plot, casket or burial. There is one, however, bound to be buried here this day. An anonymous child, a boy roughly the same age as your late son, will be laid to rest here this very evening. A John Doe; the victim of a monstrous crime. The authorities have gathered all the forensic data they need to continue their case into the lad's murder, and have decided now to put him to rest.

“The local government is fronting the cost for this arrangement; a basic plot has been paid for, along with a simple casket. Because me and my staff are handling this, we get to decide which casket to use, and may opt for a larger one—one large enough, perhaps, to house not one, but *two* children. Do you understand me, Mr. Prescott? I offer you this chance at a free burial for your son. He and the poor John Doe may share a grave here, in my cemetery. If you have his body promptly ordered here, I will see to the paperwork and other preparations myself. Your son and this John Doe will be dealt with carefully, laid to rest respectfully, and there shall be no cost to you.

“Of course, there is a caveat. No one—and I mean *no one*—must know of what I've done. It would be a matter of some legal gravity, and would doubtless cause a scandal. The way I see it is this: Both your son and this poor John Doe have left us before their time. They will be able to keep each other company on the long road to eternity, and you, in your need, will be able to rest knowing that your son's remains have been reverently interred.”

The old man held his breath and was rather gray in the face. He knew just how outre and ugly his offer was. He'd spun his share of pretty words in making his pitch, but in the end he was proposing that my son play the part of a stowaway in this John Doe's grave. It was a soul-wrenching and stomach-turning proposition.

But it was one that I couldn't afford to reject.

Having no alternatives, I reticently agreed to Lopez's terms. A call was placed to the local hospital where my son's body was being kept, and Lopez himself made arrangements to have it transferred at once.

Within hours, both bodies had been placed in Lopez's care, and the two occupants of the full-sized casket were gussied up in short order. My son was laid to rest in his Sunday's best, and in cleaning and positioning him, skillful Lopez imparted something of peacefulness to my son as he was placed within the coffin.

Then there was the other boy.

He looked about the same age as my son, though a good deal more haggard. My boy could not have claimed to have had a nice and privileged upbringing, but this other lad looked, bluntly, like a street urchin. He was covered in bruises, burns and wounds, some of them hastily sutured by investigators. He remained clothed in filthy rags, barefoot, with wild hair—just as he'd been found. Unwilling to let such a thing pass, I urged Lopez to postpone his burial just long enough for me to return home, where I grabbed up a few of my son's articles. The hand-me-downs fit reasonably well, and so John Doe was placed in the casket in a more respectable state.

The casket was sealed and the cemetery staff were not told a thing about who was inside, except that the coffin was bound for the "anon" site they'd been in the process of digging since dawn. Lopez and I stood graveside as the thing was lowered and covered with earth, and for that thirty-odd minutes I felt myself overcome with a warmth and calm the likes of which I hadn't known in many months. The relief I felt in finally interring my son's remains was immense, and I was extremely grateful to the caretaker for his strange but affordable accommodations. Lopez would hear nothing of thanks; he assured me that my boy and I would be in his prayers and asked for nothing in return save, in the future, good word of mouth.

With my son buried and his gravesite accessible for the occasional visit, I left the cemetery feeling as though the most painful chapter of my life might finally be closed.

I should have known better, of course.

In actuality, it had only just opened.

The dreams of my son began three or four nights after his burial. I remember them not only because they were among the first dreams of mine to register in those dreary, misty-eyed days, but because their frightening character served to imprint them in the folds of my brain. If I close my eyes now and silence my thoughts but a little, I can still slip back into that nighted dreamscape.

I dreamt my boy was sitting in a black room with his back to me. He twitched uncomfortably in a high-backed chair with velveteen cushions, and was apparently aware of my presence. His thin voice reached my ears as he looked straight ahead. Exactly what it was that captured his attention I couldn't say, but it held him firmly so that he didn't so much as think to turn as he uttered, "Dad, he won't leave me alone."

This lone remark troubled me much in my sleep. I wanted to reply to him, to get to the heart of the remark, but in this dream I had no mouth to speak of, no voice, and was reduced simply to the role of concerned listener.

"He won't leave me alone," continued my boy, his voice low but intense. "He won't let me sleep."

I awoke a groggy and confused mess in the middle of the night, jarred to wakefulness by the brief snippet of dream imagery. As any sensible man is wont to do during a particularly stressful season in life, I wrote the dream off as a symptom of anxiety, of course. I took no meaning from it, ascribed it no greater importance than I might any other nightmare. I treated it simply as a snapshot of my mental health in the moment; a glimpse into my battered psyche, which was still very wrapped up in thoughts of my late son.

But then I dreamt it again some nights later. The same dream, the same scenery, the same plea visited me as I drowsed, though the lattermost had changed since the first go-round. My son's tone was now timorous, his delivery quite shaky, and I sensed in him a childish panic the likes of which I hadn't heard from him since perhaps his toddler years. "D-Dad? Dad, please... he won't let me sleep... Dad! Dad, he... he won't... Oh, dad, please! Please, dad! Help me! He won't be quiet! He won't let me sleep!"

I came to from this second dream with my alarm fully raised and my son's voice reverberating in my head like a shrill echo. Much time and self-soothing, though, convinced me of the dream's meaninglessness, and when I'd had a good pace around the apartment, a glass of water and a glass of something stronger, I finally laughed to myself and made peace with the fact that I'd entered an era of nightmares. There were worse things in the world to suffer than bad dreams, I told myself, and surely, after all I'd been through in recent months, it was no wonder that my sleep was being interrupted by this less than pleasant fare.

The recurring nature of this dream, though, didn't sit too well. I worked its contents over in my mind long after awakening, and there were times when, at once agitated and over-tired, I couldn't help taking my son's plea at face value. Perhaps the boy, in some arcane way, had bridged the span between our worlds and was reaching out to me for help. I went back to work, spent my days buried in other people's problems, but returned to the substance of the dream in my down-time. The occasional web searches into supernatural topics brought me no closer to a satisfactory explanation for the dream, though, and a few nights of solid, undisturbed sleep saw it gradually slip from my memory.

It's funny, but this slow calm, this slow forgetting, set the stage for the single most terrifying fright of my life.

I dreamt the wretched dream a third time. In the first two instances, my descent into the dream space had been measured, paced—I had known myself to be slipping into it before the details had been given even an ounce of sharpness. This time, I fell straight into the black tableau—was dropped into it like a lobster into a pot of boiling water. My son's piercing screams broke through the stillness till I was sure my skull would split in two, and as I watched him tremble and sway in the same chair as before, I thought him white as a sheet. He tugged at his hair, thrashed madly, and even half-turned toward me with the widest eyes I'd ever seen on him. He did not ask for help this time, did not address me in any way.

He screamed.

And he screamed.

How long he continued screaming is beyond guessing, but the wonder of dreams is that they can occupy at once a vast space and the space of an instant. All this to say; though the vision may have only lasted the blink of an eye, I withstood my son's screams for what seemed an eon.

I awoke on the floor after that third instance, and in a sweaty nocturnal panic clawed my way across the apartment, to my son's old room. Punching open the door, I scampered in, expecting to find him within. The cries I was hearing were all inside my head, though; my ears and skull still rang with them. The room was empty, just as my son had left it before his last hospitalization.

I thought myself many things after suffering that particular fright. I thought myself ill. Depressed. Suicidal. Haunted. I marched circuits around my place till dawn with all the lights on and coached myself under my breath. Perhaps I would seek professional help. Perhaps I would call a priest. Perhaps I was coming down with some disease of my own, and this shock of madness was but its first symptom.

Eventually, though, I made the decision to call someone else. I chose to call old Lopez, of all people.

I appreciated—and, in some respects, still appreciate—what the man had done for my son, and had found him well-mannered and easy to talk to. My ultimate reason for reaching back out to him however was that he had buried my boy along with a stranger. This stranger, this John Doe, seemed to be at the very heart of my son's dream-borne pleas. Who else, if not his casket-mate, could possibly be responsible for keeping him up, for interrupting his eternal repose?

And so, extremely nervous and very careful not to sound the ingrate, I dialed Lopez late in the morning.

My reception, though, was not nearly so warm as I'd envisioned it.

After recapping the trio of dreams and chuckling my way through certain fears and doubts, the old caretaker offered what seemed to me well-rehearsed condolences, but was unwilling to offer anything in the way of practical assistance. "To be perfectly truthful Mr. Prescott, I don't know why you're calling me. I'm very sorry to hear about your troubles, of course. And losing a child—why, who wouldn't have bad dreams? But to even suggest that this has something to do with our... unconventional arrangement... Well, I tell you, I have known many superstitious men in this line of work, but I am not one of them. You would do better to contact a therapist, I think."

"But sir," I pressed, "Don't you think it strange? These three dreams have built on one another, and my son's cries are—"

"I think," interjected Lopez, "that you came to me without a cent to your name, Mr. Prescott. You wanted some room to breathe, and I did what I could for you. I tell you, one good thing about this trade is that my clients never express satisfaction nor dissatisfaction with their stay. So, if you'll excuse me, Mr. Prescott, I have things to do. Take care."

Weeks passed and the dream I have discussed never made a reprise.

This is not to say that it no longer dominated my thoughts, however.

In its absence, I thought about it more keenly than ever before, and with every passing night of clear and untroubled sleep the weight upon me grew more burdensome. I felt as though that third and final dream had been an emergency dispatch, and that the lack of further correspondence all but confirmed my worst fears: My son had fallen to some eternal suffering. Due to my inaction, he was now beyond all help.

It was easy, too easy, to bury myself in my work. It gave me something to think about, something to obsess over, aside from my son. When I was at work, answering phones or staring at a computer for twelve-plus hours, I didn't have to think about the dreadful screams, the dream scenery, the unbridled terror in my late son's voice...

But then, each night, upon clocking out, I found myself with nothing else to focus on *but* the dream.

Feeling that I had no alternative and no friend in Lopez, I decided that I would go straight to the source.

One night, when I was sure that there was no watchman working the grounds, I jumped the low fence into the cemetery and visited my son's grave.

I had not come with any sort of plan.

I'd felt moved to visit the grave site so as to be closer to my son, though I knew there was precious little I could do to bring him comfort—if comfort, in fact, was what he'd been clamoring for in my dreams. To be near to him, I supposed, was the clearest and fondest gesture I could now muster since we were denizens of two different spheres, and huddled in the cool spring evening, I sat upon the simple grave marker labeled "John Doe" and stared up at the sky.

"I want to help you," I remember uttering into the night. "I wish I could. Just tell me how, my boy, and I'll do it. I'll do anything..."

The meandering wind brought no reply, nor did the brushing of long grass against the tombstones. I was kept company by crickets and katydids, by the rush of distant traffic and the occasional hooting of hidden owls, but my son's lips remained pursed. I wondered, of course, if I hadn't gone insane. After all, only a mad man would go to the trouble of trespassing in a cemetery like this to accost his dead son on account of certain dreams.

I racked my brain for ways to ease his burden, stretched out and listened for signs from beyond. Eventually, both physically and mentally fatigued, I fell asleep upon the grave, and that was where Lopez himself would find me the next morning with an almost demonic scowl on his face and a promise to summon the police if I didn't vacate the premises immediately.

But unbeknownst to Lopez at that moment, I had not awakened that morning the same man he'd dismissed over the phone some days prior. No, my sleep had been fruitful, and in it I had seen—been shown—certain things.

With my son's grave marker for a pillow, I saw much.

I dreamt that I was walking through the graveyard, its dirt paths clotted with tentacles of writhing mist. Beside me walked a boy—not my son, but a gaunter, shabbier and quieter youth with darker hair. He stood very close to me, but in those rare instances when we touched I felt only a severe cold upon me, like a wintry gust imposing itself upon early spring.

The boy—the John Doe—was looking up at me as we walked, and I admit I met his dead eyes with immeasurable dread. There was something impossibly dark in them, a blackness beyond black, which made the starlit vault of the heavens look bright as day in comparison. He was speaking to me, though his voice only drifted into my hearing at odd turns; I caught snippets of conversation here and there, as one might do by eavesdropping on other diners in a crowded restaurant.

"... I felt the razor go in, but I thought that..."

"... the belt was so tight, there was no way for me to..."

"... the smell of cigarettes makes me sick. The burns from them are too painful..."

"... Do you know what burning skin smells like?..."

While touring the silent, misty grounds, I watched as the little boy pulled aside his ragged outfit and put his deep wounds on full display. Here, in the core of his abdomen, was a large, ragged hole—an empty thing that puckered and convulsed as if in search of its missing mass. His ruddy torso was covered in little burns—some minor, others made deep by repeated offenses. A ragged gash breathed across the back of his head, and I could see the contents of his skull tenuously see-sawing within at every step.

"... and so this was where he hit me with the bottle..."

"... the stinging was... the worst part of... and I never woke up..."

One by one, the boy quietly spilled forth his litany of personal horrors. My ears were crowded with the sordid details of his life and the hideous facts of his untimely and brutal death. To hear a boy share such things, to hear one speak so frankly of such profound savagery ripped at my heart and left me throughly gutted. This, then, had been what my son had been subjected to. Since sharing a grave with this unfortunate John Doe, my boy had been forced to listen to this disgusting history of violence night after night. John Doe had died a terrible and painful death and could know no rest; therefore, neither would he allow his bunkmate the peace of a night's sleep until he'd vented his spleen.

———

I awoke to Lopez's scowling face. He looked on the verge of kicking me, and had been muttering curses under his breath for some time before I'd even come to. I remember sitting upright, sore as could be after having spent the night on the cold ground, and meeting him with a sheepish smile despite all the horrors that had just been relayed to me by the unidentified boy.

"You've got a lot of nerve, loafing around here like this. I could have you taken in for trespassing, Mr. Prescott. Do you have any idea—"

"I don't mean you any harm, Mr. Lopez," I interrupted. "I came here to spend some time with my boy. And with John Doe here."

The old caretaker regarded me as a lunatic. "What in the world are you driving at? Isn't there some other place for you to be?"

I stood, brushing the soil from my person, and stretched. "If it isn't too much trouble, I'd like to come back here again tonight," I said.

"I'm afraid that *really is* too much trouble. You've already overstayed your welcome, and I hasten to add that trespassing laws are no joke. You're liable to be—"

"Tell me," said I, "do the authorities frown upon the expenditure of government funds on unauthorized burials?"

The old man grew redder in the face than the sun that was then breaking out over the horizon. "You dare to threaten me? After what I did for you, for your son... No, I refuse to believe that a man could be such an ingrate! You would betray me to the authorities for having shown you kindness? For having accommodated you?"

"Of course not," I replied. "That is, so long as you'll let me pass my nights here unmolested." I peered down at the grave marker and then fixed Lopez with a steely stare. "So long as you let me spend time on the grounds with my boy, as I like, you can be assured of my silence."

Needless to say, I got my way.

It was my intention to spend my nights at the graveyard—to lend John Doe *my* ear each night, that my son might rest. And on the off chance that Lopez refused to let me in, I would—with not a little shame—report him to the authorities, which would prompt my son's extrication and, ostensibly, removal to a different grave.

Either way, I would see to it that my son would have rest, and that his coffin-mate would not keep him up each night with his litany of unbelievable horrors.

Tonight, after work, I plan to return to the cemetery. Old Lopez has been good enough to leave the back gate unlocked for me. Once inside, I will make my way to that simple grave marker and wait until sleep overcomes me. And when it does, I will be there to listen to John Doe. Night after night, I'll listen, until he no longer has need of a sympathetic ear.

One day, when he and my son both know rest, perhaps I will come to know it, too.

THE POLYGLOT PROBLEM

"We need to go."

Ethel's voice rang in my ears as I held the corpse close. Skin once warm now grew clammy, and its former ruddiness had given way to a shocking white since death had tightened its grip. The limbs—Wyatt's limbs—were no longer responsive, and the joints were beginning to tighten up as though caked in ice. His heart hadn't stirred in a long while; I'd known it the instant I'd laid eyes on him in the gutter. Even so, I cradled him in my arms and racked my brain for some way to turn the tide.

"We need to go. Leave him be, Henry," continued Ethel. She regarded the two of us—slumbering Wyatt and I, splayed across the filthy cobblestones of the alley—with utter disgust. "There's nothing you can do for him. We need to go before someone thinks we had something to do with it," she warned.

"We *did* have something to do with it." My gaze rose from the cadaver's dead eyes and were briefly locked with hers. The shudder that passed through her bird-like frame did not escape my notice. "He took a walk off that rooftop precisely because he trusted in me. He believed in me, Ethel." Since our arrival, I'd studiously avoided contact with the pool of red that'd gathered on the damp stones and which seeped into the gaps between them. The slick trail whose fountainhead was the crater in the back of Wyatt's skull. "I have to help him. I have to *try*."

"Whatever. You do what you want," she snapped. "I'm getting out of here." Still, she didn't budge. It was almost as though her curiosity was too great for her to make good on her threat. Ethel didn't believe in me; unlike Wyatt, she had never seen—*heard*—me work my magic. But she *wanted* to believe, and the wish kept her rooted to the spot.

"Cover your ears," I commanded.

"What? Why?"

"Cover your ears," I repeated. "I don't want you to hear this. Not yet. Not until I'm certain I have it right..."

"You're... you're not sure if you can bring him back? You're not sure if you... can get it right?"

Taking a deep breath, I leaned down and began whispering in the dead man's ear. I kept my voice low, delivered each delicate syllable with such stringent annunciation that my throat began to ache.

And as the black words left my lips in that alley, I couldn't help remembering.

It's said that, prior to age nine, children more easily absorb foreign languages. From personal experience, I'd say that's true enough. I grew up in a bilingual household, dividing my conversations between Spanish and English. English and Spanish both had been learnt through something like osmosis, and I've often wondered what it might've been like had I been exposed to other languages during this formative period.

It wasn't until my eleventh year that I was introduced to my third language. That tongue, German, was mastered within several months of intense study. The next, Portuguese, was attained with still greater speed on account of its linguistic closeness to my beloved Spanish. By the time I entered high school and began seriously studying Japanese, I could have comfortably enjoyed the title of polyglot.

But I didn't stop there. Kanji lessons soon gave way to an interest in Chinese, which I pursued beyond high school and into university. My acquaintance with Arabic began in the spring of my sophomore year when I befriended a handful of exchange students from Egypt and Saudi Arabia; before long, I was enjoying meals of kapsa in their homes and getting on like the Shah. I picked up a smattering of French, Italian and Latin along the way, any of which might have been pursued to the point of total fluency if not for the thing I encountered early in grad school.

Upon completing my undergrad, I was the school's most decorated student in the way of language study, and even most of my professors held me in awe. The ease with which I consumed and mastered new languages was something that most linguists could only dream of, and I was encouraged, with not a little financial aid to sweeten the deal, to pursue a doctorate in applied linguistics so that I might leave a tremendous mark on the field, dwarfing even Pinker and Chomsky.

It was on my path to do precisely that that I first met Raoul Esquito. A linguist and polyglot of serious renown, I had sought him out while choosing a new university, and it wasn't long before the boatload of recommendation letters from my old professors earned me a place at his side. I joined him in his researches into the so-called "dead" languages of the Proto-Indo-European lineage. Professor Esquito was a stern and exacting character, the stereotypical severe academic, but in him I found a spark of true genius. Like me, new languages flowed into him as freely as water, and within a short while of our introduction, I dare say the celebrated professor and I hit it off. Whereas many of the other grad students working beneath him were mere careerists looking for grant money with which to fund researches into their pet theories, Esquito and I shared a love for language itself, and long were the nights we spent over coffee speaking with one another in more languages than one might hear in an international airport terminal.

A few months into my grad school career, I wound up gaining the professor's confidence, and it was then that he shared with me his ultimate aim—a thing he had been working towards since *his own* time in grad school. It was his intention to dig deep into the past and to resurrect the languages of the Proto-Indo-European peoples, languages which had not been spoken in many thousands of years, but whose far-reaching boughs entangled almost every modern tongue.

To do such a thing was no small task; in fact, though predecessors of ours had long pined to decode such ancient tongues, most had surrendered without having made the least progress towards a meaningful summary. We were seeking to understand languages with no living speakers, and which had arisen at such a time when writing was nigh unheard of. As such, there weren't any ancient texts we could puzzle over. A few experts over the years had referenced certain inscriptions in stone found throughout the Mediterranean and Middle Eastern regions, but these had never furnished anything like real leads.

Except, perhaps, for *one.*

Some years prior, a burial site had been uncovered on the Pontic-Caspian steppe in Moldova by archaeologists. On account of governmental interference and other bureaucratic headaches their findings were some time in being published. While the discovery of an ancient burial site had initially been met with some excitement, by the time the team's write-ups began turning up in journals, the vast majority of academics had set their sights elsewhere.

But not Professor Esquito.

Delving deeply into the details of the dig and corresponding with certain of its leaders over the course of weeks, the professor became aware of certain etchings in clay which had been found there, but which had not been included in the final reports. On account of the region and the suspected age of the ruins, Esquito believed that this might be a long-awaited physical trace of a Proto-Indo-European language or one of its near descendants.

The professor wasn't long in making plans to visit the site. A flight to Moldova for him and his assistants would be costly however, and at the time the area was still being closely managed by local authorities, which meant endless red tape. Ah, but when it came to greasing palms and parting donors from their grant money, none were more skilled than Professor Esquito, and within a month of back and forth he'd more or less cemented a plan to visit the dig in-person the following spring.

As both a cost-saving measure and a bulwark against intrusions by less-qualified minds, Esquito made the decision to travel with only a single assistant. After many months of the fruitful and convivial cooperation already discussed, I was very pleased to be offered that role, and in the spring prepared to set out on a trip that would change my life forever. Dreams of book deals, of lengthy television interviews and moneyed professorships at top schools filled my head in the days leading up to our departure.

Now, unless one is unduly invested in the goings-on at my alma mater, or else a keen disciple of linguistics, the sudden disappearance of Professor Raoul Esquito that spring is unlikely to have registered. In my personal circles, though, I can say only that his vanishment led to a tidal wave of attention which was, at least partially, responsible for my exit from academia shortly thereafter.

I would go on to give, after that long night, an account of Esquito's last-known movements. Whether questioned by authorities foreign or domestic my story never changed.

This is not to say, however, that I told the truth.

For, you see, there were certain things about that trip that I could not tell. There were things about it that would not have been believed, frankly. Somehow, there are times when *I* don't believe the truth of the whole affair myself, and yet I played an instrumental role in the odd horrors that took place that night on the moonlit steppe...

The dig site was quite remote, and at the time of our arrival was manned only by a small handful of semi-local workers whose English was rudimentary. After a long drive via SUV across the steppe, we were welcomed at the edge of a vast pit where excavators had tunneled out large segments of the landscape. This great space, supposed to have been a part of an ancient burial ground more than eight thousand years old, was accessible only by ladder; that is, one had to carefully descend one of three steel ladders to reach the dusty stone floor below.

Having secured access to the site for a number of days, Esquito and I were assisted by the men on site in lowering our things down into pit. We'd brought a good deal of food and water, tents, simple bedding and other necessities in tightly-bound packs, and at once began touring the ruins in search of the inscriptions the archaeologists had spoken of. These, it turned out, were in the deepest and least-accessible portion of the site. There existed on the eastern fringe something of a burrow lined only with a rickety wooden ladder. To climb down into it was to find one's self far beneath the world in a cavernous chamber some twenty feet in width and length, but with low ceilings.

Sure enough, numbers of fragile clay tablets had been heaped there by a long-dead hand, bearing the inscrutable markings of a bygone age and tongue. I remember how we marveled at them, how we ran our fingers over the ancient marks with shudders of excitement; I remember, too, their alienage, for the markings didn't resemble any writing system then known to us. At least, not initially.

To put the matter bluntly, this deep chamber was all we'd come to see, and after our arrival we scarcely exited it. Hunched and working by lamplight, the two of us carefully arranged the brittle old tablets and began a really thorough survey of them. We took our meals amongst them, slept just outside the hole that led down to them, and subjected them to intense scrutiny.

We were not long, perhaps only a day and a half, in drawing parallels between this mystery tongue and newer, more familiar languages. It was Esquito who had the first eureka moment. By studying the arrangement of the marks and finding patterns in their sequencing, he inferred—correctly—the presence of a sort of primordial punctuation scattered about each tablet. Later, while studying one specimen in particular, I happened upon a set of marks that tugged at the thread of memory, and together we established their kinship to markings in another ancient script—this one already having been translated by some of our contemporaries.

With this, we were off to the races. The deciphering of a language by this method is very much a process of trial and error, and without recourse to a native speaker one can never be completely certain of things like proper pronunciation. Nevertheless, we worked tirelessly from morning till night, connecting certain dots and finding in this forgotten language many hidden similarities to other ancient tongues. By day four, we were well and truly convinced that we had stumbled upon something far greater than a Proto-Indo-European language; this, we began to excitedly believe, could be something of a mother tongue to *all* extant languages.

One night, before we settled into bed, still buzzing with the thrill of discovery, Esquito put it this way: "Think of it, Henry. We may have just discovered the Language of the Garden!"

I shared in his enthusiasm at the time, and even now I have no doubts that the tongue we pored over was indeed ancient. I am equally sure, however, that it was *not* the language of Eden. It was, in fact, something sinister—something that had probably been better off forgotten.

The disappearance to which I've alluded took place early one evening as our work was winding down and the steppe was treated to a light rain. By this time, Professor Esquito and I had begun working out a fragmented grammar and had even begun parsing declensions; at every turn, this ancient language was showing signs of life. Our notes were voluminous, and already my mentor had been making plans to entreat both the local authorities and our benefactors out west for more time at the site. He thought our work easily the most important of his career, and theorized that, when we were through, our efforts would prove as influential and well-known as the Rosetta Stone.

As I have said, the site was maintained by Moldovan men vetted by the local authorities. These men were given to lengthy lapses in their surveillance; given that the dig site was so remote, they wagered, rightly, that it would be of little interest to outsiders and that its distance from civilization alone was enough to keep it protected. While they should have been keeping a close eye on things and assisting the professor and I with our doings, the men often stole away to the nearest village to drink away their shifts with dark-haired women—an arrangement which suited Esquito and I just fine, for it saved us the trouble of trying to communicate with them in our admittedly fragmented Romanian.

The two of us were quite alone on the site, then, when the incident occurred. Seeking after a morsel of food to fuel him during the final leg of our night's researches, he left me in the lower chamber and began ascending the ladder to the main floor where our supplies were stored. He made it only a few rungs up the thing when, with a sickening crunch, the worm-eaten wood gave way and he went crashing back down into the subterranean chamber, where he landed on his head and went immediately still.

I answered the commotion with amusement at first, believing that he'd dropped something or merely lost his footing on the crummy old ladder, but as I moved to the mouth of the pit and found him sprawled across the floor with eyes bulging and mouth agape, I understood that he'd sustained truly traumatic injuries and sought to tend to him at once. Alas, my skill in medicine is not nearly so great as my skill in language, and at any rate, there are few remedies for a broken neck.

Professor Esquito died in something of a freak accident that evening, and I now found myself alone with him in the deepest reaches of the dig site.

You may well imagine my upset and terror, and I went on to make a terrible racket from the bottom of the pit. I tried to salvage the old ladder, to claw my way back to the surface, but to little effect; even on the best of days the thing had never been especially sturdy. What's more, despite the awful cries I threw into the air to the point of utter hoarseness, no one ever came to my aid. Our local handlers had absconded to this or that watering hole as was their custom, and in doing so had sentenced me to spend the night underground with my dead professor.

A few hours passed and night fell upon me with the hardness of iron. Hunger and thirst might have nipped ceaselessly at my heels if not for the fright and revulsion I felt at my predicament; instead, I felt them only intermittently. We had been in the habit of camping within the dig site, some ten or fifteen feet down, and even from there, with the shadows of the settlement's ancient walls upon us, I had found the nights quite dark. In the little chasm that led into the chamber packed with tablets however, I learned the true meaning of darkness, and if not for my lamp and the professor's, would have thought myself blind.

I did what I could with Esquito's body, arranged it carefully and tried to show some reverence, but when shock and horror gave way to numbness in the smallest hours I retreated back into the cavern a little ways, toward the lamps, and sought to distract myself.

I had nothing much to busy myself with but the work at hand, of course—and so it was that, slowly, I resumed the effort that Esquito and I had been so absorbed in just hours before.

With the late professor's notes and my own close at hand, I continued to pore over the clay tablets, drawing still more parallels between their markings and those of other extinct languages. At first, I did it only to keep myself calm—to give my mind something healthy to fixate on in the face of a mortal fright. I admit however—with no little embarrassment—that I soon became so enchanted with my work that I occasionally forgot that my professor's body lay in repose nearby. The hours fell away and the creatures of the steppe sang their nocturnal songs. I plugged away at my translations with almost maniacal gusto, and from down below my voice joined the nightly chorus. Tenuously, fitfully I gave voice to words older than any known empire.

The tablet that I made most progress on—and which subsequently most intrigued me—seemed to have something to do with ancient burial rites or care of the dead; a most appropriate topic considering my circumstances. I tugged at every word, filled pages with conjectures about single characters, and got into the habit of fastidiously copying the original texts in my field notebook. As far as I could tell, this particular tablet was a kind of religious rite, and having made considerable strides over the preceding days I tried my hand at phonetics. Line by line, stumbling many times, I fought my way through the tablet's contents aloud. As one can imagine, with each subsequent pass, while liberally referencing both my notes and the professor's, I improved.

I imagined myself the newest in a long-line of eons-dead high priests, pronouncing an unmentionable rite in a shadowed temple surrounded only by flickering candlelight. Again and again I spoke the words, tightening my approach gradually, until I was reasonably sure that my delivery was authentic. I had, in this selection, a real triumph; a key which would make the contents of the other tablets intelligible to me, and which would allow me to resurrect the long-dead tongue. The success I'd had would surely go on to fill many gaps in other language families as well—would put to rest many doubts plaguing not only Proto-Indo-European languages, but tongues as disparate as Coptic and Etruscan. Though Esquito was dead, his labors would live on and he would become, in short order, a household name.

So engrossed was I in my labors that I did not at once notice the sudden burst of movement from the other end of the cavern. It was only when I paced slowly toward the exit, my eyes sore for hours of uninterrupted reading by the harsh lamplight, that I discovered my mentor sitting upright on the floor, his back resting against the fragments of the shattered ladder.

I had not left him in that position; of that I was sure. Neither had his face been twisted in an infernal smirk when last I'd laid eyes on him, yet there he was, grinning toothily from ear to bluish ear.

"P-Professor?" I remember crying out, though nothing in his expression or bearing any longer called Raoul Esquito to mind. The body, the general outline, was his, but in that dim hovel I couldn't get away from the feeling that something else dwelt in the space he used to occupy. With another staggered step, the lamp at my side, I discovered that the odd angle of his head—turned harshly leftward to a degree more befitting an owl's—was the result of a clearly fractured neck. The jumble of vertebral wreckage jutted almost through the skin, and the whole swollen mass palpitated with his every wheezy breath as though on the verge of violent rupture.

The professor did not respond. Instead, somehow, he gained his feet. The movement was remarkably—*eerily*—fluid for one who should have been, at the very least, paralyzed from the neck down. His gaze roamed upward, strained in search of the night sky, and when he found it Esquito did a thing which I can only recount with a queasy stomach and a shudder that can in no retelling be denied. Hands outstretched, he muttered something to me in a low, distant voice—and in a tongue, I might add, which I did not immediately recognize. From there, grasping at the smooth walls of the vertical passage with his palms and fingers, he scurried animal-like up its length, pitting stubborn feet, elbows, whatever was necessary, to facilitate his climb. In what should have been an almost impossible feat even in perfect health, Esquito fought his way up the burrow and went crawling out into the dig site proper. I heard him pace away from the mouth of the aperture, heard what I thought was the tread of feet upon the nearest steel ladder.

And then I heard nothing more. I called out to him for aid despite my fear, but my calls brought no reply. Raoul had freed himself from the underground passage and had subsequently stalked off across the steppe in the dead of night.

The professor's whereabouts ever since have been a subject of much conjecture. I, personally, have no idea where he's gone in the years since that fateful night. For a time, I was even less sure how it was that he'd moved in the first place.

It wasn't until later, when I'd had a little space from the incident and an opportunity to think, that I recalled the few words he'd spoken to me prior to making his exit and I suddenly understood. Esquito had spoken to me in the tongue of the cavern, the one that we had been working so hard to translate, and subsequent study on my part has convinced me that they were words of thanks.

Thanks, that is, for having resurrected him.

I realized in the hours after the ghoulish escape that the whole thing had been my doing. By sitting in that dark chasm, repeating the ancient text again and again, I had unwittingly performed the rite of an ancient sect with only the dead man present to hear. Esquito's dead limbs had stirred in answer to my speech; his heart had begun pumping on account of my fevered recitations. Without realizing it, I had tapped into a malefic power the likes of which modern men have only dreamed of. This black, ancient tongue was no mere antecedent to contemporary languages; it was a thing possessed of real power—power over life and death, it seemed to me.

I was not rescued from the pit until early the next afternoon. Slumbering in the hovel, I awoke to the curious shouts of our Moldovan hosts and was hastily assisted. With my things in tow, I climbed out of the pit and helped myself to all the food and drink I could stand, struggling all the while to tell them that the professor had gone in the night. It would not be until the first of many official inquiries by regional authorities that I would be really pressed for answers, and to these suited men I gave more or less the same version of events: Late in the night, Professor Esquito had unexpectedly left the dig site. I had tried to follow, but the ladder had been left in ruins after his ascent. I did not know where he'd gone, I insisted, and hadn't the foggiest about his plans.

All this was true enough, and interested parties both in Moldova and Stateside could tell plainly that I'd been blindsided by Esquito's departure. I was cleared, ultimately, of all suspicions and the professor's vanishment was latterly considered to be related to stress, mental illness or something similarly banal.

Only *I* knew the truth. Only *I* knew that the man had been clinically dead for some hours, and that he had been returned to life on account of my infernal babbling in that shadowed hole in the ground. Had I not spoken things that should not have been spoken, the matter might have come to a simpler resolution.

It is a wonder that my belongings were not searched more thoroughly, for had they been inspected clinically the presence of Esquito's personal jottings and the painstaking copies of the original clay-borne texts on my person might've raised a few eyebrows. Funnily, my handwritten reproductions of the tablet inscriptions are now effectively the originals, for in the hours before my rescue, when I realized what it was I'd done through my utterances, I ground the originals into powder so that none might ever reference them. The destruction of these precious and remarkable artifacts would not be mourned; as previously stated, the archaeologists who'd discovered the site had failed to mention the tablets in their article, making it so that only a handful of men on the planet were aware of their existence. In the event that their destruction *did* come to light, well, I figured it would be a very simple matter to pin the blame on the site's easygoing Moldovan caretakers, whose lapses into revelry had left the place unprotected from would-be vandals on many occasions.

I wish that I could say that my acquaintance with the dread script ended there. In fact, only my affiliations with academia wound to a close after that ill-fated trip. I dropped out of grad school within days of returning to the US and instead turned to a life of independent study. With what little money I had socked away, along with contributions from friends and family, I cobbled together something of a gap year while trying to decide what to do next.

The detailed notes on the black script and the careful reproductions I'd made of the tablets were always close at hand no matter where I traveled or what I got up to, and more often than not I found myself delving ever-deeper into the language.

It was no longer my goal to enlighten, however. I no longer cared for Esquito's vision, had completely turned my back on the field of linguistics. Instead, I sought to leverage the evil tongue—to somehow use it as a means of self-enrichment.

There is money to be made in necromancy. To raise the dead, to give hope to the hopeless, is to court immense riches. Who might pay a greater price for a dead son than a grieving mother? Would not a devoted widower give anything to see his dear wife again? Through careful study of the forbidden tongue I planned to sharpen my skill and monetize it. It is true that my resurrection of Professor Esquito had not gone well, but neither had the course been planned. I wagered that a greater command of the language, paired with sheer force of will, could result in a more wholesome—and lucrative—vivification of the dead. Of course, this was a degraded and filthy course; I never had any illusions about the ethics of such a thing. Playing with the dead, conjuring up imitations of the living... it was all a sordid business. Propelled by demonic curiosity and bald want, I threw myself into it nevertheless.

Eight months after dropping out of grad school, I moved across the country to a rural area. It was there that I made my first necromantic attempt in earnest—and in secret. Volunteering at a small care home dealing with the terminally ill, I kept my ear to the ground and waited for news of passing residents. There were many who'd been deposited there by distant and uncaring family, and my pleas to sit with them in their final hours were confused for goodness by all who heard them.

Instead, like a vulture awaiting the choicest pickings, I sat at the bedside of a dying octogenarian and listened for his final breath.

When the last gasp had passed his shaking lips, my own instantly began to wag with the guttural tones of the pit.

None were more astonished than I when old Mr. Parker, eighty-seven years old, bed-bound and suffering from incurable cancer, suddenly rose up from his bed and attacked his nurses after my shift was through. The local news was briefly swamped by the story, which told of the man's sudden physical vigor, mental collapse and savage treatment of staff. My little experiment happened to prolong the man's life by a few more months, and resulted in a young nurse getting one of her eyes brutally gouged and her nose broken.

Like the last time, with Professor Esquito, something had gone wrong. The man had returned to life, yes, but he'd come back different. The light had gone from him and darkness had nestled into the open spaces. Why this had occurred—why darkness and violence appeared to be the inheritance of all those resurrected by the ancient rite—was a mystery to me, but I was committed to my work. The kinks would be ironed out eventually, I told myself.

The next body I experimented on was that of a young woman—a drug addict. I had long since moved on to a big city, and had been watching the area's junkies with a certain covetousness. One night, word went round that a pretty young thing had been duped with Fentanyl-laced goods, and her corpse's presence in the back room of a club was going to make a real headache for the proprietor. A few club-goers gawked in curiosity. A few went on to dial authorities.

By the time the ambulance rolled up however, the girl was long gone, and I with her.

With music thudding in the other room, I'd locked the door and knelt beside her cooling corpse, which had been left propped against a bench. With great care, I leaned in and whispered the words I had long committed to memory into her ears. Every line of dialogue went punching into her eardrum, and it wasn't long before the rest of her body responded to the rhythm. She jerked awake as though she'd been Narcanned and flew at once from the bench. With a terrible scream, she ripped at her bottle-blonde hair and made for the nearest exit door.

I followed at her heels, waiting for the shock of resurrection to cease. It did, seemingly, after five or ten minutes, when we found ourselves hovering alone near a shuttered convenience store and bathed in the neon lights of nearby storefronts. There, twitching and slumped, she turned and fixed me with crystal clear eyes.

"How are you feeling?" I asked, extending a hand.

She didn't take it. She didn't move toward me at all, her gaze narrowing.

"What's your name?" I chanced.

"Eugenie..." came the reply in a cold and distant voice. She clutched at herself a little, chest rising and falling as she fought to savor a breath. "And who... who are *you?*"

"My name's Henry," I explained, slipping both hands into my pockets so as to put her at ease. "I heard you were in trouble and I wanted to help you."

At this, the woman shuddered. Her expression—previously unsteady with dreamy unease—hardened into something animalistic. Her clear eyes became clouded by hatred and her delicate features were quickly wrenched in service of telegraphing the same. The words that flowed from her lips shortly thereafter cannot be reproduced here—not simply on account of their filthiness and combativeness, but because they were uttered in the black tongue.

Cast in brilliant neon and seething with an otherworldly anger, the creature before me bristled with the promise of violence.

I confess that I fled before she could make good on her threat, and after a few more nights of constantly looking over my shoulder for the mess of my own creation, I quietly moved on to another city on the opposite coast.

Dozens. Over the years, there had been dozens of attempts at resurrection. Each time, I had succeeded in bringing the subjects back to life—though it was only life of a kind. I had never once succeeded in returning a person back to their natural state. Somewhere along the line—somewhere between death and new life—something integral was lost and something infernal moved in. This happened to a greater or lesser degree without exception, and each time my subject would either escape from me and vanish into the wide world, or else *I* would be forced to run.

And now, with Wyatt's body clutched to my bosom, I wondered if this time would be any different. If it ever *could* be different.

After my litany of failures, I had decided to seek outside help. The formation of a society—a cult—would allow me to share my work with others, and also to refine it through their talents and insights. Wyatt had been among the first members of this bold new group, and had seen my abilities firsthand. Ethel, a newcomer, had been drawn in by rumors but very much remained a skeptic.

Now, kneeling in the alley, I had a choice to make.

Wyatt had wished to help me with my research. "If something were to happen to me, you could bring me back, Henry," he'd opined. "It'd be cool to experience that."

"Perish the thought," I'd said with a chuckle, not knowing at the time what he'd had planned. "We'll find other bodies, other subjects. I tell you, I'm very close to perfecting this. I'm nearly fluent in the old tongue, and once I've harnessed it correctly, I'll begin passing it on to you and the others."

"But imagine," Wyatt had pressed on just nights before. "What if there was a short-cut? What if, you know, *I* died and you brought me back. So far, you've only really worked on strangers. I remember that guy in Des Moines... He wasn't that communicative or friendly even before he died. But you and me? We're friends. We get along, we understand each other... I could explain to you what it feels like. I could explain to you my impressions, and all the things that—"

"No, Wyatt. Let's stick to the plan, shall we?"

He hadn't obeyed my orders. Trusting that he was doing me a tremendous service, and that I would be able to resurrect him intact where I'd failed in dozens of others, he'd plunged to his death from several stories up.

I gazed up at Ethel, clearing my throat. "Cover your ears," I commanded.

"What?" she asked, combing a lock of dark hair from her eyes. "Why?"

"Cover your ears," I insisted. "I don't want you to hear this. Not yet. Not until I'm certain I have it right..."

"You're... you're not sure if you can bring him back? You're not sure if you... can get it right?"

I glanced down at Wyatt's face—strangely serene. I knew that what I was doing was wrong—that my meddling with life and death would leave me damned. By now, the devils were preparing a place for me in the infinite furnace—were tending coals with my name on them. It seemed a crime to disturb Wyatt's sleep. He could enjoy this peace forever, could slumber for eternity without ever having to know the pain and confusion I'd subjected so many other innocents to in my pursuit of knowledge and gain.

But as I leaned down and began whispering into his ear, I told myself that this time might be different. This time, maybe, I would get it right.

JOEY SANTIAGO WAS A FRIEND OF MINE

The man sweating in my chair was portly and red, an engorged tick of a man, really, but I could tell by the way he was fidgeting, and by the desperate ping-ponging of his gaze around the office, that he was about to make my wallet pregnant with green.

"Mr. Bohannon," he kept on, looking as if he wanted to take another inch off his already stubby nails, "I can't stress enough how important this job is to me. The man in question—" Here came the pause of one unable to lie on his feet—"Well, he's an old friend of mine, and I've had a miserable time getting ahold of him. If you can track him down for me and escort him to the aforementioned address, I would be forever in your debt."

"Forever is a very long time," I put in gently.

"Depending on your performance, I may even be willing to pay more than your base rate..."

Apparently, my wallet and I were expecting twins. "Call me Salvador," I insisted, hands folded atop the desk. "That was three-ten Bianville Street, correct?"

"That's the one, yes. Third floor."

"I know the area."

"Splendid. When you can you start?"

Mr. Henry Taggart had caught me in my tan suit, freshly-pressed, with visions of strong drink and strange women in my head. I'd stepped through a cloud of cologne not seconds before his fat knuckles had sounded against my door and my undercut was precisely far enough from my last trim to look natural. All this to say, I was looking *damn* sweet—too good, maybe, to go schlepping through seedy clubs and whatnot in search of his man. I hadn't yet ruled out the possibility of a night in, spent kissing my reflection in the mirror.

I stole a meaningless glance at my watch and sighed. "Business being what it is, I *may* be able to get started on Monday morning. If my existing jobs allow..."

"And what might it cost me to cut to the front of the line?" asked the client, teasing at the checkbook in the breast pocket of his blazer.

My Parker ballpoint all but leapt across the desk at him. "As it happens, dried ink is my love language. A seventy-five percent bonus, up-front, and I'll have him at Bianville Street in time for a nightcap."

Taggart must've wanted the guy something fierce, because he wrote me a love letter on one of those checks without blinking. "I really can't thank you enough."

"Don't thank me yet," I warned, funneling the check into my drawer. "This fella you're so keen to reconnect with—tell me some more about him. It's a big city, Mr. Taggart, and I'd like to get right to the heart of things if I can."

"Well," said the client, "his name's Joey Santiago." I hated the way he said the name; SANNEY-YAGGO. "He's thirty-eight, perhaps thirty-nine. Black hair with a bit of gray. He's been known to chase skirts at the clubs on and around Gene Tunney Avenue. He's tall, maybe a hair past six foot, with a long face—rarely shaven."

"Don't suppose you've got a photo of him?"

"I do not."

"Pity, that." I drummed at my brow with the butt of my pen. Having thrown the details down onto a scratchpad in my neatest hand, I found myself with very little to go on. "You got anything else on this beloved friend of yours? There just doesn't seem to be a whole lot of meat on this bone. How about a phone number? An address? Where's he staying, who's he run with?"

Taggart adjusted his spectacles and squared me with a funny look, half sweet and half sour. "I'm afraid I don't have that information. It's as I told you. It's been some time since my last meeting with Joey. If that's a problem, however, I suppose I could place this case with another agency..."

"Perish the thought," I said, gaining my feet and giving my waistband a hard tug. "If you want blood from a stone, Mr. Taggart, you let me know how many units and I'll bring it to you warm."

"That's what I like to hear," he cooed, hefting himself out of my chair.

It was a chill evening, early in spring. The smell of rain stole in like a thief through the shuttered windows and a molten orange sun was taking its final bow behind curtains of rolling gray. "What's he do for a living, this Joey? He married? Any family in the area that you know of? Other associates?"

Taggart looked to the door as he responded. He plodded across my rug, hand resting on the knob. "Job? Well, he's a factory man. Car parts. He might've been married, once, though it didn't sound like a particularly harmonious affair."

"Fair enough, Mr. Taggart. Seems simple as hand meets glove. I'll be seeing you again soon."

Old Henry stole out of the room. I hung back till I was good and sure he'd gone, then killed the lamp and shrugged on my coat.

I was only an instant in locking up, and had come within three strides of the stairs when I heard the bawling kid next door and his mother's frenzied hushing. The duo were pacing up and down the corridor, the kid's face cherry-red and covered with snot. His mother, a real bonnie lass from County Kildare, shot me a sorry look. "Forgive me, Mr. Bohannon, for all the noise. He's teething, you see..." A year or two in the States and the pretty young thing still spoke like she had a mouthful of shamrocks. Something about that accent never failed to charm; had she been an executioner, reading off my list of capital offenses, I might've invented new crimes just to feel her tug on my noose.

"It's no problem at all, Flossie," I replied, slipping a finger into junior's curled fist and giving it a little shake. The constant hum of noise came part and parcel with running one's agency out of a boarding house. I was willing to deal with the occasional squealing toddler in exchange for easy access to the city's busiest spots. "Now, keep an eye on things for me, lad. Duty calls."

It was a filthy place.

I don't mean that the glassware was dirty, or that the floors were unswept, or that the toilets were particularly squalid—though none of the aforementioned were pristine, either. I mean that it was the sort of place where you could prop yourself in a corner to listen to flamenco music long into the night while breathing nothing but the smoke of other people's cigarettes. The kind of place cluttered with whores whose monikers are ludicrous things like "Cinnamon" and "Velvet", but who answer to names like Daisy-Marie back home in Tupelo. The only things separating one from the wares of these tradeswomen in most cases is a whiff of lace and an unchaperoned gaze, and on nights when business was slow they'd sway along to the music like all the rest of us, sponging drinks off the somber barman and wishing, maybe, that they'd listened to ma and pa and never come to the city in the first place.

Anyhow, the music wasn't hitting the spot tonight. I knew that old Castro and his boys had it in them, but broken strings and missed chords kept the dance floor clear enough for me to stride into the back room without braving a sea of elbows. I dropped the band a few bills as I went, figuring that I could afford it—and that by tomorrow night they'd turn it all around. The world is cruel enough as it is; far be it from me to tell Picasso to hit the oil rig after one rough canvass.

The big man working the counter in back had a stiff pour ready for me before I'd even straddled the stool. "You're looking too sharp for gumshoeing, Sally," he uttered while dabbing at his sweaty brow with a bar towel. "So why do I have a feeling you're about to ask me about some case you're working?"

"A sixth-sense, maybe. You've got a gift, Rudy. You ought to buy yourself a lottery ticket."

His dark lips parted in a cheddary smile. "Well, to what do I owe the honor? Business or pleasure?"

"A wise man knows they're one and the same." I let in a tipple of the stuff and it chased out the evening chill. "I'm looking for someone, a factory-man. I'm told he enjoys chasing skirts hereabouts and that he deals in car parts."

"You've just described a hundred, two-hundred men, easy," came Rudy's retort. "You're gonna have to get a little more specific."

"Name's Joey Santiago," I continued. "He's creeping up on forty, or so I'm told. He frequents this area."

"Santiago? He may as well be called 'Smith' in a neighborhood like this." The barkeep chortled. "What you want him for?"

"Someone's paying me a small fortune to track him down. I stand to earn so much off this job that I'll be able to put my kids through college."

"Since when have *you* got kids, Sally?"

"Oh, I'm sure there must be at least a few out there by now—not that I've met 'em." I siphoned a little more from my glass. "So, how about it, Rudy? Joey Santiago. You know him?"

"I know the name," he admitted. "He's a real quiet guy, comes in every couple nights. About your height—no, a little taller, maybe."

"You're making me feel self-conscious, Rudy."

"Been a minute since he's come in. Castro's band is playing tonight, and I feel like he's hot on his eldest daughter." He motioned through the doorway and toward the bandstand, from which there drifted an uneasy little number. "Were I a betting man, I'd say odds are good he drops in tonight."

"But you *are* a betting man, Rudy," I said, slipping him a bill across the counter. "Try not to lose it all on the races."

"Speaking of races," he replied, tucking the tip into his back pocket, "if you find yourself at the track this weekend, don't hesitate to bet a little something on my girl Aurora. That horse is going to retire me, Sally. She don't lose!"

"I'll bear that in mind," I replied, taking my drink on a stroll. Like a wraith milling through a foggy graveyard, I navigated the haze of smoke and struck out toward the bandstand where the players had set down their instruments. A few sat for a smoke while others retreated to the bar for refreshment. Approaching the silver-haired virtuoso himself, I held out a hand to shake. "Fine playing, Mr. Castro. A pleasure to listen to you boys, as always."

The musician was very gracious, and perhaps amused that a chatty gringo like myself hadn't noted the faults in their playing that night. "Thank you for listening."

"I wonder," I pressed on before he could join his fellows over a beer, "is your eldest daughter here tonight?"

"Inez?" he asked.

I didn't know his daughter from a Maria or an Alejandra, but rolled with it. "That's the one," I replied convincingly enough to keep the meter running. "Forgive me, but I was hoping you'd grant me a small favor. Would you introduce me to her? I was listening from the back room and was entranced by her playing."

"Taken by her *playing*, were you?" The guitarist, undoubtedly used to fielding interest in his daughter, rolled his eyes and waved across the room. "Oy, Inez. This gentleman here would like to speak to you about your hand-clap techniques."

The moment Inez Castro sauntered over, I decided I rather liked this Joey Santiago character—thought him a kindred spirit, of sorts. A man with such good taste in women couldn't be all bad, I wagered. This nubile thing had never touched a guitar in her life—rather, the only instruments she had any experience with were those mystifying hips of hers, bound up in a sleek black dress. Her hair was blacker than the night and longer than it, too. A little impatient maybe, and tired of being approached by men every hour on the hour, she spared me a thin smile and offered a dainty hand. "Yes, how can I help you?"

"Miss Castro," I ventured, "I don't want to waste your time. Name's Salvador Bohannon. I'm a fan of this club and of your father's outfit here. Tremendous music." Pace by careful pace, I led her away from the rest of the band. The general hum issuing from the bar ensured that the ensuing would remain between the two of us.

"Thank you, that's very kind."

"Watching you guys play up there, I got to wondering something."

"Oh? And what's that?" asked the woman.

"What's Joey Santiago think of your music?"

"*Excuse* me?"

An innocent question, posed with the intention of taking her temp, revealed that Inez here had no love in her heart for poor Joe. Only hate can invite a foreign species like ugliness to a face as pretty as this one, and I knew right then that the two had a history.

"Did he put you up to this?" she was quick to add while I stood fumbling for my next line.

"I can see there's no fooling you," I lied. "Joey's got it bad, and it ain't good. He's still crazy about you, Inez." I was spinning the yarn faster than I could hold it. "I didn't mean to open old wounds there. I know things have been strained..."

"*Strained?*" echoed the woman. "That's an interesting word for it. He's got a lot of nerve, sending some pal of his out here to poke around for him. After what *he* did?"

"He wishes he could take it all back." I wasn't sure what my guy had done, or if, in fact, he was in the least bit contrite, but I was in too deep to show my hand now. "Can he make it up to you?"

"Not anymore than he can make my money reappear," she spat. "How is that bum, anyway? Still out of a job? Still hustling naive girls to feed his parlays?"

"He's looking to turn a new leaf," I said, though I myself was rapidly losing faith in the fella I was supposed to be defending. "How, uh... How much was it that he swindled you for again, Inez?"

"Me?" She laughed curtly. "Oh, he only got a few hundred out of me. I wised up quick—quicker than that club girl he was shacking up with. By the time she stormed out on him, he must have stolen over a thousand from her."

"Right, the club girl," I continued. "Remind me, where was it those two were staying?"

There's nothing quite like a woman's intuition; once they find a chink in your hull, the whole ship might up and sink. "Who did you say you were?"

"Joey Santiago and I go way back," I fibbed. "He's an old friend of mine."

"Oh? Well, a bit of advice for you, then: Find yourself some new friends. What, you on his heels now because he scammed *you*, too?"

I chuckled. "Am I really such an open book, miss? Listen..." I planted a few bucks in her palm and continued soothingly while her father looked on with arched brows. My time was running out. "I just need to speak to him. Whereabouts was he staying with this girl?"

She eyed the bills in her hand, rubbed them between her fingers. "Last I spoke to him, he was staying at the Morrison Hotel."

"Morrison Hotel," I repeated, making a mental note. "That's grand. Grand. And how long ago was that?"

"A month, give or take," she replied bitterly. "The one thing he was good about was paying up his room rent. He had it paid out in advance, so I wouldn't be surprised if he was still there." She crossed her thin arms. "What do you plan to do when you find him?"

I left her with a smile as Castro and his boys returned to the stage. "We'll share a friendly word, I'm sure."

Outside, the sun had well and truly called it quits. I paused beneath the front awning with no company except my Lucky Strike and took a few contemplative puffs. I had never paid much attention in Sunday school, but seemed to recall a line in the Good Book about the lips of babes. Sure enough, that raven-haired babe had spilled the beans about Joey Santiago, and had given me cause to doubt Taggart's initial pitch, too. I wasn't walking the streets in search of some old friend or cherished connection; I was looking for nothing less than an out-and-out conman. From the sounds of it, this fella had his hands in other people's pockets, and it didn't take a lot of imagination to figure that Taggart's were included.

Ripping off prostitutes and club girls is one thing, but you've got to be a special brand of stupid to rip off someone with the means to come after you. Taggart hadn't been shy about paying my admittedly exorbitant fee. The guy had money. That could only mean that this Santiago character was in *real* deep.

Finishing my cigarette, I found my way into the back of an idling cab. "Morrison Hotel."

The light changed and we were off.

———

The Morrison Hotel was getting a bit long in the tooth.

Her eight stories of tired stone looked about as steady on the corner of Legrand and Boothe as the winos shuffling in and out of the nearby viaduct. Busted windows wore plywood bandages, and the lights in her street-facing sign were all out. Scruffy bellhops had their feet up out front; the only baggage they were carrying was the debt they'd racked up during their most recent throw of the dice.

No one batted an eye as I cut into the lobby with my head low. There weren't any words of welcome from the fella behind the desk, and if he noticed me at all it was with the natural tension of a lazing man who fears himself on the verge of work. The lobby, quad-pillared and done up in bad carpet, opened leftward into a wide hall. You had your bathrooms, stairs and elevators there—the latter conveniently out of service—along with one thing else.

The Morrison Hotel's bar sat at the end of said passage, its doorway leaking smoke. Lights were low—as much a cost-saving measure as it was a means of protecting the kinds of men who hated themselves enough to drink in such a place from greater scrutiny. Stepping through the door I found two or three figures hunched sleepily over mounds of empties and a barman whose take-home was probably less than his tab.

A little jukebox in the corner was spitting out a Gerry Mulligan number, but no one seemed to be listening. I myself walked a slow circuit around the place, making a big to-do about where to park it and drown my sorrows. I chose a table with a wobbly leg near room's center—the one from which I could best discern the faces of neighboring drunks—and started running down the list in search of my man. At eight o'clock was seated a black man with an overflowing ashtray and eyes so heavy they kept drawing his forehead down against the table. At my six was a man in suit and tie, neither of them very sharp, who'd had enough rotgut to kill a pygmy elephant. He was a blonde, though.

The figure posed dreamily at my twelve—call it twelve and a quarter—was wearing a blue button-down and black slacks. The shirt had been left unbuttoned as if to give the furry creature on his chest some room to breathe, and his face was dusted in all kinds of stubble. I would have pegged him somewhere in his late thirties or early forties, but a whirlwind romance with hard drink had seen him wash up on the shore of something closer to fifty, looks-wise.

This, I felt quite sure, was the fabled Joey Santiago. He had the look, I supposed, of one in the habit of playing fast and loose with other people's money. You can't summarize a look of that kind in mere words, can't point at this, that or the other to make your case. It was baked into him. An alligator can't hide the fact it's a predator, and this fella had simply been born with the cast of a swindler.

The time had come for our meet-cute, and I took leave of my table, sauntering over to him. I dropped into the booth across from him and leaned in with my brow knotted in concern. "Joey? That *you*, Joey?" I asked real sweet and innocent-like. When I saw his eyes open in answer to the name, I knew I had him on the hook and started reeling in. "If it ain't Joey Santiago, of all people! Man, it's been ages. How ya been?"

The man lurched in his seat and squared me with a sleepy eye. "Who're you?" he slurred.

"Cognac got your tongue?" I teased. "It's me, Johnny—Johnny from the factory. Don't ya remember?"

Something in the lie I fed him—the common name "Johnny", or maybe the bland reference to a factory—proved soothing. He loosed a boozy sigh and nodded in weak comprehension. "Oh, uh... yeah..."

"How long's it been, now?" I had to be careful. Taggart had only given me the barest summary of Santiago's work history. I knew he'd been in car parts, but not how long or where. Though the guy was thoroughly soused, one misstep could easily blow my cover.

"It's been..." He hiccoughed. "It's been months since I left the factory." He fished around in his breast pocket for a pack of smokes but it was all in vain. "You still hanging at the plant? How's Bill? Still throwing his weight around?"

I set him up with a fresh Lucky Strike. "You know Bill. Always been a pain. That ain't ever gonna change." I lit up and leaned pensively on my elbow. "As for me, well, I actually stepped away just a few weeks back."

"Did you?"

I smoothed out my jacket, teased the rings on my fingers in a crude display. "Sure did. Found something more lucrative. Can't afford a suit like this on a factory wage."

Sensing that I was moneyed, the guy sat up a little. "Yeah? And what's that?"

"These days? I'm a gambler," I replied, letting out a little smoke with each syllable. "Three and four leg parlays. Horses, mostly, but I've got a system. The returns have been..." I let my silence do the talking.

Joey Santiago was more than interested. The mere mention of his beloved trade saw him light up like a Christmas tree. "Parlays?" he echoed, licking his chops like a hyena. "You know," he continued, "I've got some experience in that line myself."

"You don't say?" I acted real surprised. "I never knew you had a taste for risk. What've you been up to since you parted ways with the factory?"

"This n' that," he replied, still keenly interested in our earlier topic of conversation. "You say you gotta system—for bets, that is. You been working alone?"

"No. We put a team together. Real small, but we run a tight game. Our wins have been impressive. I suppose that's why we're never wanting for capital..."

His eyes widened. "You got people investing in your outfit?"

"A few. Our moneyed clients know it's a fickle game, but... nothing ventured, nothing gained, right? We've made some rich men rather richer."

"You, uh... You wouldn't happen to be looking for a new partner in that little enterprise, would ya?" He chuckled, and for the first time seemed to give a damn about his appearance. Thinking himself in a job interview now, he coaxed back his greasy salt n' pepper hair and tried tugging the wrinkles out of his open shirt. "We should team up. I think we could do great things together."

This poor schmuck probably didn't have enough cash left in his coffers to cover a cab ride, but that didn't stop him from puffing his chest out like Howard Hughes. To a man with addictive tendencies, a dyed-in-the-wool gambler, there's nothing more thrilling, more attractive, than a little more runway. Gambling addicts aren't stupid; they know we've all gotta pay the piper sooner or later. The best of 'em are masters of forbearance. They kick the can down the road at every opportunity. Sometimes, however rarely, they even win.

"Matter of fact, we've been looking for a solid man." I ground out my cigarette. "My boss has been giving it to me in the ear, telling me how we need someone who knows their stuff. It's short notice, but if you're game, I could introduce you. I'd prefer to work with someone I know. Us factory boys gotta stick together," said I.

"You'd do that for me?" he asked, perking up. He sucked his cig down to the filter and then flicked it across the room. "Y-Yeah, let's do it." He rose shakily from his seat, unable to remember what legs were for. He did a little dance between the tables before staking his heels into the carpet and slowly regaining his balance. "Lead the way, Johnny." He threw a thick arm around my shoulders and pulled me close. "Can't tell you what this means to me. We're headin' to the moon, baby," he slurred.

Little did he know, we were actually headed to 310 Bianville Street.

Joey Santiago spooked like a frightened mare when the building entered into view.

On the walk over, he'd begun sobering up. Trudging down the street, heads low, we'd made idle chit-chat and I'd kept up my facade, copping to a heavy-set wife, a disabled son and whatever else he associated with the generic factory-man he'd mistaken me for. I dodged his questions about our destination repeatedly, but once I started across the street with the four-story building in my sights, I noticed him freeze up.

"What're we doin' *here?*" he asked.

"This is my place," I lied. "We'll head inside, have a couple of drinks, and I'll give the boss a call. He'll be thrilled to meet you."

"Yeah?" Something about the spot left him visibly ill at ease, and I felt pretty sure it was all my fault. Something I'd said or done, some loose thread left dangling out of my deceitful doily, was gonna unravel this whole thing.

Would that I had brought a hip flask; snowing the guy with a little more drink would have made it easier to guide him inside. Instead, I decided to fill his head with more nonsense. Promises of money, tall-tales of unbelievable scores, began dribbling from my lips like coins out of a slot machine. "We've got bets going as we speak. Horses, baseball—why, I've got a friend in the business who's been cleaning up on dogfighting, if you can believe it."

"Dogfighting?" snapped Joey. "That's just barbaric."

Cute, I thought. Even my serial-swindler here had a soft spot for animals.

I led him through the lobby door and started hiking up the steps, recalling what Taggart had told me. His place was on the third floor. I started the trek upward, and noticed at every landing that my buddy was going paler and paler. His gaze swept the dusty floors like they hadn't been swept in ages, and he wrung out the handrail like it owed him money. I knew he was beginning to doubt me; my stream-of-consciousness dialogue was becoming too absurd even for an avaricious drunk to believe. He was one sour note, one wrong word, from running back down the stairs and making my evening a whole lot more difficult.

We shuffled our way to the third level, and I zeroed in on the door beyond the landing. He spooked real bad at that, and came to a complete halt before we'd even reached it. "Hold on... What building is this, man?" he asked. "This is 310, ain't it? Bianville?"

"No," I lied. "This is 614. And, maybe you didn't notice, but we passed Bianville and went on to Quincy."

He shook his head. "Nah, I don't think so, Johnny. This is 310 Bianville."

"If you say so," I replied with a chuckle. "Get a load of this guy," I muttered, "thinking he knows my address better than I do."

Joey had a rare moment of clarity as I strove toward the door. "Nah, look... this is the third floor, ain't it?"

I lined up another lie and thrust it at him with a toss of the shoulders. "No... I don't know what difference it makes, Joey, but this is the second floor. We've only gone up two flights."

The guy was mighty close to piecing it all together. He was in debt up to his eyeballs, and knew that this was Taggart's place—the one man in town he didn't want to cross paths with. Joey could smell the setup and knew that I was about to deliver him to my paunchy financier. "I... I don't think you really live here, Johnny," he uttered, staring me down from across the landing.

I clicked my tongue and approached the door. It was time for a little gambit, a toss of the dice. "Yeah, wiseguy? Then why's the door open, just as I left it?" I thrust my hand out and took hold of the knob, not knowing if it would turn. My bluff paid off handsomely, though; the beautiful thing turned and I pushed the door open with a satisfying creak. "C'mon, Joey. You've had a little too much to drink. I'll fix you a seltzer or something while we wait for the boss, yeah?"

With a gulp, he bought the lie I was selling. Still jittery, he glanced about the landing before joining me in the doorway. "All right... I just coulda sworn that..." He shook his head. "Never mind."

It'd been a little ballsy of me to let myself in this way, without knocking. Taggart was almost certainly in, anxiously awaiting my delivery, but I had a thin line to walk. On the one hand, I had to make my presence look natural—to convince Joey that this really was my place. On the other, I needed to give Taggart some cue that we'd arrived.

It looked to be a small apartment, sparsely furnished. Coatrack, staggered lamps, a pile of old newspapers sitting in the entryway hall. A few lights had been left on, and a pair of nice leather shoes—the ones I'd seen Taggart in earlier—were sitting nearby. "Honey, I'm home!" I announced with a chuckle. I waved Joey on and stood in front of the door as if to hang up my jacket. "Go on, make yourself comfortable," I urged.

Joey Santiago wandered a little deeper into the apartment, turned a corner.

And then he stopped cold.

I couldn't see him from where I stood, but I could *feel* the scream that came out of him before he even opened his mouth.

Someone had been standing around the corner with a club in hand, and had brained him.

Taggart or some hired thug had gotten a jump on Joey, and he was about to get shook down.

These and other possibilities jumped out at me before the man himself came bounding back toward the entrance, white as a sheet. He looked straight through me, longing for the door, but when I refused to step out of the way he threw his shaking hands out as if to drag me.

"W-Why'd you bring me here, Johnny?" he demanded. "Why'd you do this?"

"What in the world's gotten into you, pal?" I asked, giving his shoulders a little shake.

He wasn't having it. He reared back and prepared to fight his way out.

Subsequently, I took no pleasure in cracking him across the jaw. That chin of his was hardly granite; he went out like a gallon of warm milk and hit the wall stammering. Urging him back around the bend with my heel, I cleared my throat. "All right, Mr. Taggart. I've brought your man. He doesn't seem inclined to stay long, though. We square?"

Joey Santiago fell to his knees and looked out across a bare living room, hands trembling against the wooden floors. I looked along with him, and found my corpulent client sitting in a high-backed chair, facing us. His head was hanging low, his chins pressed down into his blazer, and his spectacles were sitting in his lap, one of the lenses clearly busted.

Most notable, though, was the entry wound in his left eye. Someone—and within moments I had a solid guess who—had shot him clean through the head. The wall behind his chair was painted with threads of dry gore.

I had a lot of questions just then, and I'm ashamed that chief among them was, *Is this guy's check still gonna clear?*

"Who put you up to this? Who're you working for?" asked Joey, looking like he might be sick.

I didn't have the heart—or the words, really—to tell him I'd been working for the stiff. Suddenly, I knew why Santiago had been so jumpy the moment we'd come up to the building—the reason I'd had to drag him through the door. This wasn't his first time visiting Taggart at the Bianville Street location. "All right, Joey... All right. Tell me, what'd you have to do with this? You owed Taggart a kingly sum, am I right?"

"L-Look, look, I had a few bad runs," stammered the man. "I couldn't repay him—not as fast as he wanted, anyway. I never shoulda borrowed money from a guy like him, but... When he started making threats, I decided I had to... be proactive... I had to protect myself..."

"So you came up here, earlier this evening, and shot him. Dead men can't collect. That about the length of it? Afterward, you staggered back to the Morrison Hotel to drink away your guilt."

He glared at me from down below, his whiskered face quivering. "T-This evening? Brother, I shot this bastard Thursday before last..."

Come to think of it, poor Taggart did look pretty well-established in his chair; that is to say, a dark hue had crept into his skin and his limbs looked stiff as broom handles. He'd been there awhile; a week and change seemed about right.

It was my turn to stammer. "W-What're you drivin' at, J-Joey? He was in my office just this evening! Hours ago! He paid me to track you down and bring you here—claimed you were an old friend of his..."

"*Yes, and you did a marvelous job, Mr. Bohannon,*" came a low voice from another room. To our immediate right there was what looked to be a bedroom, its door ajar. The lights were off inside, but we both noticed something—or *someone*—standing within, shrouded in darkness. The voice was paper-thin, calm, and it snuck cat-like through the sliver of open doorway. It was familiar, too.

"T-Taggart?" I called. "That... That *you?*"

A portly, nighted silhouette teased the bedroom doorway before receding back into the darkness. "*It is. And now, I will kindly ask you to take your leave. My old friend and I have much catching up to do...*"

I wasn't sure what to make of all this. Maybe it was a theatrical put-on, meant to spook Joey the swindler. Maybe there'd been a little something extra in that last cigarette of mine and I was just seein' and hearin' things that weren't there. And maybe, just maybe, something was going on in that apartment that I couldn't explain and didn't want any part of. I took another look around, my gaze settling on the dead man across the room. In retrospect, I think I must have been going nuts, because I noticed he'd moved a little since my last look at him. He'd turned his head a bit, and his good eye—yellow and bulging—had been fixed on me as if to issue a warning. "*You got your money. Now get the hell out, Bohannon.*"

I backed up immediately, all too happy to oblige. "W-Well, pleasure doin' business with ya..."

Joey grasped at my pant legs, wanted to follow me out, but a sudden burst of movement from that bedroom door saw him turn around and whimper like a kicked dog. I didn't stop and wonder what came out of that door, and I sure didn't stick around to watch what ultimately became of the gambler. I let myself out, shut the door behind me, and got as far away from Bianville Street as I could.

I don't know what happened to Joey Santiago. His name never turned up in the obituary section—and believe me, I looked. It's possible he's still out there, but if he isn't I rather doubt anyone's missing him.

Taggart, on the other hand, showed up in the papers a few days on from that incident at Bianville Street. News of his murder caused a minor sensation, and the authorities did a lot of chest-thumping, promising to track down his killer.

And now, to answer this case's weightiest question:

Yes, the stiff's check cleared, no problem.

Henry Taggart's ghost had been kind enough to back-date it for me. He'd dated it for the Wednesday before last—the day prior to his murder.

KNIT ONE, PURL ONE

There are few things in life more alluring to me than a handwritten sign at a street corner that reads "Estate Sale". Many were the days of my youth spent hoofing it through suburbia following the arrows on such signs. They lead, invariably, into winding neighborhoods, into unfamiliar corners of otherwise familiar towns. In a word, they promise *adventure.* Garage sales, yard sales, estate sales—no matter the species, a shopper with a keen eye can find great deals at these events with a bit of effort.

It was from my grandmother that I first caught the bug; living in her close-knit community for a few summers in junior high, I became a connoisseur of antiquated trinkets and second-hand kitsch. It was granny who taught me the art of the haggle, too. "Never pay full price for anything, if you can help it," should probably have been etched into her tombstone. Together, we'd set off down the sidewalks, putting in the miles with my day's allowance jingling in my pocket. Over the course of a few hours, that money of mine would slowly be transformed into collectible plushes, rare trading cards and other purchases of dubious worth which would go on to litter my grandmother's home. Each time I successfully haggled a homeowner down from their asking price, granny would be waiting in the wings with a wide smile on her face. "You're a natural, Heather."

I like to think that my haggling prowess opened a few doors for me later on—that it served me well in negotiating business deals and climbing the corporate ladder. The trouble with working for a Fortune 500 company, though, is that it leaves you with precious little time for hitting up yard sales. Over the years, my beloved hobby fell by the wayside, a memory of summers long-gone.

Until, that is, my husband and I vacationed in Michigan.

***

We'd decided to drive through the Great Lakes State over the course of three weeks. Bed and Breakfasts were abundant, and the quaint little towns we visited between the larger metropolitan areas proved charming—so charming, in fact, that hubby and I considered staying. After all, with every passing year, retirement was inching closer. Leaving the big city behind and dwelling somewhere quieter held a lot of appeal, and we treated our tour of Michigan almost as a series of auditions. Though the Upper Peninsula felt just a bit too rural for us, the lower half of the state held some real jewels.

Among them was this little city called Morenci.

The population, if memory serves, is just a hair past 2,200. The public buildings are all small and cute, boasting the interesting architectural styles of days long-gone. There didn't appear to be any major chain stores or restaurants within its limits, but there were more mom and pop shops than either of us could shake a stick at. Better still, the place was eminently walkable; running errands by foot or bike seemed quite doable. Nate and I both were in love with the city as we sailed through this final leg of our journey. It was a place out of time—as close to a generic, TV-ready suburb as one could get.

We happened to wheel into Morenci at a special time. Unbeknownst to us, the citizens there were in the habit of holding a community-wide garage sale each summer. Homeowners all over the city had put out their wares on the same weekend in early July, drawing respectable crowds and many out-of-towners. Food trucks from further north had also made the trip, and were staggered along residential streets, seeding the air with delectable scents.

"What's this, now?" asked Nate, cutting speed. "The twentieth garage sale in a row? Is this all coordinated?"

I stared out the passenger side window of our SUV like a dog, my nose smudging the glass. "Oh, babe, we've gotta stop! Look at all this!" Rolling down the window, I stuck my head out and studied the street we were on from end-to-end. As far as the eye could see, lawns were cluttered with signs, tables and other unmistakable hints of commerce. "Find someplace to park!"

"Garage sales?" My husband—the sort of man who's content to wear whatever I buy him and who seldom sets foot in a store of any kind—seemed almost offended at the concept. "It's just a bunch of old junk, Heather. What, are we gonna rifle through someone's collection of 8-tracks?"

"Maybe... !" I replied, genuinely intrigued at the prospect. "You never know what you might find at a yard sale! People get rid of interesting and valuable things *all the time.* Haven't you ever seen *Antiques Roadshow?*"

"Yeah, I have. It's great television. But I've also watched the local lottery program, and that doesn't make me any likelier to run out and blow my money on scratch-offs."

"Come on, Nate! Pull over! Let's just wander one or two of them. Please?"

He sighed, easing down on the brake as a bunch of kids went running across the street—kids with armfuls of new toys they'd probably bought for a pittance at nearby sales. Kids I could identify with. He inched forward, then hung a lazy left into a new branch of the neighborhood. Here, too, sales dominated. There was seemingly no end to them. Neither was there an end to my pleading from the passenger seat. Realizing himself defeated, Nate guided the SUV toward the curb and threw it into park. "All right, but we're going to set up some ground rules. Two sales. Maximum. I don't want to be here all day, OK?"

"Sure, that's fine with me." I went bounding out onto the sidewalk and had a nice, long stretch. Standing beneath shaggy maples and elms, the sunlight poking through their canopies and the summer wind in my hair, I felt like a girl again. Scanning the succession of sales before us was almost overwhelming. "So much *potential!*" Giddily, I took Nate's arm and hauled him down the street in search of something special.

Pleased with the stunning weather, or else amused at my childish excitement, Nate chuckled to himself. "What's gotten into you? You weren't half this excited when we spent the day walking that huge outlet mall in Auburn Hills."

I dug through my purse, ensuring I had at least a bit of cash on hand. "I'm sure I've told you about it before—the way my grandmother and I would haunt local garage sales in the summers? I can't explain it... Looking through other people's things, you get a vantage point into their lives, you know? Maybe you discover an old book—a book with an inscription in it. Finding something like that can be a little funny and a little sad all at once. Know what I mean?"

"Not really."

"Well, I happen to be a pretty mean haggler. Finding something you want at one of these sales and wresting it from the owner at less than asking-price is an art." I flashed him a grin. "Just you wait!" One of the houses across the street, a narrow two-story with a sagging roof, was particularly abuzz with activity. The grounds hadn't been mowed in awhile, and a path to the front door had been cleared through the stomping of visitors. The screened-in porch was cluttered with hand-written signs meant to draw in passersby even from a distance.

ESTATE SALE, read one, scrawled in permanent marker.

EVERYTHING MUST GO, said another on wrinkled cardboard.

COLLECTIBLES AND MORE. PRICED TO MOVE, promised a third.

I snapped my fingers and, when I was sure we wouldn't get smashed by a passing car, I dragged Nate across the street. "An estate sale? You know what this means, right?"

My husband couldn't help rolling his eyes. "Means someone kicked the bucket and now their family members are trying to turn a buck by selling off their things."

"OK, that's fair. But you know what else it means?"

"Bedbugs come *free* with the furniture?"

"You're being a real buzzkill, babe." I sighed. "It means someone probably spent years in this house. Maybe lived in it all their lives. Everything in there is bound to have a story, and there could be some genuinely interesting pieces inside!" I waggled my brows at him, adding, "If you've got a good eye, you may even be able to find something of value at a sale like this one!"

The two of us scooted past the other shoppers and made our way up the lawn. The stench of age, of places long shut-up, met our noses as we slipped onto the porch and approached the front door. From inside, I could hear so many delightful noises—shoppers and sale-runners were engaged in hushed back and forth, boxes were being rummaged through and deals were being brokered.

What we found within was, aside from the wheeling and dealing, the ultimate in coziness. In fact, the moment we passed through the front entrance and started through a small, lamplit sitting room, I felt myself thrust into the past and had to do a double-take. The house was—if only in atmosphere—a mirror image of my late grandmother's.

Sure, the specifics were different. To start with, my grandmother had lived in Illinois, not Michigan, and her yard had always been pristine. My grandfather had been a landscaper, and she'd never been able to stomach anything but perfection on that front.

The pair of recliners in the corner, their cushions defeated, weren't done up in a leafy print like the ones I remembered, but were a tackier check pattern. The pictures on the walls weren't the lush nature scenes my grandmother had commissioned from local painters, but were instead family photos.

But there were throw blankets—more than any one person could ever hope to use. And there was evidence in the room of *at least* one pampered cat. The poor thing, probably spooked by the ceaseless rush of visitors, was likely hiding in some dark corner, waiting for the sale to end. The coffee table and side tables near the sofa were all of stained hardwood, and looked, somehow, exactly like the ones I'd colored on while visiting my grandmother as a girl.

China cabinets had been left sitting open, their contents marked with colorful tags. Cups, saucers, teapots and porcelain figurines were many, and numerous shoppers had congregated before them to search for uber-valuable pieces. The kitchen counters, dining room table and other available surfaces had been ladened with large boxes for easier rummaging. In these, one could find everything from clothing, mugs and glassware, vinyl records, old children's toys and more.

Nate, attempting to be a good sport, wandered to the nearest box and thumbed through the selection of records. "You know, I've been meaning to pick up a turntable. Vinyl's back in style. Didn't see that coming."

I peered over shoulders at crystal figurines and hand-painted tea sets, and then started paging through a box of old books. A handsome set of encyclopedias sat within, almost as old as I was. "Babe, look!" I said, plucking one of the thick volumes out. "My grandmother used to have a set just like this!"

"Man, that makes me feel old... A world before search engines?" Nate suddenly brightened, happening upon something in the box of vinyl. "Hey, how about that?" He plucked a single record out of the bin and turned the sleeve in his hands. "*Pet Sounds?* This is the first record I ever bought! I played the heck out of it. Man..."

He opened the thing, inspecting the record itself. "The liner notes are here and everything!"

Without his realizing it, Nate had fallen under the spell of the estate sale. "Keep looking! I'll bet there are some other good ones in there. You could even pick a few up... You'll need something to spin on that turntable if you get around to buying one, after all..."

He grinned. "Challenge accepted."

I spent a few more minutes turning the pages of an old *National Geographic*, and then waltzed a little deeper in, where I discovered a narrow stairwell. The sale appeared to bleed over into the upper level, and figuring it less crowded than the ground floor I took the steps two at a time and made my way into a carpeted hall. Aside from a bathroom—which looked to be closed to visitors—I discovered only three doors on this second floor. One was a closet stocked with cleaning supplies. Another, on the left side of the hall, was a bedroom which hosted only a few sticks of dusty furniture. An old bed frame, a dresser, a standing mirror and a tiny ottoman had been left within, all of them wearing bright tags with handwritten prices. Uninterested in these, I turned my attention to the last door.

The door on the right was ajar. Standing in the hall a moment and listening closely, I *knew* that there was no one inside; that, for the time being, I was alone on the second floor of the house. Curiously, though, I *felt* like there was someone standing on the other side of the door. Something beyond my senses assured me it was so, though as I carefully stepped inside, it fast became clear that I'd been mistaken. How strange it was, then, when the feeling *continued* to linger in the absence of all reason.

The room was small and packed to the gills with crates, boxes and bags. A well-loved rocking chair sat near the window and a small, weathered rug—a Serapi, perhaps—was spread across the floor of what had once been a craft room. Sturdy shelves lined the walls, and these had been burdened with every manner of fiber-working tool imaginable. There were plastic bins packed with knitting needles of various sizes, bundles of crochet hooks bound up in twine, at least three sewing machines in varying states of repair, and thimbles, needles, pins and bobbins aplenty. Squares of felt had been piled on a small table, the whole mound priced cheaply, and rolls of fleece and cotton batting were also on offer—these left leaning against the wall.

I'm not the craftiest person in the world. In fact, when it comes to anything beyond threading a needle, I'm more or less useless. It wasn't always like this, however; in fact, there was one point—one of those summers in junior high—when I thought I might take up knitting. My grandmother had been fond of knitting and had made me many sweaters as a girl; in the winter months, especially, she'd loved nothing more than working up a good ball of yarn by the fire with a cocktail close at hand.

Stumbling upon all of these supplies, stored away meticulously by the former owner, I felt that old desire suddenly rear its head. I squeezed a few yarn balls, rifled through bundles of knitting needles and discovered well-loved stacks of craft magazines, their heavily-referenced patterns cluttered with handwritten notes.

It was then, too, that I discovered the beginnings of a cable-knit sweater tucked behind said magazines, the needles still holding tension as though the crafter had just set them down and would soon return to begin the next row. I drew the bundle out of its dark corner and examined the yarn—very soft and sumptuous—in the light. This was no ordinary yarn, no corner-store acrylic. I knew within moments that it was cashmere, at least three balls' worth.

The sweater, child-sized by the looks of it, had been shelved before the owner had hit the half-way mark. Even so, the work that had been left behind was lovely to behold; the stitches were all nice and even, and it was plain that the knitter had been possessed of considerable skill. I couldn't hope to match that skill myself, but came quickly to the conclusion that I wanted to give it a go.

I didn't have any children of my own, and so saw little need for knitting cute, tiny sweaters. Nevertheless, with a bit of effort,

I could undo the existing stitches and make something new with the yarn—a fine scarf or hat, perhaps. I don't know why I felt so drawn to the half-finished project. Maybe it felt a little sad to me that the owner hadn't been able to complete it before she'd passed and her things had been put up for sale. Maybe I was just feeling sentimental, filled with good memories of my late grandmother and her passion for crafting. Whatever the case, I brought the whole mess, needles and all, downstairs with me. It hadn't been tagged like so many of the other items in the house, but I intended to buy it.

While I'd been up in the craft room, Nate had picked up a few more records. He was now hovering over other boxes, and was flipping through decades-old magazines like a kid on Christmas morning. "Oh, hey," he said. "You find something?"

I nodded, holding out the mass of yarn. "It's cashmere! I'm going to make a scarf or something."

My husband eyed the bundle curiously, but didn't dissuade me.

I sought out one of the sale-runners to get a price for my yarn. Seated in the kitchen, looking out the window into the backyard, was a forlorn young woman in the ballpark of twenty-five. She'd had bleached hair, once, but hadn't kept up with treatments for some time and her black roots were showing. Wearing a baggy sweatshirt and jeans, she didn't seem to notice me enter the kitchen, and only reacted when I cleared my throat and drew very near the table. "Excuse me…" I began. "Are you… ?"

"Oh, how can I help you?" she asked, shooting up from her chair. Standing at her full height, she struck me as a tiny mouse of a woman. She met me with large, clear eyes and a somewhat nervous smile, and I saw in them both a bit of trouble. The woman had been brooding over something, and the moment she was done with me I knew she'd return to the chair and get back to it.

"Very sorry to bother you," I continued, "but I found this great yarn upstairs, in the craft room?" I held it out for her to see. "How much would it cost for this yarn and these needles? It looks to be about three balls' worth of yarn here."

"Um..." The young lady combed back her bangs and slipped her delicate hands into the pocket of her sweatshirt. "There's no price on it?"

"No," I replied.

Studying the heap of yarn more closely, she smiled a little and shook her head. "I... I don't understand. It looks like gran was working up that yarn before she passed, but she never finished the project. Y-You want her old work-in-progress?"

"Oh," I said, "it was your grandmother's project? It's really lovely work. I admit I'm not much of a knitter, but I'd like to learn. I was thinking I'd use the yarn for something else."

"I see..." She cleared her throat. "Yeah, this stuff, all of it, was hers. She, uh... she passed on almost two months ago, and we're just now getting around to clearing out the house." She shrugged, returning to the matter at hand. "I dunno... we could do three dollars for it? A dollar for each ball of yarn. The needles are free."

I'd been looking for an opportunity to haggle, to drive the price down even further, but coming away with real cashmere yarn for a mere three bucks was already a steal, and I couldn't in good conscience pay the woman any less for it. What's more, as I'd watched her glance over the pattern and discuss her late grandmother, I felt that I'd struck upon the source of her trouble. She was still in mourning, and being surrounded by her grandmother's things in this way—parceling off precious mementos for a few bucks—was overwhelming for her. "Three dollars? Sure, it's a deal," I said, digging through my purse. I handed her three singles, and from a kitchen drawer she passed on a plastic bag to help me contain the whole mess.

I don't know what compelled me to do it, but even after the transaction was complete, I remained in the kitchen and tried to make more conversation. "This is a lovely house," I continued.

"Reminds me a lot of *my* grandmother's place. So sorry for your loss."

"Yeah, thanks," she said, turning back toward the window. "It was kind of sudden. None of us were prepared, but... that's life." She chuckled and motioned to her belly. "I, uh... I was looking forward to her meeting her first great-grandchild."

"Oh? You're pregnant?"

The woman nodded sheepishly. "Yeah, just a few months along. Granny was so excited; she was planning to make all kinds of hats and sweaters for the baby." She motioned to the bag in my hand, adding, "I think that may have been one of them."

"*T-This?*" I felt monstrously guilty just then, having bought up such a thing. "I had no idea! I'm sorry! Do you want it back?"

"Oh, no," she was quick to reply. "I'm not great with yarn. Believe me. Granny tried to teach me, but I was hopeless. Better that someone else gets some use out of it."

"You sure?

"Yeah. Please, enjoy. And thanks for stopping by." Any further interaction was cut short by another customer. A man juggling several mugs came into the kitchen to ask for a box, and the woman disappeared into the basement to search for one.

Taking my leave, I returned to Nate, who'd just handed off a few dollars to a man by the door for his trio of records. "All set?" he asked.

"Yep." I gave my little bag a shake. The sting of guilt persisted as we left the house, but toying with the yarn in the car, I decided I'd give knitting a serious go—and that I'd make my grandmother proud in the process.

We wound up at a little bed and breakfast just outside Morenci. Ten small cabins had been erected around a lake so tiny it was hardly worthy of the name, and we checked in to the seventh of these after a lovely dinner at a local restaurant, just as the sun was setting. Within it, we found a comfortable bed and sofa, air conditioning, a stocked mini fridge, and a television that was perhaps *too* big for the space. We hauled our bags in with a mind towards relaxing.

Among these was my bag of estate sale yarn.

Nate cracked a beer and did a bit of channel surfing on the bed while I took over the sofa and laid out my new acquisition. The yarn, dyed a pleasing sea-foam blue, was so much fun to play with; I ran my hands against the half-finished project and enjoyed its exquisite softness. With the help of a few YouTube videos on my phone, I took a crash course in knitting and eventually worked up the courage to pluck the needles from their resting places.

It's funny, but the long knitting needles—metal, with little plastic caps on the back—didn't want to budge, at first. I tried tugging them out of the project, but it was almost as though the fibers clung to them and insisted on anchoring them in place. It took a concerted effort for me to yank them free, and once I'd loosed them, I started looking for threads to tug on. Again, though I sought to un-do the existing stitches, none of the threads I pulled on seemed to want to budge. For thirty, maybe forty minutes, I struggled with the stubborn yarn, and losing my patience I nearly reached for my scissors.

"Ugh," I complained to my husband. He was half-asleep on the bed, watching baseball highlights. "I can't do it. I can't bring myself to just cut into this cashmere. I'm going to have to try this again later, when I have more patience."

Carefully balling the whole thing up and thrusting the needles into the project chaotically, I dropped my yarn back into the plastic bag and tossed it onto the kitchen counter. Heavy-eyed, I then joined Nate on the bed and watched sports commentary until sleep overcame me.

You must understand, I'm a heavy sleeper.

Once, in college, a roommate of mine called 9-1-1 because I'd been sleeping so soundly that she mistook me for a corpse. I've been known to sleep through storms, noisy construction work and other things that'd keep most anyone up. Usually, except when sick, I close my eyes at night and don't open them again till morning. Deep, untroubled sleep is my one superpower.

That's why it was so strange when I awoke in that little cabin to the sounds of plastic being crumpled.

Shortly after the fact, I told myself that it was only because we were away from home—that something about our unfamiliar surroundings had left me ill at ease. Of course, during our three-week jaunt through Michigan, I'd slept like a rock in dozens of hotels and bed and breakfasts without incident, so this explanation didn't hold much water. It was the only conclusion I could come to, though, without entertaining *stranger* explanations.

Nate was asleep on my left side, an arm draped over his face and his even breathing filling the air. At some point, before turning off the TV, he'd put out the lights, leaving the interior filled with gloom. There was almost no light to see by; a faint glow coming in through the cracks in the window blinds, and the spectral shine of the numbers on the microwave registered, but little else.

And in that darkness, from somewhere to my right, I heard the rustling.

Slow. Patient. Considered.

I remained completely still in bed for some time, simply listening. I recalled the bag of yarn I'd earlier tossed onto the counter, and I wagered that it was simply slipping off said counter toward the floor. Clearly, I hadn't tossed it far enough, and I fully expected to hear it thump on the linoleum at any moment.

But it never did.

Instead, as I listened, I couldn't drive away the thought that someone else was in the cabin with us—and that they were rummaging through the bag of yarn. The crinkling was joined now and then by a faint metallic noise, a sound I recognized. Bafflingly, it was the sound of knitting needles being worked through yarn. When knitting, the tips of one's needles occasionally meet and rub against one another. This results in the quiet but satisfying *click* of steel-on-steel.

Sure now that something—a raccoon or squirrel—had gotten into the cabin and was playing around in my bag of yarn, I cleared my throat and prepared to wake my husband. With a shaky hand, I reached out in search of the nightstand lamp, and when my fingers found the little knob, I gave it a careful turn.

Though I'd anticipated the flight of a small animal upon triggering the lights—a fit of screeching or scurrying—I was met instead with silence. The rustling and clicking immediately ceased; the cessation of noise was so sudden, in fact, that I couldn't help but think it deliberate. That was when it first occurred to me that I wasn't dealing with an animal, but instead with a person.

There was another sign that forced me to entertain this latter theory—one that startled me terribly and saw me shaking Nate awake in a hurry.

In the kitchen, next to the counter, I spied something. A powdery shadow leaned there, just beyond the microwave—leaned as a person might lean. Any movement in the shadowy mass was too subtle for my tired eyes to track, but I noticed in it a definite human outline. Like a charcoal silhouette, the shadow fluttered there for a moment, almost indecisively. And then, gradually, it retreated, fading into the surrounding murk.

"W-What?" moaned my husband, flopping onto his side.

I sat up in bed, scanning the entirety of the cabin with wide eyes. There wasn't much to scan, really; a living area, with bed and sofa, a minuscule kitchenette with toy-like fridge, sink and microwave, and a closet-sized bathroom. I looked up and down the length of the place, from the front door to the back wall, but no longer saw any trace of the weird shadow.

"Never mind," I told my husband. "The light was playing tricks on my eyes..."

Hearing this, Nate, my absolute *hero*, loosed a great snore and tumbled back to sleep.

But I was still shaken. I knew I'd heard *something* in the dark. Slowly, I worked up the nerve to stand and walk to the kitchen. There, putting on the bathroom light, I took a look around and half-expected to find a mouse or something on the counter.

Instead, all I found was that plastic bag of estate sale cashmere yarn.

And it was open.

Fuzzy though I was, I *knew* I'd closed the thing. I'd knotted it up, in fact, before tossing it from the sofa to the counter, in order to keep it from spilling everywhere.

Now, however, it was sitting open.

I reached inside tentatively, wondering if some varmint had been cozying up to my cashmere, but found no trace of any animal. I was close to writing the whole thing off as a weird dream, a waking nightmare caused by too much wine at dinner, when I glanced into the bag a second time and noticed something very odd.

Earlier, I'd pulled the needles out of their loops, intending to un-do the entire project.

Now, the two needles were snuggly back in place. They'd been re-inserted in the stubborn loops. I pulled the project out in total confusion, sure as I was of anything that I'd wrenched the dumb things out. In doing so, I discovered that progress on the sweater—only half-finished when last I'd beheld it—had apparently advanced.

The front was completely done, and some of the yarn had been utilized in the creation of a sleeve—nearly complete.

I admit, I gasped. Everything up to that point could have been explained away by sleepiness, but *this?* There had been no sleeve when last I'd glanced at the project. I didn't have the skill to knit such a thing, and I rather doubted that my husband had become a fiberwork phenom in the past few hours.

I was bothered, and in an almost childish burst of annoyance, I went tugging at the first loose thread I found.

As before, the project wouldn't budge, however.

The stitches were perfect, even and tight. I hadn't been able to un-do the earlier progress, and I couldn't seem to unravel this latest addition, either.

Suffice it to say, I lost my taste for knitting right then and there.

Spooked, I double-knotted the plastic bag, carried it into the bathroom and threw it into the shower stall. Then, shutting the bathroom door, I shuffled back to bed. I planned to throw it in the trash before we left, and wanted nothing more to do with it.

I didn't get much sleep that night. I put on the television to keep the room lit up, and I leaned heavily on its constant muttering to drown out any sounds from the bathroom. I didn't hear anything more, and I held my pee till late in the morning so as to avoid another encounter with the stupid sweater.

It was Nate who next broached the subject, when he shuffled out of bed and decided to take a shower. "Hey, Heather, what's *this* doing in here?" he asked. My husband emerged with the plastic bag in hand. Sleepily, he clawed out its contents and inspected them. "Whoa, nice. Did you make this?" he asked. "Is this what you were working on all night?"

"Huh?" I sat on the edge of the bed and pawed at my throbbing head. "What're you talking about?"

"This sweater," he said. "It's kinda small, though. Who'd you make it for?"

Nate held in his hands a beautiful little sweater. Made of the sea-foam cashmere yarn, it featured a handsome cable-knit, and size-wise looked perfectly suited to an infant.

He chuckled, putting it down on the counter. "I thought you didn't know how to knit! This turned out pretty good—you should keep it up!"

I was at a loss for words. I tried, a few times, as he wandered off to the shower, to tell him that I *hadn't* knitted it. As though called up to examine something grisly, I crept out of bed and into the kitchen, appraising the sweater from up-close. Overnight, in the hours since I'd ditched it in the shower, the project had been completed. The sleeves, collar, hem—all of it was perfect, pristine. One couldn't have bought a cuter sweater at a boutique.

And yet it frightened and disgusted me.

Looking at it, I knew myself in the presence of something unnatural. Walking the floors of the tiny cabin, I could find no trace of the one who'd done the knitting, but whenever I glanced at the completed project I could almost *feel* them in the air, as if they were standing close-by.

I nearly threw it away. In fact, I bunched it up in a rage, first, and tried to pop its stitches, but the fibers held and I lost my nerve. I threw it back onto the counter and wondered how such a thing was possible.

Over the course of Nate's shower, something occurred to me. *This project... the deceased woman started it for her great-grandchild before she passed.*

I had only to peer at the sweater to note that the work was consistent throughout; however impossibly, the same hand had been responsible for each and every stitch—both those pre-existing and posthumous. The craftsmanship was unmistakable. The only explanation I could come to, then, was that the dead woman, realizing I was about to unravel her work, had stopped by to complete the sweater.

I've never been a full-on skeptic in regards to ghosts and unexplained things of that nature, but neither had I ever witnessed such a sure and baffling sign of their existence. Convinced that I was dealing with such a thing, I considered telling Nate the whole story. I hadn't mentioned my conversation with the young woman working the estate sale, hadn't told him about the late-night disturbance in the cabin—none of it.

After a bit of dithering, I decided to keep it all to myself, however. When you've been married as long as I have, you get to know your spouse, and you know how they're going to react to things before you even open your mouth. My husband, though I love him dearly, is as unpredictable in these matters as you can get. He would either dismiss the whole thing out of hand, or else insist that we ferry the sweater to the nearest paranormal society for further research. Wishing to spare myself dismissive lectures or future ghost-hunting TV show marathons, I kept it close to the chest.

Instead, when he staggered out of the shower, I asked him for a favor. "Before breakfast, we need to go back to that estate sale."

The woman at the door was more than a little confused when she found me standing on the porch. "Er... Yes? Can I help you?" It was the same young woman as the day before, and recognizance flashed across her face as she awkwardly answered my summons. The street was much quieter this morning; Morenci's city-wide garage sale had come to an end. "Sorry, um... The estate sale ended yesterday, so..."

"Don't worry, I'm not looking for a refund or anything," I said. With a sheepish smile, I held out the plastic bag. "I just... remembered our talk yesterday, and I wanted you to have this."

Still baffled, the woman swept back her bangs and carefully reached for the bag. Opening it, she drew out the completed sweater and studied it in the light of the foyer. "Oh... Oh, this is..."

"It's the sweater your grandmother started," I said.

"And you finished it! In a single night?" She laughed. "That's incredible! It's... It's lovely, thank you. But—"

I stepped away from the door. "Well, you're very welcome. Congratulations on the baby, and I hope the sweater fits."

Taken aback, she tried to follow me out onto the porch. "Look, I really appreciate it. You didn't have to do this. Can I at least—"

"Oh, please, think nothing of it," I insisted, trying to keep my distance from the little sweater. "Your grandmother wants you to have it."

"Are you... Are you sure?"

"*Certain.*" I spared her a final wave and then bounded off the porch, rejoining Nate in the SUV.

"All set?" he asked when I'd finally buckled up.

"Yeah, let's go."

He pulled away from the house with a wistful glance in the rearview. "You know, it *was* kind of fun going to that sale yesterday. There were a few records there that I considered picking up, but I wasn't sure if we'd have room in the car for them all. I wonder if anyone bought 'em up... I might be able to go in there and haggle for the whole lot. What do you think?"

"I think," I said, regarding the house with a frown, "we're going to throw out those stupid records you bought yesterday."

"What? Why?"

Because if granny is as attached to her record collection as she is to her knitting projects, I want nothing to do with them... I cleared my throat and cracked the window for a little fresh air. "Vinyl sucks, Nate. Just listen on your phone like everyone else."

SPIRALING
DOWN
DISTURBING HORROR STORIES BY
MICHAEL MARKS

"STRIKING, BITING, AND WICKED;
YOU WON'T WANT TO MISS THIS COLLECTION."
PLASTIC
FACES
UNSETTLING STORIES BY
MARTA ABROMAITYTE

"STORIES THAT ARE
GUARANTEED TO
ENTERTAIN"
VACANCY
R.K. KOMBRINCK
THESE LONELY
PLACES

I'VE DONE
THIS
"TRULY SPECIAL"
BEFORE
A BARRAGE OF
NIGHTMARES BY RYAN MAJOR

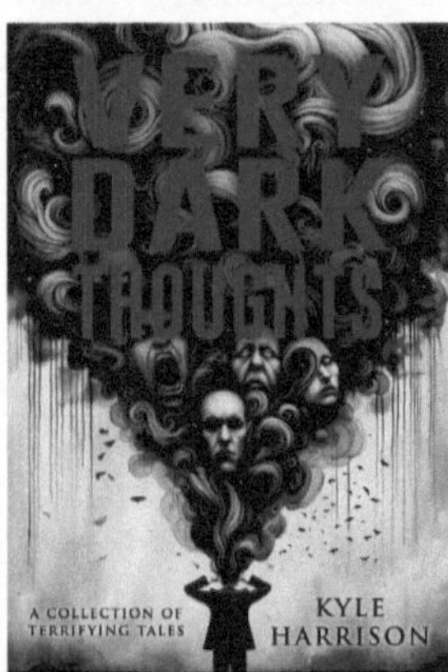
VERY
DARK
THOUGHTS
A COLLECTION OF
TERRIFYING TALES
KYLE
HARRISON

"AN EXCELLENT
COLLECTION
OF HORRORS"
IRON
MAIDENS
TWISTED TALES OF KILLER WOMEN
SARAH JANE HUNTINGTON

STRANGE
TALES
OF THE
MACABRE
TALES BY E. REYES

FACE DOWN
"A GREAT LITTLE
COLLECTION OF THE
BIZARRE (AND)
MACABRE"
IN THE
GRAVE
SINISTER TALES BY
THOMAS O.

TRIPPING
"T. W. GRIM CAN
TELL ONE HELL OF
A STORY."
OVER
TWILIGHT
DARK TALES BY
T.W. GRIM

MORE CHILLS FROM VELOX BOOKS

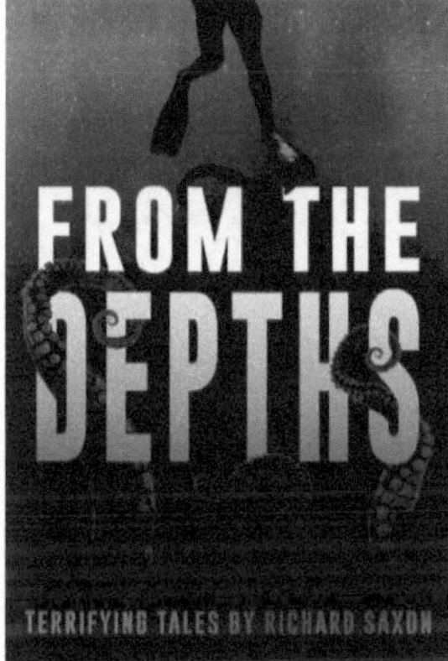